THE LIGHTS OF ALBORADA

Also by Gianni Riotta

Prince of the Clouds

GIANNI RIOTTA

The Lights of Alborada

Translated from the Italian by
SHAUN WHITESIDE

FOURTH ESTATE · London

First published in Great Britain in 2006 by
Fourth Estate
An imprint of HarperCollins*Publishers*
77–85 Fulham Palace Road
London W6 8JB
www.4thestate.co.uk

1

A catalogue record for this book is
available from the British Library

HB ISBN-13 978-0-00-717494-2
HB ISBN-10 0-00-717494-2
TBP ISBN-13 978-0-00-723342-7
TPB ISBN-10 0-00-723342-6

Typeset in Minion by Palimpsest Book Production Limited,
Polmont, Stirlingshire

Printed in Great Britain by Clays Ltd, St Ives plc

To Anita the great dolphin
To Michele the great helmsman

1

When I was a child on the Island, feast days were announced by the Alborada. At the first light of 'rosy-fingered dawn', as our teachers taught us to call it, Orazio the sexton lit rockets full of black gunpowder. Their fuses were short and hemp-grey. The explosions rang out dry and crisp, without heat or smoke. One after another, like the beads of the rosary that the old women fingered during Vespers, in the cold of the church of San Noè.

The village lived by the bloody trade of fishing and the strenuous business of processing tuna, the silvery herds of the blue Mediterranean Sea, and it was too small – just a few houses lined up along the cliffs – not to be roused all at once by the sound of Alborada. The first explosion made us all jump, snug beneath the salt-stained quilts that our grand-mothers had spent their evenings embroidering. The other reports slipped easily into our ears, but none of them rumbled in the same way. There was no fishing on a feast day, no nets to untangle or harpoons to hone to razor-sharpness, to strike the blue skin and the red flesh of the tuna. The women didn't have the bother of sheets to wash and wring in the irrigation ditch, or children to send to school, hoping that the holes in their shoes wouldn't get too big before the annual *mattanza*, the tuna slaughter, before the vital force of the tuna paid for the next year of our lives.

When the explosions brought the pyrotechnic volley to an end, Orazio began to ring the bells, short strokes through the morning air, which was clear but still grey. When the last bell fell silent the villagers would roll over in bed, the men relax and the woman begin to think about lighting the stove for a cup of coffee, when there was coffee, and when there wasn't, then a cup of substitute coffee made from barley or bitter chicory. Between Alborada and the first awakenings there lay a contented zone of Purgatory, of waiting. The feast day had arrived, and promised, in the poet's words, repose and fleeting joys suspended in a no-man's-land, a day free of the prison of duties, chores, labour. The village waited for the future, not yet awake but coddled and rebuked, like sleepy children by their mothers: 'Wake up. I'll be back in five minutes with your *caffé latte.*'

I was the only one who stopped sleeping when the Alborada sounded. As the first report rang out I slipped from my quilt and wrapped myself in a yellow oilskin against the dew. I ran. I ran along the deserted cobbled alleyways, my heart pounding and swelling against my breastbone and my skinny ribs. I flew over nets the colour of raw raffia, missed by a few inches the harpoons and the rough metal anchors. I jumped from bollard to bollard, balancing over the icy waters of the harbour, I ran my hand along the booming black gate of the school, slipping over the cobbles outside the big tuna-processing plant, the building of yellow volcanic stone that held our lives and our luck. I headed for San Noè, and behind me, on Hangman's Hill, where the gallows had stood in the days of the Saracen Turks, goats browsed the salt-crunching grass. My feet scraped the coarse turf, I grazed my knees on the paving-slabs of the market and turned to run up the hill, gliding like a happy gull over the church square of San Noè.

My challenge was a simple one: to cross the village, leaving our house at the first blast, and kneel beneath the paternal figure of San Noè – St Noah – before Orazio's final fuse brought the Alborada to a close. Once there, I would pray to the patron saint of the Ark, the guardian for forty days and forty nights of our species and of the myriad varieties of plants and animals, to intercede for me too, and for my family and for the village. What blessing I was asking for, I couldn't say. Neither did I really understand that word 'intercede', but it seemed to me that my mad, childish running, to the detonations of the Alborada, were a sacred and essential rite to be repeated every year.

Orazio came down muttering like a lonely old man, and noticed me in the square. 'This time too? You're completely mad. Have you prayed? Fine. Now go back to bed.'

I never paid him any heed. Orazio turned his bent shoulders towards me and went back into the church to prepare the altar. I waited for my heart to settle in my chest, and walked gently towards the pier. There, a rare school of flying fish, frantic dragonflies, beat the waves with the same energy that I felt had been freed in my soul. I had fulfilled my vow, delivered my request for some favour as yet unknown.

My father was no longer at home, he had disappeared out on the Indian Ocean, swallowed up by the waves along with a cargo of Arab carpets. My mother lived on his pension, and although we were poor, we weren't starving. Papa had left me the books that had belonged to my grandfather, a lieutenant of Garibaldi's in the fight for the liberation of Italy. Naval almanacs, atlases, chronicles of the military actions of Garibaldi's Redshirts in Europe and America. I read and read. Only during those hours, only while waiting on the pier, after the Alborada and before the village roused itself, did I know what my life would be like. My schooldays and my adolescence. A girl with a blue pullover and hair down to her shoulders, strolling on the beach to the sound of a guitar from a balcony, and the sad songs that our men had learned in Spain. Love, happiness, tenderness.

Can a child imagine life through an adult's eyes? We think it's possible, don't we? We relegate not only today's children, but ourselves as children, to a perennial refuge of childhood, as though toys and illusions were the only things that children knew. Whereas that isn't the case, or at least not for those of us who grew up on the Island. I knew very well, as I ran off through the echoing reports of the rockets and the steely strokes of the bells, what I wanted from my life. I wasn't only concerned with glory, with travel, the constant and amazing tasks that I would perform on tropical waters, taking vengeance for my father's shipwreck. The adventures I took for granted, the sure reward for those heroes who stood in brilliant colours on the covers of boys' story books. The disdainful Cesare kidnapped by pirates, General Desaix in the last charge at Marengo, my grandfather making coffee for Garibaldi, indolently serving him under Bourbon fire. 'General, was this morning's blend to your liking?' 'Manes, if you don't watch out for those muskets, you won't be making any coffee for me at all tomorrow morning.'

Manes is my surname, Giovannino is my first name, but everyone's always called me Nino, Nino Manes, a man who – I was sure of it as I watched the crashing festive waves – was going to make his mark on history. And I craved love, too. My childish idea of erotic passion didn't go beyond the smutty remarks of the old men who picked up cigarette stubs from the pavement, or furtive glances darted at an innocent little bride, or the moist kisses of some platinum-blonde Hollywood diva. Those feelings satisfied my heart and my imagination. I would be able to paint like my father, whose oil-painted ocean dawn hung gleaming over my bed. With a steady hand I would outline the face of my lover to be. There were her round lips, her soft, sweet eyes, a hint of cheekbone, her cheerful smile and her forehead, covered with the fringe that was customary then among girls of marriageable age. I always imagined her in a blue sweater, on the seashore at night, and in my ears I heard a song that was fashionable at the time: 'Barefoot on the beach with you . . .' My heart beat like a sparrow pecking grain; love and the future were that sky-coloured jumper and that girl who was alive only for me. But how alive she was!

I returned home damp and confused, as though I had spent my first, premature night of marriage. Mama gave me an egg beaten with sugar and the Marsala my father had left behind. SOM, said the Indian-ink label: Superior Old Marsala. My mother had resigned herself, poor woman, to these excursions of mine, and I think she would have been amazed if I had missed a single one.

My last Alborada outing coincided with my sixteenth birthday. It was easy for me at that age to scamper from the meadow to the hill of San Noè, since my legs were long, and I had strong feet that could grip the cobbles and the grass. But my palpitations at the idea that I might not make it, the anxiety of slipping beneath Orazio's bells before the final stroke, sent me off at a frantic gallop. It was no longer a children's game. It was a flight from the present, from adulthood.

For my Alborada as a sixteen-year-old, in 1937, I had donned long trousers. And I ran like mad, striding fiercely, not really looking where I was going. For the last time, I slipped into the church square, a winner, and pumped my clenched fists triumphantly in the air. I turned a half-pirouette, looking around for Orazio so that I could win his approval – 'I've done it, Orazio!' – and instead what I saw was the most beautiful girl I had ever set eyes upon. The nimble sway with which she walked set the sleeve of a blue pullover, slung lazily over her shoulders, swinging back and forth with the elegant severity of a metronome. Bareheaded, she gazed out to sea, and the breeze mingled curls and wool. My startled agitation must have produced a crunch of gravel, and she turned around to stare at me with mocking curiosity.

'Are you always running? You're in a terrible hurry at this time of the morning. What's your name?'

'Nino. And you?'

'Zita.'

And I never ran again.

2

During the fiercest war of the twentieth century twelve million soldiers and officers were taken prisoner. Former warriors, proud of their armies and their units, often convinced of the cause for which they had been recruited, spent their days behind barbed wire, vying with their fellow soldiers for a slice of bread in the mud or, when conditions were more humane, waiting restlessly for the next day, querulous and impotent. Twelve million human beings, a nation, scattered from the frozen steppes of Europe to Australia, where six hundred Japanese kamikaze fighters threw themselves against the machine-gun nests of the camp guards at Cowra, choosing bullets over the shame of detention. In Africa, the Italian lieutenant Carlo de Bellegarde escaped from a British camp in Kenya and, on foot and on a bicycle, covered over three thousand kilometres of jungle and savannah to reach Mozambique in two months. Prey to snakes by night and lions by day, he defended himself with a torch, waving it around to chase the beasts away. Two askaris, Ambekilili and Wakuru, captured him on the last bridge before freedom: '*Bwana mkubwa, Bahati mbaya* – Noble lord, a terrible misfortune!' they said sadly.

In 1915 the men of my village suspended the tuna hunt, and they went to war. The ones who survived the eleven Isonzo Offensives returned and took up their nets again. We, their sons, set off for sun-scorched Africa, the merciless Balkans, eternal Russia. When the fate of the war turned for our lovely homeland, we were imprisoned in Nazi camps, or in Siberia, or across the sea. When we came home, our children listened to us complaining about vanishing shoals of bluefish, the declining tuna population, no more tuna hearts hanging to dry in the sun, no gleaming fillets in oil. We never talked about what had happened to us.

Ettore, my father's cousin, had served on a rickety banana boat that crossed the Red Sea. Cut off beyond the Suez Canal by the declaration of war, he and his crew crossed two oceans, the Indian and the Pacific, to be welcomed in triumph by the girls of Tokyo and ended up in a concentration camp when Italy surrendered on 8 September 1943. Ettore saw the flash of Hiroshima on the horizon, survived and came home with two pearl necklaces which he gave to his daughters. But he didn't say a word about his adventures.

Uncle Massimo was captured by the 6th Australian Division in Bardia, in Africa. They stole his Vetta watch, but he didn't hate them for it. 'It's war, no point harbouring a grudge.' He ended up in Yol, in India, in the foothills of the Himalayas. They dragged him across three continents but they didn't break him. On the yellow sand of the camp he drew up a plan of escape to Manchuria, climbing mountains eight thousand metres high and then marching hundreds of kilometres to the Japanese bases in China. No one wanted to follow him (are you surprised?) and he set off on his own. When captured he was up to his neck in snow. The British colonel warmed him up with a bowl of soup, and then gave him permission, on his word of honour, to move around freely inside the camp as long as he never again tried to escape. He too kept mum about his adventures.

No one wants to listen to prison stories, so we just kept quiet. We behaved patiently, we waited like stoics, refusing to let ourselves be humiliated. And yet we were defeated. Benito Mussolini's wicked project was beaten back, the banners broken, strips of them sold as souvenirs. The most respectable kind of captivity, the bravest of lives as a prisoner, is still the mark of a battle lost. It's hard for a child to look into his father's eyes and know that this man was once young and handsome and defeated, a hostage of people who stole his chronometer, his rifle, his mother's letters, his identity, his victory and his future. We, the fathers, redeemed the honour of battle with our courageous conduct in the camps: but what about the sons? Who are the sons of the retreat, a generation without flags, avid consumers at the cinema of the exploits of the victorious Allied warriors at El Alamein, the Don, Sicily?

They listen to the stories and, puzzled and attentive, miss the moral. There's only one adventure they want to hear. Of all the escapes, real or imagined, dreamed up or frustrated by our jailers, one alone gives heart to the children born after the peace. They tell it to each other, changing or adding details and secrets every time they do so. Its protagonist is a maths student who became a fisherman. Perhaps, in this century, others will be delighted by the tale of his escape, which began in April 1944, at a bus stop in Hereford, Texas, in the great and powerful United States of America.

Four hundred thousand Germans and 50,000 Italians were imprisoned in that new continent. Only 2,200 of the Germans, veterans of Field-Marshal Rommel's Afrika Korps, patient, silent and organised, tried to get away, all of them recaptured. Thirty-five of them died, killed while attempting to escape. The Italians too, apparently more serene, endlessly singing a single song, '*Rosamunda, tu sei la vita per me . . .*' escaped as quickly as they could, as permitted by the Geneva Convention. I got hold of the figures – the American War Department estimates that 604 Italians broke out. Rather more than the Germans, on average. Why? Where were they planning to go, setting off on foot from Texas, from the Mississippi, even from Hawaii in the middle of the Pacific, digging tunnels, dressing up as priests, as labourers, eluding the patrols by hiding in haystacks? To reach a ship and be transported, clandestinely, to Europe, to Spain or Portugal, neutral countries? Or did they just want to escape the endless routine, dinner, roll call, reading, football, dinner and lights out? Where was a prisoner to go, on foot, without a word of English? The dream was the free ports, New York and Philadelphia, the only ones that allowed ships from non-allied countries to berth. The Americans had spread the rumour that Savannah, in Georgia, was open to foreign vessels as well, and thus managed to intercept the refugees who headed south.

I, Giovannino Manes, am the hero of the story that the boys listened to. I escaped on April the 17th 1944, from Camp 1 in Hereford, for hardline Italian prisoners. We had decided not to collaborate with the Allies even after the armistice of September the 8th and the declaration of war on Germany. We were strange people, fascists, most of us, but communists too, and socialists and libertarians who refused to work the fields so as 'not to help the capitalist economy'. We were confused, simple and pig-headed.

The sun was high over Texas, and the long road was dusty between the maize fields. I had fifteen dollars in my pocket, which I had got hold of by selling a guard some SS 'medals' carved from a tin of tomatoes. I knew a bit of English. The compulsory insignia, POW, prisoner of war, had been traced on my trousers in toothpaste rather than the regulation white ink, and clumsily erased, so I could not be identified by that. The plan was a simple one: get to New York, stow away on a ship and then land in Portugal and be repatriated by June the 24th. Not a day later. In my pocket I had, folded in its envelope, Zita's letter:

My dear Nino,
Of all the things I've written to you over the years when
you have been far away, and of all the things I would like
to write to you, nothing grieves me more than the words I
am about to write to you now. On June the 24th I am
going to marry Professor Leonardo Barbaroux. He wanted
to write to you himself, but I told him no, I must tell Nino.

We grew up in his house, Nino, I know. We spent the most beautiful hours studying mathematics and logic with him, when all of life seemed as simple as a theorem. And yet you joined up, and you know what Barbaroux thinks of war. We stayed on the Island, almost alone. You boys were away, and the women were at their wits' end. We went on studying, day and night, always on our own, until what happened happened, and I don't want to torment you. We're going to get married. I know it will hurt you, and I carry your pain within me. But war forces us into swift decisions, my darling Nino, we none of us know how long we will live, and where and how. Resign yourself to it. It's clear that it wasn't to be, after our magical encounter at the Alborada. Don't close yourself away. Leonardo says he'll write to you. Please don't suffer too much. Nino, my love, whom I have loved so very much.

    Zita

When I received it, I put the letter in the pocket of my uniform, opened the wooden door of the barracks, headed for the latrine and threw up.

'Are you feeling ill?' asked Captain Righi, who had lost an eye in Bir el Gobi and had a bat-like sense of hearing.

I didn't feel ill. I felt empty, like a pot scoured by my mother after Sunday lunch, or Nana's marrows, which the children scraped clean of their pulp and floated down the Scutari stream. My long imprisonment – I had fallen into the hands of the Australians in January 1941, Lieutenant Beretta and I had been the last to surrender – had made me indifferent to emotions. Nothing happens directly to prisoners of war; every event, whether it aggravates or alleviates the punishment, is caused by someone else – the camp commandant suspending your mail, the mess sergeant giving you a particularly tasty dish. A prisoner has no power. Over anybody. The world happens to him. He has control only over his own thoughts, but it's a delicate, ephemeral art, a piece of hand-blown Murano glass. Many people lost it and remained mere shadows, playing football and eating, in a state of suspension for years.

Standing on that step, I understood that I had to control my thoughts or become a victim like Ferrucci, a friend from the battlefields, who had turned in on himself, grown melancholy, stopped responding to anything and spent the seasons staring at the tumbleweed blown into the desert by the Texan wind. He smoked and looked at the prairie, unable to feel pain or to decipher grief. After reading the letter, I could have run yelling towards the watchtower where the guards were posted, the '*camans*' as we called them because they were constantly telling us to 'Come on, come on.' One idiot rookie would probably take fright and fire at my back, intending to kill me. That was what had happened to poor Lieutenant Giardina, in Africa, left by the French to die in pain with a bullet in his belly for taking a step too close to the wire. Some of the *camans* were trigger happy.

What choice did I have? Zita, my beloved, my innocent, my snow-white virgin, my betrothed, sweet blood of my heart, the lips I had kissed, the breasts I had stroked in the shade of the *faraglioni*, would be for ever the wedded wife of Barbaroux. He, Barbaroux, would possess her, love her, conquer her. It was for him, for Barbaroux, that she would give birth and smile, it was to him that she would read those mathematical studies, put his books in order and turn out the light, before slipping beneath the sheets, with him, with Leonardo Barbaroux.

We were the professor's favourite pupils. He was a mathematician and an anti-fascist, a friend of the genius David Hilbert who had withdrawn into voluntary exile, leaving his post so as not to be forced to swear loyalty to the Duce, Benito Mussolini. From a wealthy family – his father's company made the most precise telescopes of the day – Barbaroux had taken us to his bosom, his two shy village children, and sent us to university. Now I, who loved mathematics because it was free of the snares and paradoxes of the type that I had just spent a year avoiding – mines, tanks, machine guns, thirst and scorpions, and every day in the camp in Hereford, stupefying myself with masturbation, rotting my mind by gluing little models together, arguing over nothing – I was finally up to my neck in a contradiction that neither logic nor war had prepared me for. Barbaroux, who could have been Zita's father, was instead to be her husband. And she would be a rich and revered lady, and how people would smirk at me in the club! But thinking of their smiles didn't hurt me, I felt numb, anaesthetised. The fear I had felt in battle, the raging charges in the desert, the solitary humiliation of prison, had all vanished. Pain had turned me into a ghost, I felt as though I could pass through the barbed wire and fly home on the wind, unseen by anyone, not by poor Ferrucci with his dead eyes and his dead cigarettes, nor the *camans* in the Hereford watchtower. And my flight was the flight of a ghost, protected by a kindly god. I had to be in Italy by June the 24th, to prevent the marriage of Zita and Barbaroux. That was all.

And that was why I was leaning against the pole of the Hereford bus stop, in the dust and the wind, on that April afternoon in 1944. And when I saw the young American lieutenant coming towards me with an ironic smile on his lips, I thought, He's going to catch me now and put me back inside, but I'll escape again tomorrow.

3

The lieutenant leaned against the bus stop and, still smiling, rolled himself a thin, firm cigarette, tufts of blond Virginia tobacco sticking out at either end. He rolled a second one and held it out to me. I had never smoked in my life, always bartering my tobacco rations for stamps for my letters to Zita, but to say, 'No, thank you' might have scuppered my plan before it had even got under way. I nodded and allowed the man to light the cigarette in my mouth, although I didn't inhale.

The bus appeared around the bend of the aqueduct, followed by a cloud of dust and a dog that barked merrily in the hot air, with the resounding vigour of prairie strays. The driver braked, raising a cloud of dust from the beaten earth, and indolently opened the door. First aboard was a sprightly old woman, and out of soldierly habit I stepped aside for the lieutenant, who climbed the two steps and showed his papers.

'What about him?' asked the conductor, pointing to me. He looked me up and down unsympathetically. 'Are you a GI?'

The lieutenant didn't answer yes or no, but just murmured,

'Mmm,' and dropped a few coins into a zinc basin. Then he stepped aside so that I could reach the free seats.

I tried to work out where he was going to sit, so that I could find a seat as far away from him as possible. Why had he paid for my ticket? Out of kindness? Never before had I encountered kindness on the part of an officer towards a raw recruit he didn't even know. Had he mistaken me for one of his men? In that case I should have had my papers with me as well. No point standing there brooding about it, better to pretend to sleep, wait till we reached the outskirts of a town, and then feign car-sickness and run off through the fields to jump an eastbound train.

During my transfer to Hereford, beneath the awning of a little station in Arkansas, I had met a hobo, the kind that travelled the freight trains. He'd told me how easy it was to jump aboard the slow convoy of wagons. He was originally from Friuli, his father had moved to the States from Udine and he spoke a mixture of Italian, German and English. 'If tu jump ok, tu land ok. No be frightened, Italiano, if no kaputt, ok? If cop come, you know cop? If sheriff come, and hit you with electric torch, tu run for life.'

I'd stolen an old railway timetable from the American military canteen, its cover scorched by the flames from the kitchen – I had explained its disappearance by saying it had been burned to ashes – and had learned it off by heart from cover to cover, times, dates, places, Southern Thunder, Northern Arrow, Atlantic Sky Hawk, all the trains over there have wonderful, mythological Indian names.

I stretched out on the hard bus seat, resisted the temptation to watch the flat panorama passing by, the great expanses that had lain unseen beyond the camp fence, and closed my eyes. The less attention I attracted the better.

This was how I had escaped: I hid in the potato silos and didn't answer when the roll was called. The *camans* hunted for me all over the camp, then got bored and eased off. On the fifth day I joined a unit of navvies. Captain Righi winked as he pretended to count me, and I left the barbed wire behind. Exhaustion, emotion and my melancholy over Zita had now lulled me into a calm feeling of numbness: I can't imagine any prisoner of war has ever escaped with such absolute serenity, insensitive to fear.

In my sleep I heard the notes of the song '*Rosamunda, tu sei la vita per me*' – Rosamunda, you are my life, there's joy in your kisses, the more I see you the more I love you, Rosamunda my darling – perhaps because that harmless little dance tune had become the anthem of the Italian prisoners. Yes, the fascists still sang 'Youth, youth, in life and life's harshness . . .' and, after September the 8th you might have heard 'Brothers of Italy, heed Italy's call . . .' and the wonderful chorus of '*Avanti o popolo*', but '*Rosamunda*' was the song of all the Italian prisoners, POWs as we had to write on our trousers and rucksacks, in big, clear letters. POW: and we had christened ourselves '*povieri*', the poor POWs. I had rubbed out the three letters on my uniform, and was fleeing towards Zita, our meeting was sure to be stormy, violent, and at the time I had no doubt, my twenty-year-old beauty, but that it would bring me back to her, with love as always.

'*Rosamunda, tu sei la vita per me*': who was whistling the tune on the bus? I woke up gently, not stirring. I half opened my eyes, the cheerful whistle came from close by, very close. '*Tu sei la vita per me.*' I looked; the lieutenant was sitting there, still whistling and smiling. He had clearly worked out who I was, but I decided not to give him the satisfaction of catching me straight away. I would feign stupidity, to the last moment, even if it meant mooing like a mute. To get away again, at the first opportunity.

Bored of waiting, the lieutenant tapped me on the arm and whispered in Italian, 'Hey, fella, wake up.'

I gave a start like a soldier told off by a superior, and saluted accordingly: 'Don't understand, sir.' The old trick of my language exams, if you speak in a low voice it dulls the sound of mispronunciation.

'So where have you escaped from?' he asked in Italian.

Who was he? His Italian was perfect, just like the English he had used when speaking to the driver. Even a hint of Tuscan, and Texan, just to make everything perfect.

'Sir? I don't understand, sir.'

'You got out of Hereford?' he asked again in Italian. 'Which camp? Hardline fascists, Camp 1?'

He even knew our internal divisions. I tried to say, 'Respectfully, sir, I don't understand,' but I always had problems pronouncing the word 'fully', and I heard the simplest words coming out of my mouth: 'With all due respect, sir, I don't understand French.'

'French, eh?' he smiled. 'You're a sly one. Fine, as you wish, if you don't understand, you don't understand. But you'll understand sooner or later.'

He let his cap fall over his nose, rested his shoes against the back of the chair and dozed off. The journey continued for two hours, the strangest two hours of my strange life. Who was I? A fugitive in the clutches of a meddling officer? Was I lost before I'd even begun? How was I going to get myself out of this? I knew I had to avoid any kind of violence that would mean being punished or, the greatest terror of all, being sent off to labour camp in Hawaii, with no way of contacting Zita.

The lieutenant was snoring, lost to the world, and we were already driving past the first houses of Amarillo when the old woman nodded to the driver.

'Would you stop for a moment? I don't feel well and there's a lemonade stand over there.'

The brakes whistled, the lieutenant showed no sign of waking up and, unable to believe my luck, I leapt over his knees without touching him, nodded goodbye to the driver and walked past the kiosk, which was decorated with beautifully scented lemons. One of them had fallen into a ditch and I picked it up, like a talisman. The rind was fat and rough, ripe and yellow. I scratched the skin and the smell of my secondary school wafted out, sunny afternoons, a hand stuck through the fence to steal a lemon, the amazing fruit, a bit of sunlight in your fist, the juice sharp on your tongue after scoring a goal on the red clay pitch.

The lemons were stolen from Paulus, a Russian who had escaped from St Petersburg in 1917 – a baron too far on the left for Vladimir Ilyich – and who ended up cultivating the gardens of south Italy. The trees, the smell of Zita, Marseilles soap, Russia and the tuna fishing nets, the world seemed wonderful to me, full of exotic cities. As though wearing the Seven League Boots of the fairy tale, I would fearlessly travel the planet. I saw myself living in Amazonia, then in Petrograd and Hong Kong, and in Pittsburgh where they made the steel for the tuna harpoons.

It was as if, in Hereford Camp 1 (yes, the lieutenant was right, I was in number 1, with Tuimati, the tall, thin cavalry officer, with Berto, always writing on his wooden board, with Burri who drew pictures on empty sugar bags, and with Troisi, silent and elegant) I had left the prisoner Giovannino Manes, *poviere*, POW, prisoner number 8117125, 81 meaning captured in North Africa, 1 Italian and 7125 my arrival code. Now, once again, I was Nino Manes, and I could travel my life in those Seven League Boots, with Zita by my side. As if our life was not in fact determined by the belligerence of the Italian fascist regime, the tactical errors of General Graziani in Egypt, or the forces of production of President Roosevelt's United States. It was the *caman* Nick Carraway who had explained it to me: 'Our black workers, the ones the Führer wants to exterminate, can build a liberty ship in a single day. The U-boat captains show great courage in trying to sink them. But do you know who defeats their daring? The black workers who, for a few cents, can get a ship seaworthy in twenty-four hours.'

I wondered what Carraway was doing now. He certainly

wouldn't have expected me to escape. He was sure he had saved me for democracy, his democracy, a ship a day to defeat the Führer, assembled by black workers. In Texas those same workers didn't enjoy the right to vote for the upper-class president, although they still had great things to say about him. Carraway wouldn't have been pleased by my escape; basically he agreed with the theory of Colonel Rogers, the head of the camp: 'Italians, bastards, greaseballs, wops, they sing and eat spaghetti with brilliantine sauce on it, they're slaves to the Krauts. They don't even know how to work. Save them for freedom? It would take ten gener-ations.' But I didn't care about Carraway or Rogers, I was going into Amarillo. I would have a bowl of soup at the coffee shop without speaking to anyone. I'd brought the Bible with me, a gift from the Quakers. I was learning English, and in the south people always respect the silence of a soldier reading the gospel, with its black cover and its pages edged with fiery red.

I sat down at a corner table, close to the door, and said, 'Soup, please.' I only needed a few words; on my way out I'd leave a big tip to distract the old waitress's attention from my accent. The soup was good, thicker than the soup in the camp, with bright carrots and barley floating in it, among big patches of sweet grease. Aromatic pepper, the bold flavour of Coca-Cola. The bread wasn't so good, dry, crumbly, nothing like our pure white loaves back home. And yet those crisp crou-tons were exquisite to me. It was as though I had worked to savour them, forging SS insignia in return for contraband dollars to pay the bill, risking the machine gun fire of the *camans*.

I wiped my face with my napkin, a piece of worn grey cloth, and started to read the Bible. The spirit of God moved on the face of the waters, those waters I was sure I would cross, as Moses passed through the Red Sea. After endless periods of exhaustion and cunning and luck, to be able to sail on the ocean of war to Zita.

The waitress had returned from the yard at the back, carrying a big bunch of flowers. There were bright petunias and daisies, early poppies with red petals like butterfly wings. One by one the woman took them and arranged them in a vase filled with fresh water. She was never content. Now she moved the stem of a rose, now she adjusted the green grass that swathed it. She was in pursuit of a certain effect, working with the shadows that the brilliant sun cast on the white wall. When the prospect seemed a happy one, she let the stems settle. Otherwise she barely brushed them as though caressing them, with hands that were scarlet from washing up too many dishes. I was distracted, I didn't like it, and for the first time since escaping the surveillance of the Hereford *camans* I was afraid. It was as though my fairy-tale journey, my Seven League footsteps to the sea, and the Bible, and those epic lines 'The earth was without form and void, and darkness was on the surface of the deep' were not enough to protect me against being captured, *nunc et semper*, now and for ever. Only by being unaware and kind, like the coffee shop lady with her flowers, concentrating solely on my task, on both my lemon from long ago and the one that gleamed yellow on the dark table, only then would I truly succeed in escaping across two continents.

I'd finished the soup and the bread, I wanted a coffee and even, perhaps, to risk a bit of conversation in exchange for directions to the nearest railway station. There was no need to ask. The woman finally gave a nod of blessing to her geometrical bouquet, set the cup on the table and slipped my tip into her apron pocket.

'I expect you're looking for the station, son. It's past the bridge, that sloping path takes you straight there. The Eastern Daylight Express'll be going through in half an hour. You got plenty of time.'

I smiled and murmured, 'Thanks' as though my tongue was burnt by the hot coffee, and got to my feet. On a shelf behind the bourbon bottles there was a black-framed photograph: 'Tim McMurdo, Private First Class, Anzio 1944.' The flowers were for that young soldier.

Outside the sun was dazzling. I walked along the dusty white path, 'the voice of God moved upon the face of the waters', and on that slow, blue river. The stones crackled under the soles of my new shoes, bartered with the storeroom guy – 'Bums always wear good shoes,' the hobo had advised me. I wouldn't stop at the station, but would carry on to the hill where the river formed a loop and the two-lane highway climbed to the east. The train would slow down and I would hop aboard a freight car. 'Tu jump ok, tu land ok,' putting my hope in the Spirit of the Waters.

I wondered how the lieutenant had felt when he woke up to find I had gone? Was he drunk? No, it was too early in the day for that, and there had been no booze on his breath. I was about to leave the wooden barracks of the station behind me when, at that very moment, just as brazen and clear as before, the song began again: '*Rosamunda, tu sei la vita per me, nei tuoi baci c'è tanta felicità.*' The Spirit of the Waters seemed to mock me and the Atlantic coast suddenly seemed a long way away. And yet my heart didn't leap. I set my bag down and turned around: soon I would have a clearer idea of the intentions of the lieutenant who whistled '*Rosamunda*', and discover why he was trying to keep me from escaping.

4

A big blue river ran along the valley floor, alongside the plateau, a vast river unlike anything I had ever seen at home. Not even the Stagnone lagoon, with its flashing shoals of silver *ope* fish and darting rainbow-coloured *violette*, was as vast and deep as that river. At the Stagnone, the Phoenicians had built a road across the sea, which time had sung beneath the mud: in ancient times the merchants had crossed the waves in high-wheeled carts as far as Mozia, an island of temples and shops, a trading centre, as famous then as Manhattan is now. And I, who had left the Island, was to return to the real Manhattan, to try and reach Zita in time. The river had distracted me, everything on this flight was a distraction, everything distanced me from fear and confusion. The lieutenant was standing in front of me, awaiting my reply to an unspoken question. He smiled as though there were something comical in my expression, and at the same time something reassuring and familiar, like someone spotting a friendly face from a long time ago among the harried travellers in a railway station.

I could have lied, or I could have run away, back down the slope. He was the same size as me, but I didn't even think of attacking him. Not because I was frightened, quite the contrary, his features were mild and aristocratic, fair hair, an elegant profile, and I felt I would have had the advantage if it had come to a fight. I was a street boy, and I'd seen vicious stone-throwing battles between rival gangs, when the whole sky is dotted with rocks and one of them would be enough to split your head open. I could have pretended to lower my head and broken his snobbish nose with a butt of my brow, his septum opening up in a discharge of blood and surprise, an easy blow to deliver, a bit like landing a rain-soaked leather ball in the net from a corner kick, the laces imprinting them-selves on his forehead. In my mind I could hear my mate Volpe: 'A surprise punch can deck an elephant, always get your attack in first.'

I was restrained by the caution of the fugitive: attacking a uniformed American officer could land me in front of a firing squad. Who would really come here in search of a young soldier who had escaped from a prison camp? They would have expected me to head south, towards Mexico, crossing the border under cover of a storm. Or else my thirst would lead me into a cactus-filled ravine, and my bones would bleach among the skulls of cattle. If I injured an officer, on the other hand, the FBI and the Military Police would hunt me down from county to county, and when they got their hands on me they'd lock me up in one of those camps there's no escaping from, the ones they were always telling tales about in Hereford. They're on the Aleutian Islands, off Alaska, log barracks surrounded by bears, three oceans away from home.

No risks. The lieutenant screened his green eyes with the nervous hand of a cavalryman, and stared at me curiously, without rancour. '*Bella giornata* – Beautiful day,' he said in Italian. 'The sunshine's nice. The train's about to arrive from behind the mountain. Isn't it time we introduced ourselves?'

The engine whistled, already past the ravines: time to surrender. We were two men on our own, in uniform, by a river that looped before disappearing from view, high on the banks. The lieutenant appeared to be unarmed, we were equals, the same age, and out of my mouth, unbidden, came the first words I had uttered as a free man since the Australian soldier had told me to get out of my bunker, waving the barrel of his Sten gun: 'Out of the bloody pillbox, wop.'

'I'm Nino Manes, an Italian logician. I'm going home. Our countries aren't at war any more. We're fighting Hitler together. We ex-prisoners are waiting to be released. I've got to go early, for personal reasons.'

'You're going to Europe on your own?'

'Yes, sir. I'm going back to Europe.'

'On foot?'

'No, sir. In half an hour the 12.30 Eastern Express will be passing this way. It stops in St Louis to pick up connections and tomorrow, at about six in the evening, it arrives in New York, Grand Central, 47th Street.'

'So you think you're going to get to Manhattan by train, before sailing off for Europe, which is still at war, and sort out your affairs?' His voice was ironic.

'I understand that you find it amusing, sir, but that's exactly what I intend to do.'

I was speaking as a free man, as one equal to another. The lieutenant understood. 'Okay. Then you ought to know that this train, whose times and destinations you know by heart, well done, is searched at every stop by patrols of Military Police. They don't miss a thing, they check the passengers' tickets and papers, paying particular attention to uniformed males of your age, even if the uniform is, how should I put it, as *irregular* as yours. Stopping a prisoner who's escaped from the camps is a rare treat as far as they're concerned: they'll get medals and promotions. When they get their hands on you, what are you going to say? "Gentlemen, the war's over, I'm going to Italy to sort out some unfinished business." And they'll say, "Sure, my friend, we'll escort you, don't worry, can we get you a drink while we're at it?" Quit fooling. Follow me, or we'll miss your Orient Express or whatever the hell it's called.'

The lieutenant set off along the road, towards the station and the river, and I followed him. Prisoner? Travelling companion? I didn't know. For the whole of that autumn and winter I'd seen the desert wind form enormous balls of twigs and thorny brambles and drag them across the prairie, past the wire fence of Camp 1. Since June 1940 I had felt like them, blown about at random by the mistral and full of thorns, my life a barren prairie. What was changing now? Nothing but the abandonment of all desire, all wishful thinking and ambition. If I had managed to turn myself into an inanimate creature, an object that could move, one marked POW, then this was my miraculous metamorphosis, worthy of Ovid, into a tangle of twigs. The wind, warm as breath, was enough to blow me to Zita's feet, her fragrant lap, with all my thorns and all my questions. I wouldn't try to do anything, no act of daring, no strategy, I would be obvious, natural, I would allow nature to act upon me, driving me back to my home and my love. If they locked me in a cell, I would bang my head against the door until either the door or my skull split. If they forced me back behind what Carraway had taught me to call the accordion, the concertina, meaning the gleaming barbed wire, I would burst it apart with my chest, until something gave, whether it was my chest or the wire.

Now, half a century later, these reflections seem like the melancholy notions of a boy kept too long in a cage full of parrots. I wouldn't have thought that way if I'd been thinking realistically. If I'd accepted my situation with the wise fatalism of a grown man, I'd have gone mad, I'd have been broken, like so many of my comrades. Like Ferrucci, like Siviero, the radio ham who had managed, hiding under the blanket at night, to make a little radio out of Spam tins: each day he opened us up to the world, Stalingrad, the fall of Mussolini, the surrender of Italy. And after four years in the camp, they were still watching the stars at night and the tumbleweed by day, spent cigarettes in their mouths. 'Good weather tomorrow, Ferrucci?'

'What does it say on the radio?'

'Only things about the war and Hollywood.'

'Not the weather?'

'Sometimes.'

'And what does it say?'

'That spring's coming to an end.'

Neither Ferrucci nor Siviero replied to letters from home any more. I typed their letters for them, crammed with lies, and copied their signatures in pencil: for a few years those pious lies spared two pairs of old Italian parents from meeting their new son, the *poviere.*

If the wind rolled me in the wake of the lieutenant, I, like the tumbleweed, would be unable to resist. Rolling my way across the world, I would meet up with Zita once again, in time to stop a wedding which struck me – please forgive the impetuousness of a young man – as utterly obscene. Not that I hoped to persuade her to marry me. No one had ever seen Zita change her mind. I just wanted to interpose my body between Zita and reality, stop it, even for a moment, like the tiny grains of sand that stopped our gleaming Vetta chronometers in the desert. Tomorrow a craftsman will give them a good clean and the ticking of reality and the present will resume, but for a moment the sand exists and stops the measurement of time. I wanted to be like that sand. When I got depressed, spending a gloomy afternoon in silence beside Ferrucci, Sergeant Carraway would hold me out a piece of spearmint chewing gum and say, 'Face facts: remember, Nino, you've got to face facts. That's the soldier's life. Face facts, Nino.'

I couldn't face facts any more, that was enough, thank you.

I wanted to cut right through facts, and that was that. The lieutenant, unaware of my ruminations, went on ahead, leaving me to walk a few yards behind him as prisoners were regularly required to do, and whistling that poor song of ours, '*Rosamunda*', of which he seemed so fond. Soon we were at the station, and from there on to the train. And as the prairie passed flatly in front of us, the Military Police patrol, in their spotless uniforms, appeared precisely on time. 'Tickets? Documents? You, boy?'

That would have meant the end of my great escape, whatever my mystical intentions, if the lieutenant, holding out two gleaming identity cards to the Military Police, hadn't smiled: 'Prisoner of war. Italian. I'm escorting him to Manhattan, New York, 47th Street, home of Allied Radio, Italian Service Unit. He's going to read bulletins for free Italy, and for the parts of the country that are still under the Krauts. General HQ's really keen on the idea. I'm hoping to get to Manhattan very soon. There'll be girls at the radio station, you know? Girls, chicks!'

To escape the lieutenant's tiresome lasciviousness, the two Military Police giants returned the documents with barely a glance, saluted him and gave me the look of contempt that the soldiers of the victorious army – people who have never known the dry mouth of fear during bombing raids – reserve for defeated warriors and prisoners to justify their impeccable uniform and the embarrassment of telling their girlfriends the story of a war spent punching railway tickets.

I looked out the window, and got my breath back. In the

distance you could see the mountains through the mist, the fields dotted with cotton-pickers who, at the sound of the train whistle, raised their heads for a moment and immediately bent patiently back down to draw water from the channels of the majestic river. We passed by them, rattling over a bridge with a clatter of boards and bolts, the arteries of the country that was holding me back. I asked, 'Which river is this, sir? The Mississippi?'

This time the lieutenant didn't smile, as he usually did. On the contrary. His face turned very grave. 'The Mississippi? Ol' Man River? No, when we reach the Mississippi you'll recognise it all by yourself, have no doubt about that.'

5

The young waitress adjusted the belt of her white apron with small, sure, nervous movements and glanced around Restaurant 21 to check that none of the customers required her services. Captain Jim Cheever looked at the girl's hand with the serene greed of young men who have been forced to remain chaste for a long time. Unexpressed desire subsides, and the body is filled instead with a clear and formidable energy. 'That's why Catholics demand celibacy of their priests,' mused the Presbyterian Cheever. The mind is clear and clean, it moves with grace and warmth. The body, on the other hand, becomes aware of the erotic atmosphere that bathes it, as though your skin has become the vibrating antennae of a wandering dragonfly. Cheever was thinking about his new military mission, in that final – penultimate? – year of war. General Stan Matthews had summoned him, as a matter of 'immediate urgency and discretion', to Restaurant 21 in Manhattan, rather than, as protocol would have decreed, the Pentagon in Washington. Why such secrecy? And yet, as his mind reflected on the mission before him, his skin was aware that the waitress was a beautiful and desirable girl, a slender mulatto with chestnut eyes, happy to have a job, because the war kept the men at the front, giving her a paycheck, a weekly wage. Her hand ran back and forth across the embroidered linen, nervous of her new environment, sure of her feline beauty, and Cheever looked at her. He thought about the war, and his body was drawn to the girl, silent and distant. He tried to concentrate, worrying that the solitude and aridity of his mission in defence and on behalf of the United States of America might lead him into regretful sensuality. On those long afternoons in barracks, or at daybreak in tumbledown motels on the outskirts of town, he had learned to shoo away his erotic fantasies, irritating gadflies that they were. To stay prey to them was to unleash a wave of morbid longing, uncertainty about what to do, doubts about the future. And in wartime, Cheever couldn't afford to have doubts. 'So,' he thought, glancing at the mulatto girl who had suddenly moved, 'the end of the war will let us return to doubt. Love, certainly, I'll go back to my old love, but doubt is more seductive to me than love. Being able to cultivate eccentric notions, without worrying that a mistake might cause the death of good, decent boys, or even the failure of the mission, and lead in a terrible chain of events to the total defeat of the army, the end of democracy. The luxury of uncertainty: that's what distinguishes peace from war.'

General Matthews came into the restaurant, stroking the revolving door with his gloved hands: such was the power that emanated from his well-trained torso that it appeared as if the magnetism of his body was moving the massive walnut door in a great surge of prestige and energy. He frowned, not noticing Cheever at first, and then recognised him, but his jaw didn't move: everything was as it should be, rendezvous accomplished, Cheever was there, plan obeyed, the strategic operations of the Allied Armed Forces operated according to pre-established protocols.

Matthews sat down and beckoned the girl over with a wave of his fingers, and Cheever was sorry that the general had sufficient authority to enter even his guileless reverie, summoning the docile mulatto girl whom he had courted in silence. He sat back down and concealed his disappointment even from himself, feeling ashamed, as boys will, of feelings that they will later recognise as the clearest they ever had in their lives, and saw after a moment's delay that a second officer followed in Matthews' wake. He was a major in the Office of Strategic Services, the OSS, the arrogant men of American espionage, and he said, 'Good day, sir' in a curious accent, neither French nor German, a low, guttural sound that Cheever had never heard before.

Matthews nodded and the stranger sat down. The general took two large sips from the mint julep he had ordered, holding it as though he were going to snap the glass full of chopped ice, and turned to Cheever. 'What are the latest missions? Are you aware of the situation of prisoners of war detained in America?'

'I was involved with the U-boat raids, sir, anti-sub missions, particularly after 1942. A specialist in interception, anti-sabotage and code-breaking. I don't know much about prisoners, sir.'

'Have you ever met Major Cafard?'

'No, sir.'

'You'll be working together. The major is part of the anti-terrorist section of the OSS. He's just back from Europe. Now he's working at home again. He'll give you details of your mission. Listen to him carefully.'

Cafard: the name rang a bell with Cheever, but he couldn't remember why.

The major started listing figures in his gloomy accent, which sounded like the official language of the undercover war, English with a hint of occupied Europe. 'About half a million Germans, most captured in Africa, are held in prisoner-of-war camps in the USA. The first arrivals are veterans of Rommel's Afrika Korps, convinced that the war was still theirs after the Desert Fox's brilliant campaigns. They still have tans, round sunglasses and tins of Bavarian butter. Tough guys. They thump the other prisoners at the slightest infraction. They've set up a Gestapo network throughout all the camps. All it takes to get on the wrong side of them is an anti-Nazi joke, an expression of resignation or a curse against Hitler. At night they throw a blanket over the unfortunates, and everyone in the room has to join in the punishment beating. Anyone who refuses ends up under the blanket himself. And their families back home are blackmailed, too. For most of the prisoners, a stay in the United States is their best chance of survival. They eat better than their compatriots, and they learn languages and trades in the classes and laboratories that we've set up. Some of them even take courses at American colleges, and receive degrees and diplomas. But a minority hang in there, fighting a pointless undercover campaign, terrorising their comrades.'

'How can we control them?' Cheever broke in, to lighten the feeling of unease that the man's accent provoked in him.

'With infiltrators,' Matthews replied. 'By censoring their mail. Often we receive tip-offs from prisoners who have converted to democracy and want to isolate the Nazis. But the Gestapo are a constant threat. They're trying to organise a mass breakout to cover a unit of saboteurs who are capable of causing slaughter and terrorising our civilian population. It'll be a great propaganda coup in Berlin. We've set up special camps to keep the hardliners in place.'

A curious sense of menace overlaid Cheever's irritation with Cafard's accent, but he refused to be tempted into doubt. He took a sip of his coffee and listened.

'Not many escapes. A few thousand Germans, just one among the Japanese and more than five hundred Italians. On United States territory –' Major Cafard glanced at a card that had appeared in his hand as though by magic, checking that he had the precise figure '– 371,683 Germans and 50,273 Italians held in total. And it's the Italians who are giving us problems. They've surrendered. They've lost the war. They're fighting under our command in Europe, and yet they're still escaping. Only 0.5 per cent of German prisoners try to escape. Among the Italians the figure is 1.2 per cent, nearly three times more than the Germans.'

'Any of them make it?'

'Very few. They slip away. They try to disappear into the city. One Italian lieutenant, Montalbetti, walked two hundred miles through the desert. He had hidden in the camp for four days, and escaped when the guards gave up looking for him. We caught up with him on the border with Mexico, just because he'd lost his bearings and turned up at customs on the American side. Now lots of them are imitating his technique.'

Two hundred miles alone in the Texan desert. Cheever had hunted coyote and mountain lions – puma – with his father, in 1938. The hot air fills your mouth, your feet sink with a squeak into the dry turf. The only things that flourish there are scorpions, rattlesnakes and cacti. The coyotes will hunt down a mountain goat, the puma a deer that has come down from the forest; no human being with any common sense would be so presumptuous as to cross such an area. He wanted to request an interview with this guy Montalbetti who had chosen to risk ending up having his bones gnawed by the vultures rather than wait and go home comfortably once the war was over. Curious animals, the Italians. Now the Germans, devils on the battlefield, were biding their time. The other guys were escaping: why?

'At the beginning of the conflict, in 1942, we were afraid of sabotage, by the Japanese in the west and the Germans in the east. Above all, infiltrations by commandos from the submarines. You know about the U-boat hunts, don't you?' Matthews went on.

Cheever went back to the spring of 1942. The shell-covered

beach at Shelter Island, the black rubber raft. They were chasing four German raiders, silently lest they alarm the few well-to-do people who wintered on the island. A single gunshot, one broken window, and terror would flood the bright lights and the headlines of nearby New York. Sixty miles away from the deer forest, on the alert for the roar of the backwash, panic could spread to Manhattan, jazz, the Apollo Theater and the ladies who danced in their satin dresses. On Shelter Island, a saw-toothed, tempered-steel German dagger slit the throat of his friend Tom, without a cry, without a movement, just a gurgle like that of an unplugged sink, the last sound of the voice that had, in 1939, seduced the whole class of graduating girls at Barnard College, up in Broadway. Perhaps, even now, those young women were wondering, over a drink at Baker House, 'Where do you think Tom is now? We must go and hear him when the war's over,' but Tom lay bleeding to death on the beach which, once peace had returned, would host happy family picnics by the rock pools. Cheever had finished off the Germans, two pistol shots muffled by his silencer, and captured the remaining member of the commando unit, a colossus who had been lamed by one of the shots. He could have killed him like a dog – who would ever have investigated? But Tom had died precisely because they didn't want to act like Nazis. A democratic officer didn't cut throats like an SS fanatic. So he had given him a slap and dragged him by one arm to the Ford, to take him to the investigation centre. In the darkness, the light of the 100-watt bulb . . .

'Cheever, are you listening?'

'Of course, General.'

'We have precise information on the escape of a dangerous Nazi from a prisoner-of-war camp. An expert in sabotage. Like the one you captured on Shelter Island, he's off the U-boats. There's some confusion about his identity. Read this.'

The general handed him a grey file, and Cheever timidly opened it. The sheet of paper, the meticulous typing of the girls in Washington, the black stamps of the censor and the secret service, and the stout, white vellum suggested the hand of the Washington top brass, the only ones who could still afford to use such fragrant paper.

'U-boat commander from 1940 to 1942,' began Matthews. 'Six Allied sinkings in the Atlantic to his credit. His name is believed to have been Hans von Luck, Prussian Junker of aristocratic family, father a diplomat, speaks three languages, escaped from the camp in Amarillo, expert in sabotage and explosives, code-breaking, infiltrations of enemy camps, undercover operations. Sources in the Italian fascist camp in Hereford, Texas, tell us that Captain von Luck, disappointed by the way the war was going and the resignation of his fellow detainees in the USA, planned to organise a highly visible suicide operation. He trained the Italian subs at the Danzig base in 1940, and can rely on their solidarity. He's probably preparing an attack on the levees of the Tennessee Valley Authority, to flood a vast zone in the southern states, and spark the enthusiasm of the Germans. He plans to force Allied Command to increase checks and confiscations, concentrating men and resources on this side of the ocean. A massive manhunt in the south would have enormous propaganda value, and would be broadcast by radio to occupied Europe. Hitler's in desperate need of a psychological success.

'Von Luck must be found straight away, Cheever, he must be arrested, neutralised or brought back to camp in chains. I didn't want to write this in the file that I've prepared, but another source assures me that he's armed, and heading to Washington to attack President Roosevelt,' Matthews continued. 'And we're not even sure of his identity.'

'What do you mean, sir?'

'I mean that prisoners are identified by their *Soldbuch*, the paybook of the German army. But von Luck's *Soldbuch* wasn't found at the camp. He can hardly have taken it with him, it's far too dangerous. It's more likely that he's destroyed it. I'm worried that the escaped prisoner may not actually be von Luck.'

'Tell Cheever your hypothesis, Major,' ordered the general.

'The prisoners are quite capable of preparing fake American documents, creating a new identity for themselves. So why not obliterate the old one? We'll be going after von Luck, but our true prey is someone else.'

'And what about von Luck?'

'He's dead. Or he never got to America, he went missing at sea, and someone else has his *Soldbuch* in his pocket. There's a lot of confusion during prisoner transfers. And the registers are kept in order by the senior prisoners, we haven't got enough of our own men for the job. The escaped man could be an officer, but not von Luck.'

Cheever understood. 'When am I off?'

'Tonight. Cafard will be in charge of the mission. Will you be able to make it?'

'I'll have a shot at it, sir.'

Then he looked at Cafard and corrected himself. 'We'll have a shot at it, sir.'

This reassurance wasn't enough for General Matthews, who leaned over the restaurant table. He pushed the glasses aside with his massive hands, and pressed his torso breathlessly forward. 'Get him, Cheever. Get him. Once the war's over I don't want to find myself with a fanatical Nazi wandering about the States blowing up dykes and massacring innocent schoolchildren. I don't want him to organise a terrorist resistance network in the German quarters of New York. Get him before he shoots the president, get him, whether he's German or Italian.'

Matthews seemed very old to Cheever, his face wrinkled, tired and melancholy. He repeated the words, 'before the war is over', as though afraid he wouldn't see that day. As though catching the only fascist at liberty in the United States of America was not a military matter, like guaranteeing the safety of the dykes, the schoolchildren of Tennessee and Franklin Roosevelt. No, it was rather as if putting that U-boat commander behind the barbed wire of the Amarillo camp was the strategic key to the final victory, a magical challenge to the fate of the world.

'Get him, Cheever, get him. For all our sakes.'

6

What did Ulysses dream of during those nights on his plank bed on board his ship when the bright and friendly stars of the Mediterranean lit the unknown way before him? Did he draw up battle plans for fighting monsters? Or did he ask himself questions about his destiny, did he try to find a solution to the traps of Fate that had left him on his own, his comrades gone, the final mystery still to be solved, the doubt that lay within him? What is the hero's true adventure? Blinding the Cyclops, escaping Sirens, seducing goddesses, or is the challenge one of finding inner clarity, the truth about oneself, being accepted and understood as part of the nature of the world and the things that are in it? Perhaps Odysseus' bosun wasn't seeking his course up there, beyond the pulsating Pleiades and the Great and Little Bears, doubting his own vision, rubbing his salt-crusted lids, but wise in the knowledge that bound him to the heavenly vault? Faithful to his course, he would return home. Then, whatever bitterness might be hidden in his homeland, not even Father Zeus, not even Nux, the night that awaits us all, will be able to overcome us.

Back in barracks in Turin, rolled up on the deck of the rusty steamer that had brought me to Africa, in the watches of Bardia, lying on the soft sand of the desert, I had wondered about Odysseus' dreams as I went to sleep. Sleeping is hard in wartime. Even when you're completely worn out and you want only to plunge yourself silently into the darkness, you are held back by the anxiety that you might have made a mistake, and that you would die before dawn for that tiny mistake, perhaps you'd broken a little branch on patrol, forgotten about sentry duty, or miscalculated the trigonometry of the enemy's artillery camp. Or, worse, that that same mistake might cause the deaths of the men whom fate had entrusted to you. It's hard for a serious-minded officer to sleep in wartime.

Sometimes I tried to remember Zita, the professor, to meditate on logic and my sins, like Wittgenstein in Cambridge in 1911. Nothing worked. Sensuality was depressing. If it was sated, I was drained of energy, while if it was the object of my contemplation, it led to a painful comparison between my two lives, the happy one of earlier times and the present, piled with my comrades on a haystack that the British General Wavell was about to set alight along with our little fortress. It was then, at five o'clock on a freezing morning in December 1940, two weeks before the Australians caught me, that I dreamed the dreams of Odysseus. Wasn't he perhaps like us, a soldier in a war who had tried everything he could think of to avoid fighting, feigning madness and sowing his fields with grain? Perhaps he wasn't our sainted protector, the leader who stormed Troy, but simply one who gave his own name to a poem about the desperate, proud, shrewd, legendary need to return home. Thinking about Ulysses gave me courage – he had landed in Ithaca, after all, so why shouldn't I? On the afternoons spent on the liberty ship that took me to America, on the train that loudly crossed the new continent, bringing us prisoners to Hereford, I meditated upon Odysseus. He knew that power required violence, and abstained from it. He didn't like Agamemnon, he wanted to sail and live in the sun without any trouble. He won the war, he routed the suitors because he had to, but then he went to dwell far away, in search of peace.

My head banged hollowly against the wooden bench, and my thoughts and dreams became confused. What, in the end, did Odysseus dream about? His strategy for returning home, or the path to self-knowledge, the only voyage that everyone undertakes, even if they don't move an inch?

'Cigarette?'

I opened my eyes. In front of me I saw the soft face of the lieutenant in his American uniform.

What language had he spoken? Italian? In English, his officer's English, clipped, staccato, without the Texan drawl that I had learned to recognise in the speech of the *camans*? Or had he just held out a cigarette?

I took it, thanking him with a nod. The lieutenant got to his feet and gently closed the door of the compartment. He turned the knob, and came back to sit down. His uniform fitted him more comfortably now, it looked more like the gym kit of an adolescent athlete than the uniform of an officer in the most powerful army that had ever gone into battle in all the history of the world.

He took a single, intense drag. 'My friend, when are we going to start playing, you and I?'

His voice was deep and persuasive, the voice of a school-mate to whom you could confide your concerns and anxieties. I could have told him about my torment, I could have told him all about Zita and the professor, my escape, the war we had lost, and even asked him about the dreams of Odysseus, he might have known something about their nature. I opened and closed my mouth, as tuna do on the point of death, and not a word emerged. My life was beginning over again that day, and I didn't know it. The lieutenant brushed back his long, fair, feminine hair. 'You're an escaped Italian prisoner, I'd say, from Hereford Camp. I don't know how much money you've got, or what kind of papers you're carrying, but you've got one hell of a lucky streak if they haven't spotted you yet. Take a look at your trousers: you can still see the letters POW that you've tried to hide. What trick did you use? Toothpaste? Bicarb? I've seen them all. Listen, you've only got one choice: as I said when the Military Police came round, I'm going to New York. The armed forces have organised a radio station on 47th Street. Boogie-woogie, you know? Datadatadada-datata. It broadcasts in several languages including Italian. It reaches your country, both the parts that have been liberated and the parts still occupied by the Germans. But I didn't tell the MP everything. I was accompanying an Italian prisoner to New York, a goddam raw recruit. In civilian life this bastard was an actor. Beautiful voice, great diction, already famous. My mission? To escort him across the mighty United States, God bless them, and set him down in front of a microphone so that he could use that lovely instrument, that lovely bel canto voice of his to convince the people of Italy of the soundness of our cause.'

He fell silent for a moment. 'Of the Allied cause.'

'Where did you learn Italian? You've got a Tuscan accent.'

They were the first words I'd spoken in my own language, and I knew he'd got me.

'My father was the American consul in Florence, then a diplomat at the Court of St James in London, and that's how I learned my languages. I know half a dozen, including Hungarian, which is so difficult that it counts as four. Listen to me. I'm in trouble too. Not as much trouble as you, but in trouble nonetheless. And since we both speak the lovely tongue of your lovely country, give me a hand. This actor I was escorting, a little fascist who probably never fired a gun in his life, slipped through my fingers, as though plastered from head to toe in brilliantine. He used to keep that stuff in a little green tin, Linetti, two drops on the tips of his fingertips and off he went. I show up at the train station to give him his travelling document and he's gone. Vanished. I should have called the Military Police and given them a report, but I'm about to be transferred to Washington, to military headquarters, and then everything'll be fine. If I confess, who knows what's going to happen. They might send me off to the Pacific to fight my way through the jungle as a punishment. We've won the war, what's the point of stirring things up? Communication between Hereford and New York isn't good. I'm your luck, and you're mine. Luck, you know, fate. Did you go to high school? You did? *Ananke*, fate: that's me, my friend. Now we're heading for New York. You think the Military Police are going to stop us? Don't worry, I'm sorted for travel documents, and so are you, so we'll escort each other. If you say no, we're finished: you in a cell, me in Japan.'

I looked at him in silence.

'And when we're on 47th Street . . . ever been there? Most beautiful street in Manhattan, art galleries, bookshops and cafés full of German girls who have got away from Hitler. We'll go to the radio station there, you'll follow me meekly, I'll go in and get the permits released and you stay in the foyer. After they've stamped the receipt, mission accomplished, I open the door and, bingo!, you've gone. Except that I've got the documents validated, and you've made it through the bureaucracy. A free Italian in Manhattan, ties with Brooklyn, find yourself a mama to load you on to a Portuguese cargo ship, and you'll be in Naples before the feast of San Gennaro.'

I was fascinated by his perfect Italian, which was full of catchphrases and high-school-teacher Latinisms. I didn't reply. This time his smile was drawn, but convincing: it concealed real anxiety, perhaps even fear, for something he was about to lose.

I waited and looked out the window. It was no use. 'We haven't got too much time, my friend. Look.'

He threw the door open abruptly and pushed me outside. Two compartments further along was a new and immaculate patrol of Military Policemen, soldiers so tall their heads grazed the lights in the ceiling. 'Papers, papers, please, sir.'

The train slipped into a tunnel and my memory is full to the brim with that one shrill whistle.

7

My journey with the lieutenant lasted for forty days and forty nights. At the time I didn't realise that between our first meeting and its distant epilogue on the Atlantic coast, precisely forty dawns would pass, the time that the Bible assigns to the all-engulfing flood before the pale dove returns to Noah's Ark with its olive branch in its beak, after crossing the watery world, bearing witness to the end of divine wrath. Nor did I see the rainbow, an earnest of the covenant between man and God. But I did see the great Mississippi River and the Ozark forests, populated by fabulous snakes – 'They can swallow a whole kid and spit out its horns,' Sergeant Carraway confided to me. Aboard that long train I passed the dykes of the Tennessee Valley, the pink clay, the dark blue lakes and the trees that bend over the still water, so still that their leaves fall gently and stick perfectly to the surface. I ate in station coffee shops, creamy potato soup, watery black coffee, octopus ink, my grandmother used to call it, still caffeine-rich enough to keep me awake, eyes open to look at the clear sky. Not so the lieutenant: he slept, unconcerned with the dreams of Odysseus. For forty days and forty nights I saw him sleeping motionless like that, as though he just had to flick off the switch of a lamp to be dead to the world. We endured dangers and worries, passion and grief, each of which would have been enough to fill the whole lives of many human beings. And yet, as on that day with the Military Police, the moment the lieutenant closed his eyes, sleep settled on his mind like a black shroud. Who he really was and what drove him across the United States, eastwards today, westwards tomorrow, I didn't understand at the time. But even today, from the false and reassuring position of someone judging the past from the perspective of the future, the lieutenant, with his motives and intentions, still seems to be beyond my comprehension. The only memento I have of him, the only proof that our forty-day migration across the great continent was not a dream, a fabric of my imagination, is a souvenir that I am holding here. A pinch of sand. I look at it again, and it's as though I sense that he contained a seed of all the virtues that make the human soul magnificent, an ounce of every noble and dignified feeling, the Virtus and the Gratia that a father and mother would always hope to recognise in their children.

It wasn't like that at the time. Then, he was an officer of the Allied army which had defeated my boys in Bir el Gobi and Bardia and which would shortly – I had no illusions on the matter – govern the whole world, the Europe of my youth and my mathematical calculations and the America that passed quickly before my eyes: the sharecroppers at work in the fields, the chain-gangs working their picks and shovels at the side of the railroad track, skinny soldiers in khaki uniforms, lined up under every railway awning kissing their emotional girlfriends goodbye. That army was a giant washed with white soap, ignorant of the ways of the world, tranquil in its decision to battle for freedom.

I had spent my childhood in La Tonnara, looking on enchanted as the master-carpenter launched the *gozzi*, the brightly coloured fishermen's boats, with pretty names. *Maria*, *Laura*, sweet names that contrasted the harsh fates that awaited them, tossed about beneath Orion in the Sicilian Channel, fleeing storms in pursuit of swordfish and finally, when the summer heat prevailed again, hunting down the joyfully swimming tuna. The carpenter carved the wood, engraving with his gimlet, planing severely, shavings fell like snow on the sea, bright dots of sawdust in the December wind and then, when the Christmas fireworks were forgotten, glazed the skeleton, fixed the keel and the planking, painting with precise brushstrokes the colours of the rainbow: red, indigo, blue and yellow. The pungent smell of varnish filled my nostrils like a drug. I looked up, it was summer already, and the boat, or lovely *Maria* or *Laura*, was sliding into the water to feed a family.

Here, in America, the steel ships were stamped in the morning, at the hour of the Alborada, and launched at Vespers. They were called liberty ships, and, however speedily the U-boats of our German allies dispatched them to the bottom of the ocean, where Thetis and the Nereides danced, the war still would be won by those housewives and unemployed blacks who built them, sisters and brothers of the sharecroppers bent over the cotton that I saw from my passing train.

Now my memories run by me in fragments, the lieutenant and what I saw of the wagons and the locomotives, the stops on our forty-day journey and my recollections as a little boy, a vain nostalgia for another world, another sea. Far away, chaotic, terrible. A prisoner and yet at the same time a safe conduct for my guard, who said he had lost his first Italian quarry, I lived in a state of perfect, constant lucidity, every moment of my life present in the wide-open spaces of America. The colours of the tuna fishermen's boats poured over the grey steel of the liberty ships and I, a prisoner, saw my resignation and disappointment in Hereford Camp 1 making way for an obsessive, nervous awareness. I had to get to the coast, to New York. There I would escape the lieutenant's attention, before he had second thoughts and broke our agreement. If he tried anything smart, I would tie him up, I would smack him right between his courteous eyes and get away.

Zita was a shore, Europe a coast, my memories drew me there, waves that had floated me over the barbed wire and beyond the guards, and would take me all the way to Italy to put a stop to Professor Barbaroux's wedding.

I had probably gone crazy, afflicted for forty days by a form of early-onset dementia. Hunted down on the pier, I would calmly try to walk on the waters of the iron Atlantic. Dying, escaping, performing acts of madness, nothing seemed ridiculous or impossible to me. And in any case, when I had left for Africa with my regiment, hadn't I thought it impossible that Italy might lose the war, ending up divided and occupied? And yet that was what had happened.

The lieutenant stared into my eyes, reading my thoughts. 'You know Plutarch?'

'Yes.'

'The *Life of Brutus*?'

'No.'

'Read it when you have a moment. And tell me what you think of it.'

He handed me a green book, a Loeb. Plutarch, Greek text on the cover. Our train slipped through the night and I read about Brutus' youth, his rebellion against Caesar's hegemony. The ambush, Casca trembling as he struck the hero with his sword, Brutus taking his weapon and running it through the body of his adoptive father, and the conspirators lurching back in horror. Brutus strikes first, Caesar falls, he could have shouted – 'Stand back, dogs!' – his voice had once given heart to the legionaries below the walls of Alesia and aroused terror and respect in the barbarian forests. Caesar could have grabbed the sword from the cowardly Casca, and defended himself as he had in his fray with Vercingetorix. Instead, he wrapped his toga around him as a shroud and allowed himself to be felled. Only then did the terrorists take courage and strike, and when Antony shows the cloth to the crowd, every rip a dagger blow, like a Lucio Fontana canvas painted by political savagery.

Then comes the war and the defeat of the democratic illusion. Brutus meditates on suicide, and before he dies he studies the firmament, praying to heaven with two lines, 'Oh Jove, do not forget the man from whom this mischief flowed!' The second line of Brutus' farewell to the world has not been passed down to us, the medieval copyists accidentally left it out. What might he have written?

The lieutenant looked at me, and I lost myself in the muddle of my uncertainty. How could the boatwright's coloured vessels have subdued the democracy of the liberty ships?

The lieutenant said, 'That forgotten line that Brutus spoke – what do you think it might be? If we discovered it, in a dusty codex in one of your southern Italian abbeys, we'd understand which is more important, Luck or Bravery: I'm sure of it.'

Thus began our forty days across America, 'rich in Virtue and poor in Luck', as the infantrymen wrote on their memorial at El Alamein. The lieutenant looking for his line of Brutus, me looking for a ship to save my shipwrecked love and my life itself by interpreting the dreams of Odysseus in the lost war.

8

The girls were sitting at the corner table of the coffee shop. The slimmest one was drinking black Coke from a frosted glass: she sucked gently on the straw, eyes fixed on a point straight ahead of her and then opened her red lips and sucked again. The fairest one struck her fingers lightly on the gleaming table, tap tap tap, the middle, ring and index fingers, then the middle one again in counterpoint, tap tap tap. She was wearing a skirt that bared her knees, soft and round. Last of all, in the shade, a glimpse of her, the smallest one. Not the prettiest, perhaps: she neither drank nor followed the rhythm of the big band brass section that blared from the Bakelite radio. Her hair was short, and hung in a fringe over her slanted, oriental eyes. She filled the space with her face and her hands and her breasts and her thighs, as though the air were water that could support her and make her float. As though, all of a sudden, she might swim: a little dive on her cork-soled shoes and away, with quick and lazy strokes up to the fan that flapped on the ceiling, slothfully stirring the hot air. The girl would brush the beer bottles on the highest shelf with her skirt floating, she would swirl out of the bar, away over the burning earth of Hot Springs in the dusty state of Arkansas.

Her energy was apparent from her perfect stillness: like a swamp alligator, ready to strike from its motionless tree-trunk stability, descending with a whipcrack on its prey, and yet a moment before framed and lost in the hot mud. That was what the girl with the oriental eyes was like, or at least that's how I remember her now as I write about my first moment with her. Rather than trying to imagine her face again, I'm trying to feel the heat and emotion I felt then, which some of my gentle readers will have felt on at least one day of their lives, when they met their 'twin soul' as Plato would say, the other sexual half that we all have, from which we were parted at some time in the distant past. Today I feel that emotion again, in its entirety.

I looked at her, I fully expected her to dive away and swim in an erotic crawl, free from gravity, in that banal café in the shadow of the wild Ozark Mountains. It's certainly possible, even likely, that my memory has been falsified by my forty-day journey, and by what I later experienced with her. The reality was probably quite different. An ordinary Italian fool, defeated in the desert sand, broken in the Bardia winter, was seeing beautiful young girls for the first time in years, was free to observe them without hierarchy or hindrance. A prisoner of war spends his time thinking about women, forgets what women are really like. In the camp, I would wake with a vision of Zita before my eyes, summon the patience to stand in the queue for the latrine, keep a firm grip on my memory of those hours of mathematical analysis on the creaking wooden table because Zita and her perfume and her flesh existed beyond the sea and, in darkness when I was in the Texan sun, in light while I slept in the breathless night of the camp, she too trod the planet with feet that I would greedily have kissed in the shadow of the *faraglioni*.

That was how I had lived, as a free man and a prisoner, until she had decided to marry Professor Barbaroux, and then my fate too had been captured, along with my future as a POW. No one could possibly bear that two-fold imprisonment, knowing that one was a prisoner in the present and the future, without paying the price of madness or resignation. So I had escaped, into the great concentration camp of real life and the jokes it plays, vaster and more cruel than Hereford.

The lieutenant's voice rang out in a singsong: 'Here we are in Hot Springs, in Arkansas. This is where the wounded and the convalescents of America come to regain their lost health. Europe cripples them in war, the springs restore them. No one will notice us here. We can rest. We've a long way to go before we get to New York.'

He got up and winked at the table of girls. 'What kind of GIs are we if we don't cat around? Chastity will get us noticed.'

The three girls gave the lieutenant a chilly welcome, edging up to let him sit down. The most spirited of them shook his hand and started to chatter.

I was left alone at our table. A prisoner or free man? I couldn't work it out, but I wasn't willing to lose my only true feeling of independence: my pain over Zita and the decision to cross the USA in captivity, all for her.

The coffee was good, the apple tart fragrant. From the back of the gleaming wooden room came the notes of a song that one of the girls was singing in a low voice, accompanying the radio. One of the songs in vogue that spring, with the kind of sweet refrain and sentimental words that made girls cry. 'I heard that lonesome train whistle blow . . .'

Better to stay and look at the light outside the door, Main Street shining in the sulphurous dust of the springs. Then I felt the smallest girl's hand on my thigh, just where I had traced the three letters POW with toothpaste, then rubbed them out as I prepared to escape. The fabric was worn away by washing with the regulation fatty yellow soap and hours flapping on a line over the prairie, a banner of forgotten poverty, while we sat on a step with a letter clutched in our fists and our eyes lost somewhere beyond the water tower. It was as though the girl's hand was Zita's, and the soft veil of military beige heightened its warmth, its gentleness, its life.

No one ever touches a prisoner's body except to inflict violence, or some kind of punishment. The responses of the *camans* to a vague gesture of protest, the rough jostling of your comrades as you queue for an egg, the acrid stench of disinfectants, the thorny blankets and, when you're in transit, the hardness of the benches, the bumps of the wagons, the steel needles of the vaccine that welcome you to the camp.

Months without seeing, or speaking to, or breathing the air of a woman. There were the girls employed at the camp orderly office, resolute and cheerful Texans. They considered the Italian men with a certain fascination. Certainly they despised us – 'Happy go lucky!' they called us – but then some of them fell in love with the lieutenants and sergeants with their glistening hair. The Italians sang, they were nice, they didn't kiss as though they were chewing gum, and when it was dark they knew the names of all the stars, or if they didn't know them they knew how to name them passionately after Mary, Lucy or Joy. After the war, many American girls went to join their heartthrobs in Naples, and emotional nuptials were celebrated.

One day two secretaries came to Camp 1, where the hard-liners were kept, and sat down on our benches. They stretched out their nylon-clad legs on the freshly swept floor, forcing us to climb over their calves and gleaming heels. Perhaps it was a bet, perhaps it was indifference, or perhaps one of them was in love with one of the prisoners. Then they left, in their best regulation posture, and Fefe, the funniest one of all of us, Fefe who had seen his Captain Urbani in Africa sodomised in an act of reprisal by Moroccan guards, French Souaves, stretched himself out on a bench groaning, rubbing himself on the wood and whimpering while we laughed.

I didn't see the hand that drew its fingers across my leg as though drawing a tattoo. I kept my eyes on the sulphurous road, and felt the blood stirring inside my pants. But before the sense of excitement, which ran free and strong, I felt tenderness and compassion for my skin, recruited in Rome, battered by sea-storms, tanned in two deserts, leathery skin that knew the corrosive sand and the tough showers and the hasty thread of the Venetian nurse who sewed me up. 'Christ alive, it's just a scratch, the poor guy in the bed next to you hasn't got legs to mend.'

And now, just below the white marks of that scar, sharply drawn by British shrapnel, like the footprints of a steel-footed sparrow, the girl's hand lingered. Almost imperceptibly she tightened her grip, and the shiver that followed did more to open me up than the sudden explosion of a grenade, a cry for help, a barked command. It pierced my resignation as a prisoner, it cut through the pain at my abandonment. However my hunting season might have gone, I still had a heart. Was that good or bad news?

Recalling her now, the girl, H.S., that was her name, seems liquid to me. At night, when the cold mistral splits the shutters of my bedroom and wakes me, I find myself thinking about her once again. Her diaphanous weightlessness fills my empty mind. I run through our days, few in number but crucial in our lives, and H.S. ethereally expands, like a piece of origami, the beautiful swan with the sinuous neck that she folded out of paper after making love. Like the few poetic words she prayed to her Buddha. In the pockets of her silk trousers she had a little Buddha of Happiness, who crossed the world smiling, his bag of suffering held tightly on his back. 'He gives me my courage,' she said.

We made love immediately after our meeting in the coffee shop. There were two rough rooms upstairs, and the lieutenant, with a wink, had gone ahead of me. She took me by the hand, and when she did so her hand didn't seem to touch me.

I wasn't a great Casanova, and twelve hundred nights of war had done nothing to sharpen my skills as a seducer. I lay on the little bed, a basic affair like the one on which I slept next to Ferrucci, and kept my hands behind the back of my neck. She opened my khaki shirt, one button at a time, and exposed my chest. I was lean, God knows, muscular, smooth, strengthened by privations and effort, my body was like a weapon. H.S. took off her clothes with a single prima donna movement, a tunic that weighed no more than a scarf, and was suddenly naked on top of me. I can't recall, scouring my memory, whether she rested on my crotch or my thighs, or whether she floated around me like a hummingbird. She rose to lick me and – I had to do something, or at least that was what they had told me on the Island – I sought the buckle of my belt with trembling hands.

'Let me,' said H.S., and unhooked it by herself. She moved her body as though merely rearranging her hair, a brief shadowy movement and I was inside her.

They still come to me on nights when the mistral blows. Why are memories so weightless? Even the tragic ones, even the painful ones? If I think of Bardia, when I fell into the hands of the Australians, at the age of twenty, all I hear is the machine-gunner whimpering, 'Do we surrender, Manè? Do we surrender or do I fire, Manè?' I don't remember when I had fired all the rounds in the magazine, in accordance with military regulations, 'Fire to the last round before surrendering', and I really did fire the last cartridge, yes, sir, I, the student of the socialist Professor Barbaroux, fired until the barrel of the Breda was red hot and we were out of ammunition. I remember none of that. I only remember the silence, what could be sweeter than silence, what could be harder to reassemble in the memory? And my gunner lying face down on the sand, arms open, motionless and cruciform. I saw the sand thrown up by gusts of wind, one, two, three, and I didn't see the enemy. Faceless and nameless: they would acquire faces and names only in prison. Not in war, just being the enemy was enough, they fired and we fired back. Finally the outlines come, the target shooting – mortal targets – assumes the guise of humanity, they strip us of our watches and pile us up in open railway carriages, so that the indigenous people can spit on us, the only chance they will ever get to humiliate a white man.

So: to remember those moments I have to make an effort of reason, I have to use thought as a compass. If I close my eyes and look out the window on to the unlit gulf, both within and without, and then open my lids, nothing changes, the darkness enfolds me. Of the girl, H.S., I am aware of the lightness with which she unhooked my belt, the sparrow's flutter with which she settled on my chest, and the lightness with which she made love to me. Of my capture, I see sand flying suddenly from the crest of a dune, then again, every second, and the machine-gunner embracing Mother Earth and praying as he awaits a Mediterranean divinity, while the enemy advances cautiously and victoriously towards us, certain prey in the desert.

We are all prey to memories, which we cannot alter, and which wait for us like bookkeepers, precise collectors of debits and credits. Are they worth more than real events? No, what matters is the story we forge for ourselves in our memories. At Camp 1 my gunner – 'Do I shoot, Manè? Do I shoot?' – never spoke to me again, he didn't want to poison our battling past with our captive present. Ciao, and that's that. So I can't tell you if the girl was as graceful as I remember, or whether I only perceived her carnality, her taut skin, her slanting oriental eyes. I was sure, and I still am, that H.S. was the most beautiful creature that the Lord God had ever put on earth. The privilege of finding her and the perennial bitterness at losing her will be the last memories to abandon me in the few days I still have left. In 1944 I didn't think that way, I was young. And yet when the girl circled about me, my body tensed and I thought, 'You're happy now, remember, remember, remember.'

You might think it wise for a boy to be so precisely aware of his states of mind of sorrow and happiness. But I bitterly regret it. It's true: rare among human beings, I possess a precise memory of happiness, a lucid awareness of having perceived vivid joy. But searing within me I also feel the regret, the emptiness that comes afterwards.

Perhaps the girl was carnal, her womanly ardour certainly was. And perhaps I was innocent, my eccentric escape for love certainly was. That lightness means everything to me: it is, and will remain, my life, the life of Giovanni Manes.

The next memory, a flash after her hands on my belt, is the

mocking blond head of the lieutenant: 'Still here? What a fuss you Italians make!' And he starts singing Puccini, to my horror, in the purest Italian: 'Oh! Sweet kisses, oh languid caresses, and I, trembling, unveiled those beautiful forms . . .'

We paid the girls. I hadn't even asked her name, if weightlessness has a name. We took a bus at six o'clock, perhaps a day later we would make it to Nashville and from there to Baltimore, Washington and New York. The sun was high, the wooden footpaths deserted. The lieutenant and I the only ones who walked them, in our light shoes, in silence, drained by love after so much solitude. My head was bowed in confusion when I felt a gentle touch on my arm. A dark-coloured car was coming towards us. The lieutenant pushed me maternally into a grocer's shop full of dried-up vegetables. He picked up the bowl that was used to weigh the green, green peas, and plunged it into the big brimming sack. As soon as the car had passed he led me to the next shop, through the door and into the post office. 'They're after us,' he said gently.

'But aren't your documents in order?'

I looked at him uncertainly. What had gone wrong with his perfect plan?

'It's better to stay out of trouble.'

The flight from shop to shop couldn't go on for ever: the Buick stopped to check the crossroads that led to the bus stop, where two Chicanos were waiting.

The lieutenant set off in the opposite direction, but that part of the world was a papier-mâché chessboard, white, black, white, a few moves and checkmate. Reflected in the glass of the barber's shop, I saw our pursuers' car heading straight towards us. The air filled with a mechanical hubbub: a farmer's truck, fully laden with crisp bales of yellow hay. It braked in front of us, and the right door opened. The driver was the girl, H.S. Barely moving, she beckoned us in. Lying on the truck floor, we slipped by, invisible to the street. I looked up, and in the rear-view mirror I glimpsed two officers, at the wheel, a mean-looking dark-haired man with a thin moustache, beside him an uneasy-looking adolescent. Leaving a trail of yellow dust behind us, we headed into the desert light. A haggard coyote barked a warning, but didn't bother to follow us. He hobbled away, one of his legs stiffened by an ancient trap.

9

They reached the prisoner-of-war camp in Amarillo, north of Texas, at about three in the afternoon. Colonel Downing brought them into his study with a great display of energy. 'Gentlemen, I won't waste your time. There's no point in my repeating the life story of the man you're after. I know that General Matthews has already outlined it for you. He escaped from this camp ten days ago. He changes languages the way he changes shirts. He's pleasant and stylish. Everyone here loves him. Read the report by our inside informer: I haven't yet had a chance to pass it on to the general.'

He handed them a sheet of thin paper, with holes typed in it corresponding to the letters 'e' and 'o'. Out of respect for his rank, Cheever let Cafard take the sheet first, but Cafard handed it to him without so much as a glance.

'Our agent, Dieffe, maintains that Lieutenant Commander Hans von Luck is heading for the Atlantic coast . . .' Cheever was still reading, and Cafard mockingly questioned the colonel. 'How can your agents, locked away in a camp, tail a fugitive many miles away?'

'Don't underestimate the Nazis, Major. They have under-cover radios, they use secret codes.'

'The Italians have a radio that we haven't managed to confis-cate. I'd never heard that the Germans had one, too.'

'They can prepare any kind of fake document. Look.'

Downing, irritated by Cafard's incredulous tone, opened the box and took out half a withered potato. He handed it to Cheever by way of reply: carved into the tuber was the security stamp of the American Military Command, the precious mark that guaranteed members of the armed forces free transit across the United States.

'You want a hunting licence? A passport? A few fresh po-tatoes and they can reproduce the whole fucking Washington bureaucracy, you bet they can.'

'Can we interrogate this . . .' Cafard tried to find the right phrase for a moment, feigning uncertainty, and Downing wondered, 'Is this bastard having me on?'

'. . . this agent of ours?'

Cheever, disciplined and embarrassed, handed him the perforated sheet of paper, which Cafard stuffed into his pocket.

'Ah, no, that's out of the question. Are you kidding me?' Downing saw himself regaining his advantage, and used it skilfully. 'What did you have in mind? Call him into the main barracks and expose him in front of his comrades? Within a few hours the Gestapo inside the camp would have him in the blanket. I hope you know what I mean by the blanket?'

Colonel Downing smiled grimly: tough cops from the spy

department, you talk and talk, and then all of a sudden you drop the psychological warfare in favour of actual violence.

'General Matthews mentioned that. Can I ask you, Colonel, how you tolerate such practices in an American prisoner-of-war camp, governed by the rules of the Geneva Convention?'

Cheever had spoken unexpectedly, thrusting his chest forwards: and Cafard made a mental note of how young he was, or at least how young he looked when he blushed.

Downing dropped the third lump of sugar into the white and blue ceramic cup, sipped the piping-hot tea and stared at the young upstart. 'Captain, I hope that in your months of service they have taught you that our job is to obey orders. In my thirty-three years in uniform I think I've learned that discipline is more important than anything else. You know what my mandate is? To keep order in this camp, do you understand that? I'm not playing politics, I'm not talking about values. I have two thousand prisoners under me. So far not a single escape, not one revolt, no trouble of any kind. And if the Nazis help me do my duty, so much the worse for them. Have you talked to my friend Rogers, who's in charge of the Italian camp in Hereford? He thinks along the same lines as me.'

'I thought von Luck escaped . . .' remarked Cafard.

'Apart from him, apart from him, of course,' Downing butted in harshly. 'But you're going to catch him, aren't you? If the Gestapo can keep the hotheads under control then everything's okay. The result isn't always positive. Often the Nazis are the best ones at keeping the camps in order. You transfer them somewhere else and out come the socialists and the communists. They hold discussions, they debate, they print fliers and newspapers. And they argue, God knows they argue. It gets impossible to enforce the rules. A good Nazi colonel behind the barbed wire and everything runs smoothly, from reveille to lights-out. Have you ever visited the camps where our compassionate President Roosevelt has gathered together the soldiers who call themselves anti-Nazis? Take a look, gentlemen, believe me, it'll be a fine experience. Debates, newspapers, even film screenings. There are communists in there! You know that Hitler, finding himself short of men, sent the *Strafbataillon* to Africa? It was a punishment battalion formed from socialists held in the camps, freed and set to work in uniform. Well, the moment they saw our men they surrendered: "We're not going to fight for the Nazis," and their camps are a bedlam of demonstrations, meetings, university courses. Set the Krauts free, and that mechanism that led them to Weimar and Nazism? They'll set it in motion all over again. I have no doubt that your generation will be able to repeat all those problems in Europe once the war's over. But not in my camp, no, sir. Everything here is in order. Gestapo or no Gestapo. You cause trouble, you're finished. Finished,' repeated Downing, satisfied by his tirade.

Cafard interrupted him, as though he hadn't even been listening. 'Commander.' His accent sounded sinister to Cheever's ears. 'You will be aware, I hope, that for all we know this informant of yours might be a provocateur, a double agent. You won't even allow us to see him and he's pulling our leg on behalf of the Gestapo. With your permission, I'd like to show you my orders.'

He set General Matthews' letter down on the table: 'Grant Major Cafard and Captain Cheever full and unlimited access to the prisoner-of-war camps, to identify traces and clues relating to the escape of a dangerous Nazi prisoner of uncertain identity, perhaps Lieutenant Commander Hans von Luck, and leading to his capture.'

'Now you will let us get to work, thank you.'

Having said which he got to his feet, making Cheever leap to attention, and walked out into the sunlight.

The camp was organised around a central unit, designed by some rational bureaucrat in Washington, and from there it spread out to all the various prisoner centres. A wide, central, dust-covered avenue, narrow wooden boardwalks like the ones you see in Hollywood westerns, a sports camp, a canteen full of merchandise adjoining the mess, the rows of barracks and, in the distance, the gleaming concrete punishment block. Directly opposite, the chapel for religious functions.

A game of football was being played in the square. One team wore the khaki jersey, white vest and baggy trousers of the German Afrika Korps. The other, bare-chested and in green shorts, all of them tanned by the sun of two continents. Germany against Italy.

The khaki winger dashed rapidly down the white touchline. He tackled an opponent, who fell to the ground with a grunt, then pelted to the end of the pitch and, from there, with a twist of his chest he fired off a light cross. His mate in the middle of the field made as if to jump, caught the ball with his fore-head and shot it into the net. The joy at the goal was fierce and exasperated, the joy of people accustomed for years to emotions of cruelty. The scorer was hurled to the ground, and the team piled into him, mocking the defeated men, who stood gloomy in the midfield. The referee's whistle signalled the end of the game. The furious goalkeeper kicked the ball, which rose straight up into the sky, hovered for a second and fell back heavily towards the two American officers. Cheever tried to block it with his hands, but Cafard stepped in front of him like a shadow, softening the sphere's parabola with his left heel and sending it gently into the arms of the German winger who, exhausted from running, was still sitting on the ground. 'I didn't know that Yankees played with the back heel.'

'Come here,' murmured Cafard, with the tone of someone who's sure he will be obeyed.

The man came over, the leather ball held tightly in his strong, broad fingers. He confronted Cafard fearlessly. 'Yes?'

'Salute,' ordered Cafard. The rules decreed that military prisoners always saluted enemy officers.

A smile spread across the footballer's lips. But salute he did. It was the German salute, which was envied by the American officers at West Point Academy, and which the great mass of Allied civilians, geometers, rationalists, teachers of grammar, uniformed assistants in the major stores, found unbearable. Harsh, stylish, starched, the body tending to attention, respectful of hierarchy, in the calm anxiety of the war machine.

'At ease,' Cheever said quietly, embarrassed by the scene.

'Where do you come from?' Cafard launched in.

'Danzig, sir.'

'I asked you where you came from.'

Without answering, the man rummaged in the Saharan jacket he had left on the ground and, with a sun-bronzed hand, held out a little grey card, his identity *Soldbuch*.

Beneath the dry wrinkles, his eyes were green and hot. He stayed silent, looking covertly at his comrades, who were heading for the mess in noisy clusters.

'You know Commander von Luck?' Cafard asked in German, nodding to the boy to give him the ball. He quickly chipped it at him. Cafard checked it with the inside of his foot and softly, with the instep drive, returned it.

'So?'

'I know him.'

'Were you together in the submarines?'

'You'd have to check the date of capture. We ran out of fuel off Long Island. If that hadn't happened you'd have a few bathtubs less, and I'd be playing football in Kiel.'

He checked the ball with his thin chest, and turned to face Cafard.

'Are you fond of him?'

Cheever was astounded: Cafard was interrogating this boy, playing football with him and asking him if he was fond of the escaped man.

'Have you ever served in a U-boat, sir? It isn't a good place to be fond of your comrades. Too cramped. It's hard to like people you recognise by their stench.'

'Are you fond of him or aren't you?'

'Yes, I am.'

'Friends in the camp as well?'

'I'd got used to his stench.'

'Why didn't you escape with him?'

'Why? He's escaped? I didn't know.'

Cafard caught the ball on his forehead, let it slip over his right shoulder, down to his foot, flipped it up and caught it on his other shoulder, slid it on to his knee and back to the ground. 'Son, Americans don't know how to play soccer. Hungarians do. So listen to me. Whatever identity von Luck has managed to assume during his stay in the camps, having himself transferred and assuming new names each time he moved on, I have good reason to maintain that you do know him.'

'Like what?'

'Like he's your brother. You were on the team together at Florence University. You played on the right wing, your brother was in goal. In a friendly in 1936, in Rome, you beat Cambridge.' Cafard held the ball towards the boy, staring fixedly at him. 'You scored a fine goal. And your brother did some great saves. In the last minute of play, they tell me.'

'I've got to go, excuse me. The mess is great, but the cook hates latecomers, and we're having sausages today.'

Cheever followed him carefully, concealing his embarrassment. Where did Cafard get his information from? What game was he playing? The ball landed in the German's hands.

'You know Sergeant Carraway? He's from your parts, he's

on our side, but he speaks your language. He's busy developing links between the German and Italian camps. If you get any clearer ideas about your brother, talk to him. There's no need to have a meeting in front of the other prisoners. Carraway won't refer you to Commander Rogers, or to your man Downing and his tittle-tattles, who would end up alerting the Nazis. Just a quiet chat, you, Carraway, me, three quick passes, just like in a game of football.'

The boy smiled. 'You know everything already. My brother, the story of the game, whether the linesman had piles. What am I supposed to inform you about?'

Cheever was horrified to see, exposed to the hot sun, the secret sheet of paper, the prize of Colonel Downing's counter-espionage campaign. 'Read this,' said Cafard, 'it's a coded message from your guys. It's about your brother, it calls him a dangerous terrorist, on a mission to sabotage military posts and spread panic among the civilians. Whoever supplied this information, one of your fellow prisoners, perhaps someone on the team here in the camp, is begging us to condemn him to death. Take care, he's a dangerous saboteur, shoot first, ask questions later. Message received: whoever catches him is going to kill him. Of course that may well be how things are. Colonel Downing's sure of it. And on the other hand, perhaps the Gestapo in the camp want to throw us off the scent. To make us give your brother hell. Could be, I'm not sure. Carraway says that's the state of play. You know more than I do. If you felt like helping your brother, him, not me, I have a sense that this time you'd be the one to save the penalty kick. Talk to

Carraway about it. Me, you, him. Quick game. By the way, you are Italian, aren't you?'

'Yes, sir.'

'So how come you've got a German *Soldbuch*? Is it fake?'

'No, sir. Some of our submarines, and all our crews, were seconded to the Germans by Italian Navy Command. I don't think I'm giving away a military secret when I say that. I was with them, and when they took us prisoner I chose to stay with my comrades. None of them have ever asked me any questions. I speak German, and I organise these matches among the ex-Allies. That's all. Any problems?'

'No problem,' said Cafard sardonically. 'And von Luck was with you at Danzig. Sooner or later you'll tell me who he really is. Don't hold out, or he'll be killed. Remember: we will win the war not because we're better fighters than you, quite the contrary. But because democracy works better than dictatorship. Your courage doesn't make you right. Trust me.'

Cheever didn't know how to conduct an inquiry using these unorthodox methods. But he was a good psychologist, and his kindly soul read fear and uncertainty in the eyes of the Nazi, the Italian, or whoever this strange prisoner might be.

10

The sun was setting behind the wretched asbestos-roofed shacks. A Baptist preacher was reading in the church square, shading himself from the last rays with a straw hat. The breviary in his hand contained the whole of his faith, but the man broke off his prayer and gazed wordlessly into the distance. The girl drove carefully, neither too quickly nor too cautiously, changing direction by instinct, along the red clay tracks between the fields and down the steep mule paths, into the hills. She seemed to be driving entirely at random. Several times I thought I saw the boulder from which the lame coyote had mocked us, but we weren't lost. H.S.'s spiral led us to a remote and sheltering canopy of yellow branches. It was impossible to spot from the road, while we had a wide view of the horizon. The door creaked unsteadily on its hinges, an old varnished plank served as a front door. It was the boundary between two worlds. Outside, the southern USA, hot and brightly coloured. Inside, the Orient. No furniture, apart from two tatami mats unrolled on the floor, a dark-coloured wicker box and three silk-screen panels, decorated with a fishing junk vainly pursuing a silver whale. At the end of the room, the ash from some incense sticks burned in honour of a Buddha that cast a knowing eye upon our fugitive group. I knew who he was from my school books, but I'd never met him before.

The lieutenant lit the cigarette between his trembling fingers.

'You'll leave as soon as you can. For a few days the cops have been in the streets. They've been looking for new faces. The only ones I've seen are yours,' said the girl.

'Thanks for the lift, miss,' said the lieutenant, 'but we aren't actually escaping. Can't you see? I'm an officer, and I'm escorting an Italian prisoner.'

'Really? It's the first time I've ever seen an officer allowing a prisoner to visit a whore.' That was what she said, 'whore', and my heart clenched. Didn't this girl's grace defy such a word? She sat down cross-legged, wrapped in her dark purple tunic. In this place she was the boss, the queen, the desert nymph.

'You'll sleep here. Tomorrow I'll take you as far as the pass, and you'll get to Memphis by coach or train. When the Military Police stop you, just tell them you're an officer, and tell them what language you use in bed. But if the OSS officers catch you out there, it isn't going to be so easy to pull the wool over their eyes.'

The lieutenant blushed. I didn't understand and, to mask my embarrassment, I asked, 'Where do you come from?'

'My father was American. My mother is Japanese. I have two brothers in the army, in Europe, and a sister in California, in the concentration camps set up for us

Orientals. I managed to escape all that, I've got a western face. I can get on with my life. My brother, who is Japanese as well, used to play the piano. I expect he's dead somewhere in Italy. The Military Police came to get him, they wouldn't let him take his musical scores with him but he didn't care. "I'll see the Greek temples at Paestum," he said. "It'll be beautiful."'

H.S. didn't look either at me or the lieutenant, concentrating instead on a point in the distance that was invisible to us. 'I hate Washington and the Military Police. If they're after you, I'll give you a hand.'

I stared at the lieutenant. If he really was an American officer, why didn't he arrest the girl for treason? In wartime you can be put away for less. He stared back, smiling as ever. 'Nino, our mission is unusual. If we start showing our papers to any stupid cop, how long is it going to take us to get to Manhattan? This isn't about playing by the rules, it's about saving our skins. Time is moving on, and in a few days our travel permits will be invalid. Look –' and he held them out so that I could see them.

They looked real enough to me.

We slept separated by the silk-screen whale hunt. I said to the girl, in a whisper, 'Will you come with me to New York?'

'Why?' she said, leaning on one elbow, amused.

'Life's terrible here. The war's about to end.'

'You want a lover to escape with?'

'I don't even know why I am escaping any more. This lieutenant picked me up, sure, but now he says we have to stay together and that we're going to make it. I'm following him, and we've made it this far.'

I told her about Zita and Barbaroux. She smiled with pity. 'You're following someone you no longer know, across an enemy country, towards a love you've lost, but you're sleeping with me. You're either a madman or a saint, or both.'

She touched my forehead, as though taking my temperature. 'Whichever it is, let me stroke you: saints and madmen bring good luck.'

'Why do you say my love is lost?'

'Because you're running away. You're not trying to stop her getting married to this professor.'

'Then where am I going?'

'You're chasing the boy you were before the war. We were all different then. Young, clean. We didn't know what men were like. I'm resigned to it all. You aren't. You're running away across the sea, hoping to interrupt the marriage ceremony of a woman who doesn't belong to you, and magically rediscover yourself as a boy. You can't succeed.'

She still held her fingers pressed hard against my face: and it was the only time in all the memory I have of the hours I spent with her that I noticed gravity in her gestures, ardour, the heavy material that is our lives, and of which she herself was happily free.

'The only thing that's lost is us. The children we were before the war. The past doesn't belong to us. We believe it does because we are foolish and frightened, because the feeble darkness of memory terrifies us less than the light of the coming dawn.

Think of the magicians, the oracles, prophecies and horoscopes that we consult. Look at my cards, the I Ching, the signs of the water diviner: we are seeking the keys of the future, which is light and doesn't weigh us down, and we escape the past as quickly as we can. Memories confuse us, the future eludes us. My sisters are held captive by their past, just as you are. And yet you are escaping in order to return, to become the boy who had no memory of the barbed wire. You won't find him again.'

I had before me the most beautiful woman I had ever seen. It was quite natural for her to crouch above me and take me tenderly inside her. And now she was explaining to me that everything I was doing was in vain. Why?

'If you turned up before the wedding, what would you say to Zita?'

'Don't do it. He's not the man for you. He's a maths professor. Think, don't love.'

'All negative: don't do this, don't do that. You should be saying, "Be with me, love me, choose me."'

I blushed, but in the candlelight she didn't notice. I was young and sincere. 'That's what I'd have said before I met you. Now I'm confused.'

'You were more confused before, believe me.'

The little flame danced beneath my eyes, and cast enormous shadows on the bare wall. The lieutenant was breathing behind the screen: he was either sleeping or listening to us curiously, greedy as ever for life.

'If I asked you to keep me here with you, to hide me until peace came, would you do it?'

'Yes, but you won't ask. You know I'd say yes, and you're afraid of that. What would you do in this room, waiting for the war to end? You would ask yourself who you are, what you want, what to do with your future. Much easier to let yourself be dragged along reluctantly through time. You know what I think will happen?'

In the semi-darkness her oriental eyes were as sharp as a blade. And from those gleaming slits I read the future, my future.

'They won't catch you on this flight of yours. The lieutenant, whatever identity he may carry with him, will be caught. You won't. You're a ghost, a mirage. The real Nino Manes stayed in the camp, in the sand of Africa. Or perhaps he's still studying maths in La Tonnara. The Military Police at the roadblocks won't even see you.'

I had barely told her anything about myself, and now she was weaving my life together as though she were in charge of it.

'Will I get to Italy?'

'I'm not a magician. I'm a student who has become a whore. You're Italian: did they make you read Horace at school? Are you surprised that I know Horace? Why? I studied too. "*Coelum non animum mutant qui trans mare currunt.*"'

'Epistle to Bullatius, I, II, with the three most beautiful lines in classical poetry: "*Neptunum procul e terra spectare furentem*" and "*Coelum non animum mutant qui trans mare currunt/ Strenua nos exercet inertia.* A perennial frustration wears us out. Live as though watching the sea from the land, as the storm rages. He who travels across the sea changes the sky, not his heart."'

A furtive shadow appeared behind the injured great white whale. It was the lieutenant, sitting up on his rough tatami mat. He was in his underwear, the girl was topless, but neither showed the slightest embarrassment. I alone pulled the sheet up under my chin, like a virgin.

'Horace,' the lieutenant explained politely, 'teaches us that flight doesn't change your nature. The starry sky changes above your mind, but your heart is still fixed within you.'

'Horace is wrong,' said the girl. She spoke quietly, and her little breasts moved from side to side like a hypnotist's watch.

'That wonderful line is his excuse for not leaving Sabina. Even if he did, he said, only the sky would change. Piffle. When you leave, your heart changes for ever. And you find yourself spending the rest of your life chasing the souls you abandoned in this world, by accident, out of covetousness, out of ambition, out of need, out of a spirit of adventure or love.'

'Are you in search of lost souls?' asked the lieutenant.

'Yes. I was a student mad with dreams and illusions about life in Hollywood. And who didn't end up in the camps like her sisters because she has western features and a lover in the Alien Office. Where are my souls? Better to lose them. Or at least that was how it seemed to me until I snatched you out from under the nose of the police.'

I didn't understand a word. Perhaps I was dazed by the exotic smell of incense, which until then I had only smelled in church, as an altar boy, or perhaps it was the two naked bodies beside me, both so serene, as though I myself were a ghost. If they had started making love I wouldn't have been surprised. And in fact the lieutenant put his hand on the girl's and said, 'I'll accept a lift as far as the stop for Memphis. I'd rather avoid those people.'

'I'll come with you to New York.'

The lieutenant wasn't pleased. 'We'll be too conspicuous. I can pretend to transfer one prisoner, not two.'

The girl, almost closing her eyes, licked two fingers and ran them carelessly over her nipples. 'I'm coming with you. You seem quick to cope with new situations, Mr American Army Lieutenant. You'll tell the police that I'm an alien who's escaped from the camp in Long Beach, California. My name's on the register. They'll give you a reward for capturing me. How much money have you got?'

'Thirty-five dollars. Nino has twelve, I checked when he was asleep.'

'I've got a little, and we don't need much. We'll go together.'

It had been a long day, and the fragrance of H.S.'s strong tea emptied my head and my chest. I couldn't stay awake, I struggled but fell asleep. Was I dreaming in the darkness, or was it jealousy? I thought I could hear furtive movements on the tatami. I tried to wake up, to shake off sleep, but it sucked me in. The girl's incongruous gesture, the loving fingers she had just licked, and the silvery thread of saliva that drifted from her mouth to her hand to her breast, imprisoned me more than the barbed wire in Hereford had done. I couldn't wake up, and let myself fall into the darkness.

As a boy in La Tonnara, I had grasped the top of an anchor and swum hard towards the depths, like a gymnast climbing up the rope of an inverted world. Then the blue water had swallowed me whole, and I had disappeared from my friends' view. I crouched on the bottom, to worry them, and when they – alarmed – tugged on the cable, I came back up, lungs hurting, to be welcomed by laughter and insults.

Now no one waited cheerfully for me at the end of my journey to New York. I was a ghost. But when the world is turned upside down, aren't ghosts the ones with flesh and bone, while men and women have the destinies of ghosts?

I was worried. There was no point in struggling against the darkness. It came as a great relief to feel the girl's hand on my forehead, like my mother's hand taking my temperature in the winter. It was gentle, soft, I loved it. It felt damp to me, and full of humours. It had an effect of immediate peace. For the first time since the night on the beach of Bardia, watched closely by the Australian riflemen, I slept as a free man.

11

'Tell me about her?'

'Her?'

'The girl you love across the sea.'

The truck was running along the red track. The lieutenant had changed the wheel, and we weren't making for Memphis, we were heading south to throw off our pursuers, who thought we were going straight for New York.

'Thanks to H.S., we've got a few dollars. We shouldn't head straight for the Atlantic. That clearly isn't going to work. They're probably looking for you, Nino: and how am I going to explain that I'm escorting the wrong prisoner? We'll go the other way and give the cops the slip. Head south, Nino, south.'

We set off for New Orleans, in the state of Louisiana.

'Gas is rationed,' the girl objected, 'I don't think it's worth the risk of wandering about.'

From his case the lieutenant drew a permanent supply permit, authorised by headquarters. Whether it was real or not, it looked perfect to me.

'Is she beautiful?'

'Very beautiful.'

'Do you make love with her?'

Yes, on Professor Barbaroux's sofa, while he took his after-noon siesta and left us on our own. It was the only place in the Island where we could have any intimacy. The professor's library, the little damask-covered velvet sofa. Could I say that she now made love with Barbaroux in the same place? I'm an islander, and I didn't reply.

'Hurray!' The lieutenant clapped his hands in response to my silence. 'Nino's a virgin.'

I glared at him. I couldn't bear his jokes, I couldn't under-stand what we were doing together. I was bored.

'Talk to her, leave me alone.'

He smiled. 'Don't be cross, Nino. Honestly, you Italians! Life isn't an opera.'

I suddenly yanked up the black handle of the handbrake, and the wheels locked with a hiss. I'd had enough of this journey. Three was a crowd. The pickup slid along the mule track.

I turned to the girl. 'Excuse me, I've got to get to Italy. Goodbye, Lieutenant. This is where we part company. If you want, you can report me to that MP. You seem more desperate to get away from him than I am. See you.'

I jumped from the cabin and set off with my bag over my shoulder, in the dust. There had been dust in my life for four years, as there was in the Buddha's bag. Except that the pain was in my heart, and my bag was full of lost joys. It was a crazy thing to do. With the lieutenant I was already halfway there, and now we had the girl, the truck, the money. Perhaps

I was really running away from her. I was confused, I was in love with her. And loving her meant giving up Zita, giving up running. Too many doubts. I wanted to prevent that wedding, and I would do just that. I slipped my hand into my bag to root myself in my innocent madness, rereading Zita's last letter:

> *I'm thinking about the time we carved those words in the bench: 'Inimicus Plato, sed magis inimical falsitas'. Yes, Plato was our enemy with his phony world, but even more of an enemy was the lie, falsehood. With you, I have always been real. With that same reality, I am writing today to tell you that the wonderful love is over.*

Where was I? I had hurled myself headfirst, sliding down the slopes to a salt plain furrowed by the railway tracks. I would reach them, and hop a northbound freight train. A few miles away from me, a small and dirty-looking hill covered with dwarf bushes forced the track to take a wide bend. There, the interminable trains feeding the war effort slowed down for a moment. I slipped, rolled, bounced back, the bag striking my back and my neck. At great speed, I left the fine sand path and the calls of the lieutenant behind me, and H.S. and the truck were soon swallowed up by the pale hillside.

'Now they'll escape together,' I thought, without the merest hint of jealousy in my stomach. The emotional tricks that prisoners learn: feeling pain, knowing how to take it without tears. Perhaps I was finished, perhaps I had ceased to exist.

Condemned for losing the war and for losing my freedom, I had to wander about aimlessly for ever. Goodbye to the girl, goodbye to the lieutenant, my flight my only remaining identity, the only suggestion that I was a survivor. I was getting away from them, comforted by the idea of being unarmed and desperate, at the mercy of anyone able to unmask me. I had fled from everyone, but above all I was fleeing myself. Free, but from what? From being nothing.

Getting to the hill wasn't easy. Behind the hump of land was hidden a tall, dense field of maize, impossible to get through. I had to flank it to the east, and when the stalks of yellow corncobs and crisp leaves thinned out, I glimpsed an irrigation ditch full of sluggish water. I could cross it with the current at chest-level, but it would mean getting mud all over my only uniform, which was indispensable to me. I resigned myself to walking along the channel until I reached a walkway of nailed boards. They creaked shrilly under my weight, which meant at least that I existed, I had a material body, I wasn't a spirit, and the moment I set foot on the other bank, the dew-drenched ground sucked my boots into the mud, sucking them in up to the calves. I would never get through that bogland.

I hopped limply back to the ramshackle little bridge and tried to find another ford. Beyond the loop in the river I spotted a colonial house. Three sharecropperers were beating grain with long leather straps, singing, 'Oh God, oh Lord, why have you abandoned me? You cry on the Cross and leave me in the valley of bitter tears, grey dawns, mute nightingales, and the serpent, master of evil.' All of a sudden they saw me and pointed at me. They stopped their work and waved big straw hats. I hoped that the distance would help to mask my pronunciation. 'How do I get to the hill?'

They waved me down towards the bottom. 'You go back, sir, Mr Officer, go back, sir.'

Why did they want me to go back? I shrugged and continued on my way.

The three men pleaded with me: 'Not this way, sir, go back.' The oldest of them ran his hand through his white hair and tried to attract my attention by beating his big hat against his thigh.

Night was falling. The sky had turned light blue, and a family of quail, with the mother at the front and the little ones following in a row behind her, trotted fearlessly across my path. This was the hour when Zita left Barbaroux's study to hide in a boat below the *faraglioni*. I passed through the thin scrub, the clay on my shoes forming sticky clumps. Darkness fell suddenly. Venus, the star of the morning and the evening, was bright in the sky. I asked her the way to the hill, the railway and home. She passed indifferently across the mocking sky. What was H.S. doing right now? What was she doing with the lieutenant? And what about Zita? She would be waking up in Italy. Would she go to Barbaroux straight away? There were two women in my life and I was losing both of them, just as I was losing myself.

Because there could no longer be any doubts that I had got lost. It was childish rage that had made me jump down the slope. Whenever I was seized by jealousy or pride, or an impulse of dignity, I was capable of doing the most stupid things. Once Barbaroux wrote on the board, '"Zita is the loveliest of my pupils" is a phrase that can be formulated into "for every x there is one single y such that y is to x."' Piqued, I didn't go to classes for a week. And he had to come to my house, in person, to apologise.

And hadn't I perhaps gone to war because Barbaroux hated it so? Hadn't I ended up in chaos deliberately, to feel more of a man than he was?

I stopped in a moonlit clearing and thought for a moment. That business with the blackboard had shown me Barbaroux as a man, who could look with longing at Zita. Rather than taking offence like an idiot, I should have reacted like a man, confronting his rivalry, without whining. Who but a whippersnapper could get himself lost in the Arkansas scrub, alone and confused? Soon I would stop to ask for help, and in doing so I would give myself over to the prison guards. Wasn't that what happened to all fugitives in the end, wasn't that the end of all those failed escapes which, in my arrogance (Carraway called it bravado), I despised, when their protagonists talked about them in the camp? Hadn't Pulera, a lieutenant in the *bersaglieri*, handed himself in to the parish priest of Sant'Isidro with a forty-degree fever? 'Would you be so kind, *monsignore*, as to give me a glass of water?' In the evening in Hereford he had commented, 'A fine state, this Texas, perhaps a bit flat,' and swallowed the quinine tablets given to him by the *camans*. Ghirri had been handed over to the police by an old housekeeper with a sawn-off shotgun. 'I thought he was a Yankee, sheriff. I didn't know he was an Italian!'

I had hoped for a different kind of escape, a real one, and my bravado had reduced it to nothing. For all the mystique of a ghostly escape across a whole continent, I had ended up trapped in the mud. I hadn't guessed that Barbaroux would steal my girlfriend, and had allowed myself to be caught out by my rage, *ira furor brevis est*, rage is a brief madness, losing myself in the bushes.

In the darkness the toads croaked, a guttural chorus of imprisonment. Their croaks were accompanied by the share-cropper's warm voice: 'Come back, officer, come back.'

'When you get lost in the desert, Lieutenant Manes,' the askaris taught me in Bardia, 'the only thing to do is wait for nightfall and take your bearings from the stars. There's no point wandering about like a mad dog.' I tried: when I looked up, the directions became perfectly clear. Beyond the mountains lay the cold north, the place I was aiming for; there was the west, and the sirocco-blown south I was escaping from; and there was the east I would reach by travelling with the north-easterly wind. I knew where I was going, but I didn't know how to get there. Every step was impossible: the sage brush trapped my feet. The dew drenched them. If I climbed on to a hump it was only to see an even rockier one further along, between myself and the railway. I should have taken the askaris' advice and stayed where I was, but that would have meant admitting my mistake.

'I'm more of a prisoner out here than I was inside. I've

managed to get trapped again all on my own. The girl was wrong: rather than escaping myself, I'm imprisoning myself.'

I thought of the things Carraway said when he wanted to frighten us: 'Rattlesnakes, my dear Italians, in the prairie there are rattlesnakes with mouths so big they could swallow a kid, horns, hoofs and all, and digest it in peace among the bushes. So quick that when you take aim at them with the rifle, they slip into the undergrowth fast as arrows.'

Looking back, it's easy to laugh about that night. As lost as a rookie recruit, drenched with sweat and dew, my clothes caught on thorns. Unable to think about what to do, as I had been trained, forced to continue my parade ground march in 1940, eyes right, quick march. I'm still ashamed of it today, but I'm a logician, someone who had never in my life been afraid.

When the British Captain Taylor, captured on a reconnaissance mission, had said bluntly to Colonel Paoli: 'I admire the Italians as humanists, less so as leaders', I had accepted a similar mission behind enemy lines. Two days and nights in the desert, hidden and burning in the sun, teeth chattering with cold in the darkness, among General O'Connor's trenches and tents. Having spotted the British positions, I had told my mates to wait for me. Eluding the sentries, I had got into a camp and stolen a crumpled copy of the London *Times*, a copy of the *Oxford Book of English Verse* with a blue cover and, out of spite, pocketed from a rucksack a medal for valour, bearing the face of Queen Victoria.

Back at the camp, I dashed to the Englishman, who was

still waiting to be evacuated behind the lines: 'My dear Captain, I paid a visit to your men, they've sent you something to read, and this medal, to reflect on the valour of the Italians.'

He hadn't actually reacted, he had just asked if he could have the medal I had in my breast pocket, like a believer taking a precious relic from a heretic. And Colonel Paoli, a sainted man, had me confined to barracks for three days, reprimanding me: 'You put your mission at risk for an act of bravado. This isn't an act of courage, it's just braggadocio. You can stay here and reflect on the nature of discipline, which alone will win the war.'

If only I had done so; instead, for three days and three nights I brooded about the indefatigable Taylor, who couldn't even bring himself to admire me. If only I had learned the lesson that pride and narcissism are treacherous, the fighter's eternal enemies.

I was filled with fear and discouragement. I was in a glade consisting of just a few trees, rough with undergrowth. Behind every dark patch I saw the wide-open jaws of the rattlesnake, which could have swallowed me whole. Two hundred yards away a solitary tree stood out, branches spread like arms. I stumbled over to it through the darkness. Like a madman, I climbed to the top, where the branches could still support me, far from the monsters in the scrub.

Venus and the moon lit up the horizon, and I was hanging from the top of the tree, which groaned and swayed. And now? Would I go to sleep in the branches, like Mowgli? Or in Manzoni's novel *The Betrothed*, like Renzo, fleeing from

Milan, caught by the police as he tries to reach the free territory of Venice, dreaming of the River Adda, the territorial
boundary. Until, exhausted just as I was, terrified by the darkness and only then, his anxiety at its peak, he hears the kindly
rush of the river that saves him. I had always wanted to retrace
Renzo's journey from Milan to Bergamo on foot, in search of
the Adda. So like him I prayed, in the pagan way that only
people who have grown up in La Tonnara pray. I prayed to
God, the most powerful and paternal of the gods, and to the
prisoner god of the Gnostics, weak and defenceless but dear
to the fishermen, and I prayed to my kind grandmother and
my godfather, I prayed to Giovanni, my bench mate at school,
who smashed himself to pieces on the 'king's rock' after a dive
he took as a dare to me, and the water all around turned red
with his blood. I vowed to all of them: 'If you get me out of
this night, and back to La Tonnara, I will walk from Milan to
Bergamo, as Renzo did, as soon as this war is over.' That
foolish thought gave me heart. The Christian and the pagan
within me revived the courage of the rationalist.

The noise was like the rustle of the Adda in Manzoni's
novel, a vague chug-a-log, chug-a-log, chug-a-log, the train,
the train I was looking for. It was far off, it was nearby, beyond
the knoll and the tree in which I was going insane with fear.

In the lee of the tree trunk the spring rain had opened up
a gully, a channel now covered by stones and wet sand. It led
straight to the base of the hill. It was steep, like a children's
slide, but its sides were rocky enough to break your neck, as
had happened to my friend Giovanni.

I climbed back down the tree, reached the opening of the gully, crossed myself, *in nomine Patris*, and hurled myself down it.

Three long slides on my heels and a couple of mid-air cartwheels – as a boy I would have cartwheeled like that in the sun, just for the hell of it, imagining myself invulnerable. In the darkness my somersaults were heavy and interminable. My heels hit the rough sand, whirling me over, fine dust beneath the palms of my hands as I reached out for balance. Finally I glided down, flat and torn, on my back. Reaching the bottom, I got up slowly to dust myself down, touching my bones to check that they were still intact. A fox carcase gleamed in the gloom, its round skull and sharp teeth, its yellow tail flapping inertly, the banner of a lost army abandoned after the defeat.

It was too late and too dark and I was too shaken to make it to the railway. I decided to wait for dawn, and it was a decision that saved my life. I don't know whether the choice of gods and humble folk that I had invoked was the right one. But had I moved a single step beyond the fallen fox, I would have shared its fate, without even a red fur banner to honour my memory.

12

I slept like a log. In Bardia, I had curled up on the sand and slept like the desert animal I had become. I had been spoiled by my months of imprisonment in America, the camp bed, the sheet, blankets, lukewarm shower and cornflakes for breakfast. In my brief, black sleep it seemed to me that the lieutenant and the girl were repeating my name, 'Nino, Nino Manes', she in terror, he transparently laughing, pushing back his soft hair. In the darkness the fox's narrow muzzle pointed straight at me, a disappointed grin glittering on its canines in the moonlight. 'Once beautiful, yellow and proud, happy to hunt the venomous snakes, have lost my fur, nothing now but a leathery quilt, carrion cast to the edge of the gulch, gnawed by the rats that I used to catch and gulp down by the mouthful.' That was what the dead fox said to me, and his voice was harsh and melancholy, the voice of a romantic fighter.

I woke at dawn. Sunrise was hot, as it had been in Hereford. I instinctively tried to stretch my legs from the camp bed, and in my ears I heard the constant rumble of the water tower, the cathedral that gave us prisoners our bearings. My aching bones reminded me of my insane flight of the day before. I was in a kind of compound surrounded by barbed wire. I must have entered it by blindly dodging two chevaux-de-frise that had been knocked down by the storms. A hundred metres from me, a white signboard clattered in the breeze. I could have gone and read it, my eyesight was blurred in the first light, but I couldn't bring myself to take another step further. The ground was beaten hard, like concrete, dotted with little piles of earth like our poor cemeteries back in Africa, two blows of the spade to break the desert crust, the body of a friend, a fellow soldier or a recruit whose name not even the chaplain could remember, buried without ceremony, and the Sahara swallowed up the inexperienced invader.

The dizziness of my sleepless night, and my funereal memories, kept me far from the other animal carcases, flaps of gummy skin. Those mortal remains would prove to be the only safe steps on my path, only by walking on them would I be safe. Instead I instinctively wanted to steer clear of them, out of pointless disgust: so, ludicrously, we move away from safety and drift instead into the darkness of perdition.

This time the echo of my name, 'Nino! Nino Manes!' rang out in broad daylight. It was the lieutenant. He was standing a quarter of a mile away from me. H.S. was with him: she was waving her arm rapidly up and down, to say, 'Get down, get down!' Beside her the three black sharecroppers were waving their straw hats: 'Watch out, sir, you better watch out, sir, for Christ's sake . . . !'

With a creak, the zephyr stirred the white signboard, the one I had ignored before. I focused on it in the light, and this time I saw a black skull, decorated with the crossed thigh-bones of the Jolly Roger, the banner of the pirate Long John Silver. Underneath, the words 'Minefield US Army Danger Keep Out'.

I was in a huge minefield that the American army had set up to train the troops before they travelled to the front. I was living a suspended death sentence. I looked for my footprints behind me, to follow them one by one to the fence that I had passed through unawares. Impossible: this soil, baked flat by the heat, erased all evidence of my passage across it. I made no more impression on it than on a city sidewalk. The past was no help to me. I would have to follow a different track if I were to save my life.

The lieutenant came running downwind, and his voice reached me clearly, speaking English so as not to alarm the farmers. 'Nino, I'll get you out of there,' he said firmly, certain that he would succeed.

My freedom seemed to have reached its end. If even an echo of my escape attempt could have reached Zita, she would have known how much I loved her, and I would have died content: but who was going to tell her about it? No one. My body wasn't disappointed, it had brought me down that hellish gully, fully believing in existence, in the flow of blood and the humours, all alien to the dead fox. Now I was motionless in self-defence.

'Nino, these gentlemen have done work for the army, they were the ones who laid out the minefield. They say they know where the mines are. They've drawn me this map. Can you see it?' and he unfolded a big sheet of paper decorated with blue lines to reassure me. 'When you see the body of an animal you're safe, because the mine has already exploded and you can walk without danger. You should try to retrace your steps. Gently. They're most densely arranged in the zone where you are at the moment. Look at three o'clock, you remember the clock-bearings the Americans used? So, come forwards at three o'clock.'

'Sir, perhaps if he threw himself on the ground . . .' suggested one of the sharecroppers.

I was drenched with perspiration. I asked, 'On the ground?'

The lieutenant raised his arm, fist closed. 'The mines are primed to go off under the weight of a man wearing boots, Nino. If you spread your weight, it will be more evenly distributed and you won't set them off. The animals trigger them by digging for food. Try it.'

I knelt down and put my hands on the ground, gently, as though they were the plates on my grandmother's stove on baking day. It was logical – bigger surface area, less weight per square centimetre, less possibility of explosion and death. I stretched out my foot and lay on the ground, my hands were sweaty and filthy with earth, I would set my muzzle beside the fox's and wriggle like a rattlesnake, no, not like that, I wasn't going to die on my belly. I jumped up once more, carefully treading in the footsteps I thought I had left behind me. 'I'm fine standing up.'

'The farmers say there's a logic to the field.'

'What would that be?'

'W and M. One row of mines set out in the form of a W, alternating with the shape of an M. Easy, isn't it?'

'As ABC. Now where am I right now?' I yelled.

'About two feet from a mine, I would guess.'

My knees started to give again. I twisted my torso. 'And what if I turned back?'

The farmer with the white hat spoke loudly. 'Sir, I'm Hosea. Listen to me. Please don't go back. At the end of the job we were tired out, and the W-M sequence isn't exactly perfect where you're standing right now. The Angel of the Lord protected you with his wings last night, and got you here alive. Please just try and come on.'

His logic wasn't much use to me. I could understand, I could deduce, become the lucid student I had once been, and then die because of a layabout who had got his Ms and Ws mixed up in the heat of the sun. There was no point listening now, I had to act. War again, eternal war. Arm your heart. 'Okay,' I shouted, and the loudness of my voice took me by surprise. It was my voice in unhappy Bardia, the Breda, hot and empty of rounds, the machine-gunner shouting, 'Manè, don't surrender, Manè, everyone to the guns, Manè, ammunition right now, ammunition, Manè, do I go on shooting?' And the only cartridges in sight were tied around the waist of Salvatore, his body smashed by a tank of the British Empire. And I replied at the top of my voice, 'Beretta, the shells are coming, they're coming,' and reached out beneath the fire of the enemy Thompson guns to recover the ammunition. My fighting voice, heard again for the first time since the surrender.

'Don't surrender, Manè! Last of the last, we'll be the last, Manè!' he said because I wasn't lying down on what the sharecropper called the field of death. On all fours beneath enemy fire, that was fine, but here with the girl and the lieutenant and the three fine Americans, what honour was there in that? Listening to my firm voice and drawing courage from it, I asked again: 'How many steps at three o'clock?'

'There's just one problem.'

'One?' I couldn't manage a smile.

'The bearings aren't marked on the map. The bastard who drew it must have known it, and didn't bother writing it down. Do you understand?'

'I'll just have to take my chances, then. What use is a map without bearings? I'll blow myself up just as I think I'm making it to safety.'

'Hosea says he remembers the bearings. We've got to believe him.'

'Are they German-style mines? If they were, we could find them with a probe and defuse them.'

'They're American anti-personnel mines. Hosea and his men remember them as flat and metallic. Nasty stuff, Nino.'

Horrible. Easy to prime and a bastard to disarm. I was familiar with them. The Americans had passed whole truck-loads of them to the British. But the land here was hard, not sandy as it was in the desert. It might just support me. Perhaps I could levitate across the field, like Jesus on the waters of the Sea of Galilee.

The girl still hadn't said anything. I looked at her, and her first words reached me clearly. 'Go on. You're too far away for the devices to hurt you.'

Can you be jealous even if you're looking death in the face? Yes, if you're young and foolish as I was then. I didn't want to cut a poor figure in front of the girl and the lieutenant, who were close to me by now. I wanted to make myself look brave, I wanted her to see me solid and manly, *más hombre*. I took a deep breath, as I had when I was diving off La Tonnara. 'How many steps to three o'clock?'

The lieutenant's voice was martial now, clipped instructions, no mistakes: 'Ten and no more.'

One, help me, Christ. Two, Saint Anthony protect me. Three, Hermes, god of thieves and luckless vagabonds, remember Nino. Four, Athena, wise goddess to whom I have never prayed before, help and inspire me as once you helped Odysseus. Five, Giovanni, watch me from heaven. Six, my grandmother who filled me with lentils when I was little, *Ora pro nobis*. At seven I stopped. I had thought of praying to Piero Grande, a fine, gentle comrade from Bardia, a real wizard with electric cables and technical contraptions. We were in darkness, our unit had been surrounded by Australians, and it was probably only a few hours before we had to surrender. Colonel Paoli cursed: 'In darkness, we're going to have to surrender in darkness!' I called out to Piero. 'Grande, the colonel needs a bit of light,' and he nodded his fair, Norman-Italian head, picked up a wire, gripped it between his teeth, and disappeared among the armoured positions and the dunes. All of a sudden the lamp came on, casting a violent yellow light on the table covered with maps, testimony to the desert we had lost, hopeless blue and red arrows. Grande came back into the bunker, hammered on a wooden wall to fix the cable, and sat down, drenched in sweat. 'Where the hell did you find that wire?' asked the colonel. 'Courtesy of the king of England, Colonel. I slipped into their generators. It won't last long, but at least you won't be signing in the dark, I promise. And when they find out what I've done you'll hear some language, believe me.' 'God bless you, son,' said Paoli. The next day Piero decided to take the same cable to the field hospital, to lend a hand to the exhausted doctor trying to operate in total darkness. A sniper struck him in the temple, zing, fatal blow. He was our last casualty. I hadn't ever spoken to him much, but I missed his industrious gentleness at Hereford Camp, when the lamps failed. Among the mines, at step number seven, I was nervous of invoking him. He was a man of darkness, would he have listened to me in that dazzling blue sunlight?

I looked at the earth where I was about to set my foot. I leaned forwards to stroke it, it was rough to the touch, like the sand I had collected from the grave dug for Piero to send to his mother. I was ashamed. 'Piero won't let me down.'

I moved my legs stiffly and, walking like the little tin monkey my godfather had given me, I hopped paces seven, eight, nine and ten. I don't remember if I managed to pray to my godfather, to wrap me in the turquoise, talismanic smoke of his Edelweiss cigarettes, to let me live, or rather not to entrust my fate to that clockwork monkey. I had spent the afternoons of a whole summer rewinding that toy, knowing that with only a few turns of its tiny key I could bring it to life. The little animal came alive with pirouettes and little jerks, danced for a few seconds and then sank back into clownish immobility. I watched it leaping about with great vigour, slowing down almost imperceptibly and finally dying in my hand. Gone for ever, like Piero Grande: but then I was a little god, and could set it off again, overcoming the melancholy of the colourful plaything, the cute red hat, the gold decorations, the little muzzle folded into a smile, leaping and defying gravity when its spring unleashed it, then sinking back supine on to the tiles that my godmother washed with Marseille soap till they shone.

Perhaps it was my godfather Fernando who protected me, or perhaps it was the monkey. Step ten fell where it had to fall, and a few inches away from me the dust revealed the round percussion fuses of two mines. Gleaming in the sun, like eyes, they indicated the first bottom corner of a W. I called out hoarsely, 'There are two of them. I've found my bearings.'

Stating this was like claiming to have deduced a theorem on the sole basis of two figures noticed in a forest of unknown variables. I could but try. 'Do you think I can go five steps to the left?'

'Do you believe in God, Manes?' was the lieutenant's reply.

'I believe in the gods: St Noah and Hermes. Jesus is the most respectable of all the divinities, and I believe in my godfather Fernando who prays for me.'

'Fine, although in cases like this, my dear Manes, you're

better off with an Italian kind of faith, Mother of God protect me, and a kiss to the medal.'

He climbed over the barbed wire and began to move circumspectly across the minefield. He was coming to save me. That courageous gesture, resolutely lifting the thorny fence with his hand, bending his chest and passing from life to death, prompted an enthusiastic response from the three farmers. They crossed themselves and applauded, 'God speed, sir, brave man!'

Hosea approached the boundary, and he in his turn entered the field of hell, staying close to the fence like a cautious swimmer holding on to the bollards of the pier, bathing in troubled waters. From there he could pass on everything he remembered about the minefield to the lieutenant.

The lieutenant had a plan. 'Perhaps there is a logical pattern, as you think. But it's a pretty ramshackle kind of logic and, if God wills, we may have a corridor open ahead of us. Let's see if I can slip into it.'

When I finally learned the lieutenant's story, I understood his courage and his valour. I was impressed that he would risk his life to get me out of a situation I had only got into because I was stupid and arrogant. But I didn't want to lose face. 'Beware of logical schemes. They always conceal a paradox. And beware of simple ones, too. If you had grown up on the Island like me, you would know that the Madonna protects us with the power of the whole of Mount Olympus. What about you, do you believe in God?'

The lieutenant lifted the tips of his feet like a ballet dancer, and brought them down again nearby, gently stroking the ground. He didn't take his eyes off the brown earth except to glance at the white map, although he didn't put much trust in it. He relied on his instinct and on our chattered words: 'Once, when I was a submarine commandant, I lost control of a sub and it sank to the bottom of the sea. The rudder was broken, and the Lord God put a bank of sand beneath us. Why he wanted to save a good-for-nothing such as myself I don't know. The crew deserved saving, they were good men, but they all died on the next mission, while I was put in command of another ship. I repeat to myself every day: "You deserve the light that the good Lord gives you. Don't waste any more time, as you're so good at doing."'

I too began to edge forwards. Whether the hole in front of me contained a mine or not I didn't know. As long as I got to the edge of the crater, without going inside it, I would have gained a few paces. 'In prison I often believed in the God of the Gnostics,' I panted.

'I don't know anything about him.' The lieutenant stopped to get his bearings, squatting on his heels like the Arabs in Africa.

'An early Christian sect. Convinced that the true God, good and merciful, had been captured by the jealous and surly creatures, the Archons, who kept him hidden away in a celestial cell. Preventing him from communicating with us, his creatures, left here to languish in fetters and pain, at the mercy of the cruel Archons. Somewhere lost in the depths of our hearts, the divine spark shines. We dream of being reunited with our God. This time we must free him. But how?'

'Who told you that story?'

'Barbaroux.' I glanced in the direction of H.S. to see if the wind had carried my words to her: her hands gripped the wire, her palms resting like swallows in the spaces between the twisted hooks.

'I prefer a free God. We're already prisoners on this planet.'

He lurched over, then stopped, a bloodhound sniffing for a scent.

'Am I too close to the tip of the next W?'

'Yes.' My lungs were already filling with air to call out, 'Stop!' and he had stopped by himself. We were turning into an animal that tries to save its skin by discussing theology.

'Go back.'

He didn't breathe. He trusted me. Dragging my feet slowly, I murmured, 'Thanks for coming to get me.' I was happy to have said it, as he was to hear it.

'Why does a nice Italian boy complicate his life, and not pray to Jesus and Mary?'

'Because of the Resurrection of the Dead.'

'Now there's a pertinent subject.'

'Why do you think multitudes of pagans left their good ancient gods, those lovely nymphs, sweet divinities lost between the pools of water and the woods, beneath the governance of Jove the Father? Why did they convert to Jesus?'

I pointed to a white boulder that lay across the line of the W, too heavy to be lifted up by lazy recruits in the summer heat. A safe spot. He reached it, sweating, and stopped to breathe. Each step was as exhausting as a marathon.

'Because,' he answered gently, 'Jesus is a god who consoles without asking where you come from. The pagan gods inspired heroes, but they didn't speak to the slaves.'

'Quinzio, a prisoner in Hereford, doesn't see it the same way as you do. He thinks that the Christians converted in such huge numbers because they were sure of resurrection. The risen Christ conquers death. Remember the *Odyssey*, the wonderful hero, Achilles, dead, caught in Hades, whispering to Ulysses, "I would sooner be the last slave on earth, in the light of the sun, than the King of Shadows here." Not so the Christians: they believed that the last slave would sit on the right hand of God the Father in the Kingdom of Heaven.'

'Why *believed*? We still do. Now let's try to jump. One, two, three.'

I shut my eyes and jumped; as I slipped I felt the lieutenant in my arms, and we fell together on to a crevice split by the heat. I have no brothers and sisters. A baby sister was born, Giulia, who remained my mother's secret pain. And yet, clutching the lieutenant, hands grasping the khaki fabric of his uniform, I felt as though he were my flesh, my brother who had come to save my life.

'Little brother,' he said, reading my mind, 'when you're in trouble like this, you don't go through the reasons of whether or not you should believe in God. You just believe in him and that's that, hoping that he too will deign to believe in us. I pray to him every day, whether he be a bearded father or a pure spirit, to help me escape madness. To make me like the individual he created from the chaos of darkness. My

111

innocence is lost and I'm not complaining. But why lose all feeling, all instinct of goodness, of dignity? We are lost not through God, but through ourselves.'

'Are you talking about the war, or about this field?'

'What's the difference? This is war. To pass through evil without any choice in the matter, you entrust yourself to chance, counting on the benevolence of the Creator. But the blows, the wounds, the lacerations, what wrong can we have done to deserve divine indifference? It can't be as simple as that.'

We were back on our feet, our legs entwined like lovers, to occupy as small a portion of the planet as possible.

I looked at him. 'When you entered the minefield the war came to an end. It was an act of peace. I'm your enemy, remember.'

'The journey brought us together. I saw you falling in love with H.S. I know you're fleeing to save Zita.'

'How . . . ?'

'The letter hidden in your pocket. I checked it when you were sleeping. Sorry: right of censorship approved by the Geneva Convention.'

I wasn't sorry. Better to die clinging to someone who knew of my sorrows, rather than a stranger. And to die talking about Zita, beneath the oriental eyes of the girl, struck me as a luxury, as though I, lonely as a dog within the boundaries of Louisiana, could still boast a family, a cohort of affection.

A prairie sparrow with ruffled feathers, brother to the ones we shared breadcrumbs with in Hereford, settled on the ground by our boots, staring at us with lively black eyes.

'If only we were as light as him,' said the lieutenant, 'we'd be free in a flutter of wings.'

'The birds of the air sow not, neither do they reap, and yet they belong to the Kingdom of Heaven. The question is: how are we heavy humans to get to the Kingdom of Heaven?'

'And out of the minefield?'

We were twenty metres from salvation. Halfway, like a buoy, there gleamed a concrete block, perhaps used to rest the boxes of mines on while they were being laid.

The sparrow flew low over the ground, circled over H.S. and came back to settle in front of us. It flew back and forth, gliding curiously over the girl, who followed its pirouettes with enchantment, then suddenly clapped her hands and shouted, 'Look to the right. To my right.'

The wind muffled her voice. To the right we could see only earth, baked biscuit-hard by the sun.

H.S. rummaged in her pocket, took out a white handkerchief and with her scarlet lipstick drew with perfect grace the print of a foot, and held it up to the sun.

'A footprint?'

Cut into the clay were nine prints of a military boot, deep, clear, imprinted into the mud when it was still soft from the rain. You could tell the heels from the soles, and even make out the words 'US Army'. They were the prints of a giant. The sparrow, joining in with the girl's encouragement, flew over one of the tracks and began to peck benevolently at some grains of corn.

'*Manu ductu*,' the lieutenant said.

'Led by the hand?'

'*Manu ductu*, led by the hand. The monk, who guides you by leaving his own prints in the sand so that you can follow. Your own choice, your own responsibility.'

'I see the footprints. I don't see who's leading us by the hand.'

'I don't know about you. But you're leading me.'

It was true. I had gripped the lieutenant's left hand with my right, as my godfather Fernando had done at the feast of San Noè when the crowd gathered on the pier to see the effigy of the saint, aflame on a little boat, drifting away through the darkness. I jumped from one fishing boat to another, vying with the adults for the finest view. Behind me, the boys called out ribald remarks, the sparks exploded in brightly coloured parabolas, and the black sea stirred restlessly. On the boat furthest out I was calm, balanced on the prow, my hand gripped in the perfumed palm of my godfather, a fearless helmsman who had travelled up the steel-grey Hudson River.

'I'll go first. You stay. If I don't make it, change direction, it would be a waste for us both to go.' I placed my shoe in the imprint of the paternal, reassuring sole of the giant who had come ahead of us on that damp spring day. I heard a faint rustle behind me – the sparrow, nervously darting towards the next footstep – and in the same instant I saw the lieutenant beside me.

'We'll go together. Otherwise, who are you going to finish your theological dispute with? I have to persuade you that God isn't a prisoner. He's free.'

'And what about this war?' I took a step forward. The lieutenant followed me, as a ballerina follows the male lead in intimate and elegant movements.

'Forget the war.' Sweat-drenched, we were dragged down by the weight of the earth.

'God could have created a world of goodness and happiness. But goodness exists in opposition to evil, and on this earth God makes himself true by his opposition to evil.'

This time he was the one who stepped forward, bracing himself against my side to leap half a metre ahead. 'And is it because of that challenge to divine pride that we must spend our lives surrounded by the chill of evil?' I asked. 'If we do good, God wins. If we prefer sin, the Evil One exults. No. This Via Crucis between the mines is our punishment for capturing my prisoner God.'

'Is there a logic in the arrangement of these mines, or are they distributed at random?'

'There's a logic.'

'Random, I'd say.'

'If you're right, God exists for us. Because without logic and without footprints we'd be lost.'

'What an easy God you want! A God who holds a network of good and evil under your feet, so that you can measure out your moves like a chess player, black and white, the knight, one square forwards, one diagonally. Believing in God means being God, remember. Reading the Scriptures means loving them more than the One who inspired them. If we believe in God, God believes in God. Otherwise he's lost, you see? Vanished into the void.'

I didn't understand. My religiosity was pagan. The tuna fish crucified in the blood of the harpoons, in their chamber of death, to guarantee a year of life on the Island, sacrificial victims offered up to the blue sky. San Noè, whose mighty statue oversaw the haul from the red boat to the main trawler, was our broker with God. We worked, he worked, to persuade the Eternal Father to send the river of tuna in the right direction, with the right sea and the right wind, on the right day. The tuna fish were good. Evil was a dead calm sea, famine, slack nets, a few little fish splashing about in the bottom of the trap. That was why I had converted to Barbaroux's Gnostic heresy, faithful, like him, to a prisoner God, noble but unhappy. And that was why I talked about him to the melancholy fishermen.

We were now ten metres from the wire. The girl pointed to the footprints: the last one was missing, as though the giant who had been guaranteeing our safety till that point had taken one last leap to the fence, freeing himself in a single bound and leaving us to rack our brains. Right? Left?

I was sweat-soaked, tired and confused. I confess that I would have headed straight for the sparrow perching on the barbed wire ahead of us. The lieutenant held me back. 'Wait. If this is the tip of the last W, there's a mine here.'

'And what about the giant's footprints?'

'He might have walked on before the last mine was laid.'

Without any further delay, the lieutenant took my arm with his thin fingers.

'There's a bomb down there. I can smell the stench, the power, the death and the metal. It's lying in wait to blow us to pieces, and send us to see whether we're praying to a free God or a prisoner. My good God is free, free to let me croak with the first step I take, free to let you die six inches away from the girl you yearn for but don't take, faithful to a girl a thousand miles beyond the sea, who is about to marry an embalmed logician. To the right now.'

'Don't go straight on and don't go to the right.' The voice of H.S., clear and silvery in the blue of the prairie, sent the sparrow flying up into the air. It flew a wide circle around her and the three sharecroppers, and came back to grip the iron wire with its little feet, as though holding up the endless line of barbed wire all by itself.

'To the left?' We began to protest, and the girl cut us short with a gesture. 'To the right is the real tip of the W. Our friends here remember the man with the footprints burying a gigantic mine in the middle with his own hands.'

Perhaps it was fear, or perhaps the Evil One wanting to belie our disputes about Good, his eternal enemy. I took one step forwards, the lieutenant one to the right, already far from one another, no longer brothers, in a sudden scattering of intentions.

We would have gone to perdition like that, had not the girl repeated her clear cry: 'Stop!'

Beside her, the head of the sharecroppers was training a pair of binoculars on us.

'If you take a single step you'll be blown sky-high. Hosea says there's a mine there. Laid outside of the diagram deliberately. To the right you've got the first point of the W, so you only have a single way through to the left, tight and straight as a gangway. You take that one, in Indian file. Now!'

At crucial moments, the voice of someone who has suffered assumes a resolute, peremptory tone that you can't but obey. The lieutenant and I were on the brink of nervous exhaustion. We asked only to leave the chessboard of death, or to stay there for ever. Our theological limbo had left us drained. We arranged ourselves in single file, he in front, me behind, holding his slender sides. It wasn't much, three steps, although I think I can describe every breath, every twitch of muscles, every drip of sweat, the grain of the leather belt between my fingers, the alert hopping of the sparrow, the earth crunching beneath our shoes, benign when it yielded without tearing us to pieces, terrible when lying in ambush. The blue of the sky, the wind on the wet shirt, the three sharecroppers in their work clothes, Hosea with his Winchester levelled, and the girl, with the sparrow flying over her as though she belonged to it, finally resembling the bird, light, no one's woman, in charge of her own destiny and, at that moment, of ours.

'To the left, to the left.'

The lieutenant came through first, then me, and the girl ordered us to crouch down with our hands over our heads. At the signal, Hosea fired one to the right, where I was about to place my feet, and another to the centre, where the lieutenant had calculated there was a safe passageway. Two mines exploded noisily. Were they the threat of evil, ready to grab us at any moment, mocking our fleeting escape, or a firecracker of good, a cheerful celebration of our liberty? We raised our heads from the ground and left the field of death, freed from everyday evil.

13

Jim Cheever had a girl of his own, back in a world that was still young. A pretty pier and sailing boats, the bright canvas of a jib to leeward. The girl sat on the veranda of the Hobson's Choice Hotel, and behind her the laughter of the linen-clad guests accompanied a game of bridge. The ocean rocked the keels of the boats, making the chains of the anchors creak. A white-uniformed coastguard presided over the billiards, bent over the table to shoot the ivory spheres in impossible trajectories. The war was reduced to a civil exchange of salutes, coloured flashes, respectful springs to attention.

Cheever had a fiancée a long way away, Emily van Heusel, drinking gin and tonic and translating Stendhal. For two summers both he and George Hoffel had wooed Emily. George had always beaten him at tennis and overtaken him in the regattas, but he had won the girl. She had said yes in the moonlight, and he had given her a silver ring. In the Pacific, at the same time, the Japanese had been bombing Pearl Harbor, and President Roosevelt had sworn on the radio, 'A day that will live in infamy. War.' Jim Cheever had gone to Washington, joining his crusade of secret fighters. George Hoffel had been mobilised as a pilot in the Marines. His plane was shot down almost immediately by the Japanese over San Fernando, defending Manila. Missing in action, lost at sea. When his mother wrote to him, Jim was pleased that he had lost in the regattas, and Emily was sorry to have denied George a moment of joy. 'As far as she was concerned,' Cheever thought now, 'George and I were twins, same college, same sports, same war. There must have been a flip of a coin. Now I'm alive, George is gone. I can come back and order a whisky at Hobson's, and the barman will serve me with a sad smile. "What a loss, Mr James, the death of Mr George, we watched him grow up here in this circle." I have plans, I can hope, write, read, marry Emily. George is dead: no plans, never again. Perhaps he lives in a Christian paradise, elect in the spirit, he has said goodbye to our life, the pier, caulking the deck, the gull passing under the tree squawking, hungry and happy to be alive.'

Jim, too, feared going missing like George. He knew he had lost at sailing and tennis for the same reason that he had made Emily fall in love with him, his only victory over his dead friend. Because he lacked the winning spirit, the serene sense of concentration and suffering that leads to success. His incompleteness led him into double faults in the crucial game, or made him hit too heavily and send the ball off the court, or he had let George win out of shyness, aiming at the white line of the net. He would spend whole regattas neck and neck with George, only to reach the finish half a prow behind him. Emily had chosen that element of doubt, that hint of anxiety, preferring his adolescent serve to the manly perfection that George carried within him, complete even as a boy. When Jim won a game of tennis, he asked how many mistakes his opponent had made. When George lost, he calmly examined his own errors, and vowed to do it better next time. Before leaving for the Pacific, he had said goodbye to his friends in the choir of St Bartholomew the Great, in which he had sung as a child, giving each of them a blue silk tie. 'Thanks, gentlemen, for letting me sing with you. It made me very happy. Keep me in your thoughts, and in your prayers.'

Jim was ashamed to see Emily in her white dress on the pier, to hear her laughing at the piano. 'I'm lost too, unable to find my enemy in this vast prairie.' What stories would he tell after the war, what adventures, what intrigues? Cheever tried to understand all that, his heart still tied to the landing stage and the grass of the tennis court, and his new adult heart, which frightened him, and which he didn't recognise. It was his heart that forced him to hunt Nazi U-boats, and win admiration for his cool in the War Room at the Department of Defense. It was his heart that wanted to tear itself out and return to 1938, to see the ball thudding against the net, losing yet again to George, 30–40, and drinking iced tea in the club, sated with imperfection.

Jim didn't know it yet, but the war had changed Emily, too. She wanted to live in Europe, translating the Latin classics, and no longer thought of matrimony, of fair-haired children romping in the sand of Cape Cod. In those long, lonely afternoons, she had met Melanie Wessel, the literary critic of the

Pall Mall Gazette, and had decided to follow her to Paris, after the Liberation.

Lieutenant Cheever was fighting his war in America, living a past that no longer existed, unable to accept the future that frightened him. He wrote letters to Emily, which piled up, barely glanced at, on Melanie Wessel's table, and was consumed by a life that had grown too complicated, in which the dead alone seemed capable of coherence. 'You're one of our best men, Cheever,' Admiral Cunningham had said to him. 'You understand that you win a war by losing yourself in it, by cancelling yourself out in the fight.'

'If I came back I wouldn't play tennis and I wouldn't compete in regattas. I'd go out at dawn, close-hauling, I'd brush the horizon, I'd see the backs of the whales in the fog, with the cormorants. My life would be wood, sail, wind and waves. No finishing lines, defeats and victories, no character to be forged, no strategy, no fighting, no wars, no maturity. Just the wind as far as the horizon. To come back to port, moor the hemp rope and clean the boat, the deck gleaming with copal resin beneath the soles of my feet. I wouldn't have to hunt down fugitives, persuade Cafard that I'm a serious man, do my duty so that America could defeat the Thousand-Year Reich.'

He didn't imagine that his life would be as he dreamed it then: he would complete his task, he would drink a toast to the final victory, he would come home, he would briefly inhale, with some embarrassment, the smoke of Melanie's Turkish cigarettes, he would speak in a whisper with Emily, who would make the wooden terrace of Hobson's echo beneath her heels, leaving him on his own and Emily a citizen of Europe for ever. He would study at Oxford for two years with the GI Bill grant. On the death of his father, in 1948, the family bank would be run by his younger brother, Benjamin, and he would spend the rest of his life sailing on his own.

The Ghost of the Bay, the Sunday trippers called him, a part of Nantucket like the albatrosses and the backwash. In those days in 1944, his vision of a peaceful, seaborne life seemed clear to him, pure, and void of vulgar cruelty. In the winter dawns of the future, with the breakers crashing, he would be a bitter judge of his stubborn pilgrimage. Each wave that fell upon the beach was like a ball on the top of the net in a match with George. Unable to live as a leader, and yet commendable as a warrior. Disappointed by Petrarch's *De vita solitaria*, '*Nec metuit solus esse, dum secum est.*' Never fear being alone while you are with yourself. Perhaps there had been something to be afraid of. Fear. Cheever remembered the ambush on Shelter Island, that night of thrusting daggers in the darkness, fear fills the hours and makes them pulse, either you let panic destroy you, or you sublimate your terror into courage. Alone with himself, bending beneath the boom in the wind, he wasn't frightened: he was disappointed, by the smallness of his life.

Lucky the man who manages not to be alone when he is by himself. Cheever could never manage that. His life was long and clear, but no sail, shroud or mast, no daring manoeuvre, no propitious tradewind, could bring him within sight of that intimate and desired horizon, once glimpsed with Emily and then lost for ever. The daring route that lets you overtake yourself when you have lost your past, and accept rebirth in life's uncertainty. Humble and close to those around you.

14

Louis Cafard had put away the papers from the von Luck case. Every night he said goodbye to Cheever and went into his room to go through his notes for the following day. The weather forecasts, to work out whether the fugitive could expect rain or sun. Railway timetables: south, north, towards the free ports, New York or Philadelphia, towards the country's strategic positions, aqueducts, dykes, railway stations, arms deposits. And he reread the reports from the Military Police, whether anything strange had cropped up, a detail, a little fact that might finally put him on the right track. When every-thing was recorded, everything observed, he put the papers away, opened the skylight, hung on to the cornice and leapt nimbly on to the roof. The nearby town was in darkness, a blackout against air raids. The stars were brilliant, high Cepheus, the Great Bear and Polaris stood out clearly, Cassiopeia a bright sigma, the pulsating Pleiades.

Before the European war had broken his life, Cafard had practised astronomy. He knew that beneath the stars, in the darkness, a battle was raging, more titanic than the one turning our tiny planet red with pain. The distant stars, which his blue eyes followed in the American sky, yielded heat and energy to the frozen, sterile cosmos. When they were exhausted, when the force of creation had dissolved into the cold 'thermal equilibrium', as his professor in Lvov, Janina Osiasson, called it, it would all be over. Suns, planets, comets, our fleeting lives, everything would make way for an empty darkness, free of existence. Something so perfect in its uselessness that it would make even the gods feel anxious. Not even the divinities will be spared the terrifying solitude of thermal equilibrium. God will be forced to return to creation, feeling himself, his own strength and perfection, threatened by the coming nothingness.

'Perhaps the Evil One,' thought Cafard, 'is this sterile darkness that absorbs colour and erases everything for ever, without giving anything in exchange.' Those stars, so precisely fixed in the firmament, Betelgeuse, Perseus, the omnipotent morning sun, are suffering a perennial loss, they are melting into the cosmos. And Lynx, twinkling beneath the Plough and Arcturus, shining so proudly in Berenice's hair: to the fighters of Russia and Africa they all seemed perennial. The boys, terrified by the scream of the Katyusha rockets, petrified by the whistle of the heavy artillery, looked enviously at beautiful and conceited Boötes. Far from the mud, far from fear, far from their everyday misery.

But the envy and admiration that the ragged little soldiers felt for the northern sky were misplaced, and Cafard knew it. The war of Polaris and Yildun, the stars in the Plough to which he had raised his eyes as he fled the camps of Europe, hunted down by assassins, was already lost. In 1939, hearing the nearby roar of the truck full of Gestapo agents, he had lifted the collar of his raincoat over his face, leaving only his eyes uncovered to look from Cassiopeia to Draco in search of reassuring Polaris, and had walked along the railway to the border, unhurried, taking long and careful strides. Not even the stars were eternal, they were candles while stock lasted, like tallow sizzling in far-off cottages, not even they could withstand the darkness for ever.

Soon, in a tiny flicker in the cosmic chronometer, the war of the stars would itself be consumed. Thermal equilibrium, Professor Osiasson wrote on the board, in the Polish university that no longer existed, its lecture theatres transformed into a barracks. And Janina Osiasson, the studious, sorrowful girl with such intimate knowledge of the cosmos? Swallowed up by a camp: Oranienburg or Sachsenhausen.

None of the stories told about Louis Cafard at the officers' club was true, with one exception. And anyone who had burst into this bare room as he meditated on the roof would have worked out which one that was. But Cafard only opened the door to Janos, the Bohemian night-watchman, and to Ana, the Mexican cleaning woman to whom he gave his rations of Spam. On the table he had a photograph of his mother, the most beautiful princess in Budapest, who had married, in Paris, Maurice Cafard, the polyglot American poet. Louis Cafard – they said at the club – spoke half a dozen languages, and had in his youth been an active anti-Nazi in Berlin. The piece of black obsidian that he uses as a paperweight, they said, is a present from Bianca, the Marxist he loved, who ended up in a concentration camp. But no one has ever seen the stone or the photograph of Bianca.

During his last months in Europe, Cafard, American passport in his pocket, had married Bianca, a fellow student, to bring her to safety. He hadn't succeeded, she had missed their last meeting in Yokohama. She had to get to San Francisco, via Moscow. The Gestapo had arrested her in a café in Amsterdam. Tipped off by a spy. That was the only other photograph in Cafard's little monastic cell, a faded, yellow clipping from the underground newspaper of the Dutch Resistance. 'Sachs Gestapo agent, collaborationist, only picture known', read the headline in wretched, greasy letters.

Cafard was only forty-three, but he felt like a survivor. Like the Latin poet Horace at the Battle of Philippi, he had no more dreams. He knew that the war of Polaris was lost, its only prize for having shone for millions of years, pointing the way northward to fleets of disheartened sailors, would be darkness. Like Polaris, Cafard fought and lived because that was his fate. He fought out of duty, no longer out of hope.

From his roof above the blacked-out city, Cafard gazed out at Corona Borealis and the brilliant Gemma, and imagined himself at one with the sky. Not alive to see Bianca again. Not alive to see peace again, and justice, and goodness in the world. Cafard had understood that observing the life of the universe and reading the case notes of defeat meant accepting that no strategy, not even a divine one, can save us. Apart from a new covenant with the gods, a pact that Cafard didn't expect. Future generations might be candid and generous and lucky enough to persuade the gods, imperfect as those in Petronius, or loving and pure like the Christian Trinity, to set out a new agreement with Creation. The stars would be lit without going out, love and wisdom would flourish without being enclosed by the fences of hatred, like Osiasson and Bianca.

No one understood Cafard. No one loved him. Even had he known how to ferry Bianca out of the hell of Europe, Moscow and Berlin, through a tunnel in space and time, what – he wondered as he sat up on the roof – would that have changed? Nothing. The pain and the silence of those years were perennial and constant, much more so than the firmament. A benign God could cancel out the war of the cosmos, and give the stars the power of eternity, saving them from fusion. But no god, Cafard believed, would have been able to make anyone who had ceased to smile forget their tears, bring children back to life, restore a belief in goodness to anyone who had stared horror in the face. 'That is the power of evil,' he thought, 'its scars last for ever.'

On this basis, Cafard had built himself up as a perfect fighter. The Defense Department had shown good judgement: if there was a man capable of capturing the brilliant enemy refugee, it was Cafard. He would pursue the trail tirelessly, until he had fulfilled his mission.

Unlike Cheever, the shy soldier he was beginning to like, Cafard had no dreams beyond victory. His beloved stars lit him up with light born centuries before. He was already staring at the distant past, and he could do nothing to change it. If Aldebaran were suddenly to explode, freezing the Hiades and the Pleiades with light, it would be painless. It might already have happened, in a distant past of which we were unknowing witnesses.

No one, in the Allied army, worked for victory with more scrupulousness and dedication than Cafard. But no one had fewer illusions about the future. Cafard was aware that breaking the Axis forces would prevent fresh sorrow. But nothing would heal the pain and entropy already endured.

If they had ever talked to one another, and they were never able to do so, Cafard and Cheever would have been surprised to discover that they were brothers, just as Nino and the lieutenant had become close kin in the minefield. The darkness that swallowed Jim Cheever's vivacity in his long afternoons of solitary navigation, twilight after twilight, had fallen early on Louis Cafard one clammy night, while the Gestapo truck drove on with its headlights blazing, two bright points, a cruel constellation. As he fled, Cafard had not taken his eyes off Dubhe and Merak, and had managed to make out Polaris. It pointed him northwards to salvation and silence, but it left him on his own. He would always be proud of the instinct that told him to look up into the sky, even when he was nothing but a hunted beast. A simple act, linking himself with the infinite cosmos so as not to die like a dog among the tracks of the European railway system, a relentless war against evil, with no chance of victory, no practicable escape route. That was the life of Louis Cafard, Nazi-hunter.

15

As I write this story, I have with me the radio that was concealed in my bag during my flight of forty days and forty nights. It's no bigger than the Spam tin, cleaned of its grease, from which it is made. I pick it up, it weighs next to nothing, its edges are slightly eaten by rust. There are two black-painted switches made from women's hairpins. At the centre is the dark galena crystal. The headphones are held together by a leather strap, worn with use, the wire is grey, rolled and coarse, like an old piece of string. To tune it, you have to put on the headphones and rub the crystal gently with the hairpins. The contacts and the relays are in the base of the tin, frail and precious.

I scratch the crystal and hear a faint buzzing noise, the distant crackle of voices and notes against a background hum. 'This is Radio Budapest broadcasting on short wave, Mozart's Oboe Concerto. This is Radio Brussels. Fighting on the African front is still intense.'

I close my eyes: it's night on the Island, a warm night in the new millennium, the blue of the sky comes down to the sea and the boats plough the black waves, leaving a line of foam behind them. Standing on the rock, a girl calls out brightly once, twice, no one replies to her invitation and she dives into the darkness. She is calling to someone who doesn't hear her, and although I'm listening I can no longer see her among the waves. She doesn't mind being alone, her own company is enough, she's a happy dolphin, a force of nature. Below my terrace lies the landscape of a European summer evening. In the piazza, where the only remaining nets now adorn the interior of a restaurant, teenagers dance together, row by row, in a kind of contredanse directed with cheerful authority by a tanned DJ. Their grandfathers stood in rows on the sergeant's orders, these young people smell of musk, healthy and clear, and we know nothing of the thorns that lie within their hearts as we touch each other's arms. '*O masi malele su pampa, pampa,*' booms the loudspeaker in the little square. And everyone jumps and dances and laughs, but I can't hear them, I'm trying to switch on, after half a century, the little radio that belonged to the boy Nino Manes, made for me as a present by my fellow soldiers in Hereford Camp 1 before my escape. All I get is whistles in the dark and good-byes in distant languages. 'That's the end of transmissions for this evening.'

I go on rubbing, as though striking a match, and nothing happens. I try to prick the crystal, still nothing. So am I being cross and clumsy, can these arthritic hands make nothing but silence? And suddenly the headphones are filled with lively music, a German voice breaks in with the warm intonations of Bavaria, then more music, the Red Priest, Vivaldi.

The speaker might be plugging a detergent, I can't quite make out the words, or encouraging listeners to buy a car on hire purchase. It's as though the radio were a tunnel through time, able to link up with the secret waves I became aware of in the desert, as I hid with my head in my bag. The girl swims over to a boat. Vivaldi echoes in my ears, a memory of genius, fortitude and courage for us Italian prisoners in North America: a radio built out of refuse.

Tonight I see myself again with great clarity: there I am, hidden in a narrow gorge, while the lieutenant and H.S. try to interpret the train timetable. By now my English had greatly improved, so I understood perfectly, on that far-off day, the news broadcast on the frequency reserved for the Military Police. I have Vivaldi in my head, and before my eyes I have the girl, happy with her solitude on the Island, but the crystal radio is tuning irresistibly to the past.

'To all territorial bases. An enemy officer, highly dangerous, has escaped from Amarillo Camp. He may have disguised himself as an American officer. He is certainly armed, and predisposed by his training to commit acts of terror. The search is concentrating on the valleys of Tennessee and along the banks of the dykes, which he may want to mine to provoke flooding. A submarine captain, an expert in explosives and sabotage. He speaks fluent English. He may have another prisoner with him, either an accomplice or a hostage. His name is von Luck, but it is possible he is travelling under a false name.'

I switched off the radio with a twist of the hairpins, and

worked out that the lieutenant, the man supposed to be my guard, was the officer being hunted by the Military Police. Back at the minefield, hadn't he mentioned that he commanded submarines? So what was he doing in the infantry? He was escorting me to New York, using me as a screen for his own escape, parallel to mine. The radio mentioned terrorist weapons, but I had only seen his regulation pistol, which he had never taken from its holster. Perhaps his weapons were waiting for him in a secret storeroom guarded by the American Nazi underground network, the ones that Colonel Rogers used to tell tales about back in Camp 1.

In my ears I can hear the voice of the Military Police network, measured and regular, just like that of the German announcer, a German who is forever interrupting the *Concerto Grosso* tonight. My poor radio, picked up again after half a century, in this mild and peaceful summer, brings together remote periods of time, young people on the run yesterday, enjoying a sensual holiday today.

The boys brush the exotically patterned wraparound skirts of their companions with their khaki shorts, to the boom of the bass from the loudspeakers. To which of them could I tell the story of Nino Manes? What magic would I have to unleash to bring them back for a single moment to the Island as it was before the deafening notes of '*O masi malele su pampa, pampa*', in the days when women weren't naked even in bed? If I went down to the beach with this frail relic, if I found the solitary swimmer and fitted the headphones over her lustrous curls, what would she understand? Would she be able to hear the voices of the past?

I think so. I think the dancing would stop, she would form a circle with her friends on the pebbled beach, beckoning them with her golden hand and, passing the phones from ear to ear, she would listen wordlessly with them to the past, broadcast live, stories from yesterday, the time of their parents.

We are only young for a few days. And in those glowing moments we feel contemporary with all the young people who have come before. With my boyish intuition, I picked up the Military Police broadcast just by chance. As the boys on the beach tonight would understand, I understood. I needed no proof. The lieutenant was a fugitive like myself, fleeing across the American continent; he was being sought with greater precision and force because he was considered dangerous, while no one cared about me, Nino. I could tell the boys how, once I had learned the true identity of my companion, I took off the headset and put the radio carefully back in my rucksack, wrapping it in a rag so that it wouldn't get damaged. I turned around and in the faint light of the American sun, standing guard on the bare rock, I saw a mountain lion. Standing proud on the grey granite, heedless of the strong wind, it swung its heavy tail from side to side, as an acrobat might move his balancing pole, strong and happy to be alive, a magnificent, dappled, young mountain lion.

16

The sun was low on the hill. The pines, smelling of resin, rustled in the wind, shedding pungent needles on to the red earth that squeaked and groaned beneath our feet like winter ice. There was no turning back. The lieutenant and the girl had joined me, and were looking with amazement at the mountain lion.

H.S. murmured, 'Don't move, and don't try to escape. It's a puma. It must have left its cubs in the forest to go hunting, and we're in the way.'

'It's very beautiful,' said the lieutenant. Remembering him, even now, I think of his enchanting capacity to recognise beauty, wherever it was. 'Look at the light, Nino,' he said, as we crossed a sunlit canyon. The previous night, as we had slept under a station bench, waiting for the Southern Thunder Express, he woke me all of a sudden with a kick to the shin, and pointed to the moon with his elegant index finger. 'Look, Nino, look how big the moon is, when will you ever see it so big and bright again?'

He was right. The moon and its craters looked full and bright in the Prussian blue of the night. The warmth of the prairie made its white surface tremble like a breast. A glow-worm passed, and the lieutenant caught it in his hand. He showed the girl the insect's phosphorescent light, and the moon was in his fist. He stared at it with blissful concentration, the intermittent green of the glowworm flashing against the green of his pupils. Stroking it, he freed the glowing pearl, which curled up into a spiral, twisting up as humans do when captured, and was lost in the night. 'It's already on Selene, on the moon, my handsome Nino, where our brains end up too, lost in madness.'

With his nervous, athletic gestures, he slipped his pack of cigarettes from his pocket, rolled one and threw it across to me. The cigarette assumed a life of its own, like the glow-worm, like the sensual, greedy, chirping cicadas, exhausted by the heat. The lieutenant knew how to instil conscious life into inanimate objects, in the animals of the prairie and even in those who, like me, had been drained of the essence of life.

He rolled a cigarette between his fingertips, sent it flying into his mouth, between his moist lips, took a deep breath, his very life seemed to depend on sucking on the breast like a baby. He exhaled the smoke hard, looking into the sky: he didn't just breathe out, he blew fiercely, powerfully, happy, sure of reaching the Sea of Tranquillity.

The mountain lion breathed just like that and, despite the primitive fear of confronting a wild beast, I looked at the lieu-tenant, and he breathed at the creature through his nostrils, responding to the challenge.

'How beautiful it is.'

The animal rested its powerful claws on the ridge and crossed a narrow space about five metres long, turning warily back on itself and repeating the patrol. Whiskers nail-straight, tail swollen, tense: it was preparing to leap across the gap that separated us, and tear open our throats with its claws.

Since then I've read everything that has been written about the American mountain lion, almost extinct today but once lord of the New Continent. The Hopi Indians considered it divine, the white men called it puma, cougar or mountain lion. In the south it's a jaguar. It can bring down a buffalo by leaping at its jugular, it is unafraid of bears or wolf packs, it can cleanly sever the neck bone of a big, strong man, using its weight, the fury of its leap and the ferocity of its claws.

'If it attacks you,' the girl murmured, 'crouch face downwards and pretend to be dead. It may flay you, but if you lie on your back it'll rip your belly open in a flash.'

I took two steps back. I was horrified at the idea of being disembowelled by a big cat, after ending the war in the desert unhurt.

I wanted to reach the Island alone. I had gradually been altering my plan. Seen in the sunlight, in the rain, in the light of a lamp, the message in Zita's letter was unshakeable. She would never yield. If it were the last free choice of her life, she would marry Barbaroux. I had accepted it and found it unbearable, like grief over the death of a relative. Now I only asked to reach the Island and astound them all with my ghostly apparition. A harmless phantom, a little spirit like the ones at the abandoned mill by the saltworks, which dodged the stones we threw, shrieking as they did so. They appeared right on time, at full moon, at the cry of the owl and the cheerful hoopoe, the Uncle, the Aunt and the Little Nephew, big and fat, snorting powerlessly at the village boys. Who had damned them I didn't know, whether it was a god or a goddess of the past or, more humbly, a scornful witch of the caves, behind the hill of Impisu. I had been brought down to their level, a spectre who had survived the rigours of the war and the misfortunes of love, to make my appointment with the mountain lion, dancing its ferocious foxtrot, striding between a clear spring and a red canyon, a swift patrol. The lion sniffed the air with its whiskers tensed, looked as though it were solidly planted in the air, but then, like squirrels that jump from larch to larch, it sprang lightly, flying over us with its muscular abdomen, and landed behind us with a resounding thump.

The lieutenant broke a knotty branch from a tree and twirled it over his head a few times. The green twigs, still attached to the wood, whistled like a cat-o'-nine-tails. The puma paid no attention, and I had the unfortunate idea of throwing a stone at it. I didn't even want to hit it, just frighten it to make it understand that it had to get out of our way, because we were free and sovereign in our flight. I threw a pebble washed up by the roaring February floods, when that red gorge became an ocean of water, now reduced to the little spring that the puma had elegantly leapt over.

On the Island, only Volpe could throw a stone better than me, Volpe who, by the age of eighteen, had not got beyond the second year of secondary school, hero of all of us school-boys, capable of shattering the white ceramic isolators on the street lamps with a precise blow, leaving the hooks naked and shameful in the sun.

On the abandoned jetty on the Island it was Volpe who taught me the fundamental principles of survival. We had been locked in the cold warehouse, heavy with the stench of rotting grape must, by the gang led by Terrasi, the vicious orphan son of the bosun who had drowned with my father. 'First we'll nick your jackets, then we'll beat you up, and last of all a good salting,' Terrasi had announced, relishing the attack in anticipation. Salting us meant that they would grab us by the arms and legs, he himself would open the flies of our trousers, gripping our cocks with his hands and mali-ciously pulling back the foreskin. When the red tip of the penis had appeared in the freezing air, among the laughter and the nudges of our tormentors, Terrasi would rub it hard with the sea salt that spilled from the jute sacks, ready for the curing of the tuna. For days afterwards, urinating would be torture.

Volpe looked at the semi-circle that was closing in around us, and murmured resolutely, 'If you stay close to me, they'll hurt us but, with a bit of luck, we'll get out alive. If you escape and they divide us, they'll catch us on our own, they'll get their courage up, cowards that they are, and salt our throats *and* our willies.'

I remained glued to his bony shoulders. As we charged together towards the door, a bedlam of slaps and blows rained down on us, so Volpe called out to encourage me, 'Hit them, Nino, hit them!' And we lashed out as swiftly as we could. 'Always get your blow in first, always.' One last clash and we found ourselves back on the jetty, bruised, battered, scratched and happy. Outside the warehouse, Terrasi and his henchmen wouldn't risk attacking us again. They vomited insults, but the salt fell uselessly in clumps from their hands.

Volpe taught me how to throw stones as well, and how not to get caught in a hail of rocks. In a stone-throwing battle, he explained patiently, instinct leads you to cover your head with your hands without looking up, out of fear. In fact, the only way not to end up with your skull split open is to look up into the sky, fighting against your nature, and keep your eye on the sky, dotted with stones. Ignore the ones that are far away and harmless, and make sure you dodge the one that's about to split your forehead.

So it was that we got away with only a few scrapes and bruises, back in La Tonnara, when Terrasi and his henchmen, furious at the mockery of our courageous charge in the warehouse, ambushed us with stones. Volpe, bleeding copiously from his swollen cheekbone, took aim with his one open eye, ignored the pebbles that were showering at his feet and, from twenty metres away, flung a flat stone straight at the head of the gang, the most incredible throw I had ever seen, bent low and whirling like a baseball pitcher, launching the stone mid-pirouette, hand and target united in their trajectory. Volpe saw the blow and sensed it, felt it in his heart even before he threw: what a great Zen-like gunner he would have made with the field howitzer in Africa, but he barely knew how to read, so instead they set him to work as the stoker in a corvette that was torpedoed by the British in 1941, and there's not much call for stone-throwing at the bottom of the sea.

In the prairie, oh dear yes, I wanted to frighten the puma, as the lieutenant hadn't succeeded in doing. I threw the flat stone at its muzzle, the girl shouted, 'No!' and something strange happened. The animal stared at me balefully, and in its eyes I read the horror and the cruelty I was running away from. I was seized by an uncontrollable frenzy, an unreasoning hatred, and I threw another stone, lowering my shoulder towards the ground. I aimed at the animal's eyes and hit it right between them. That ruling creature was forced for the first time to feel the sting of pain and defeat with the flow of blood on its powerful muzzle. The beast was too proud to bear the humiliation. It scraped the red ochre with its claws and rose up as though on wings. It soared above us, fur bristling, jaws already gaping. I looked up, hoping that Volpe was there with me, and saw the beast attacking H.S., rolling her as a house cat does a ball of wool, felling her with a roar and then turning towards me, flecked with blood and foam. The lieutenant rained blows down on the creature with his stick, I had just enough time to strike it in the flank with two stones, but the lion laid us both low with its claws, opening up an escape route for itself, emerging as the sole victor. Crazed with pain and excited by blood, it wanted to finish us off. It charged, planting its claws on the sand, tail straight as a rod. As I lay on the ground, the wind brought me the smell of blood that I knew so well, mixed with the stench of a wild animal, flesh and fur, the smell of a carnivore, nature without hope or charity. It would have torn our throats out right there, before dragging the girl, lighter prey, to its lair to devour her. It leapt at us. A blast of rifle-fire froze its limbs in mid-air. Thrown aside by the impact, it rolled on top of me, hot and heavy, to die, proud and stunned, defeated by an invisible enemy, on the man it had so nearly killed.

The beast groaned and died, incredulous at having lost dominion over the mountain pass beneath the bright sky, and yet wise and resigned in giving up its savage soul, aware that all powerful things must pass this way, all subjugated by fate in the end. It died on top of me, crushing me, and its protruding tongue, red and damp, seemed to want to console me, a mother cat with her kittens once again, imparting to me the lesson it had just learned: 'Beware, Nino Manes, beware the treacherous flash that destroys your dreams and your life, as it has done with me, for I too felt arrogant with the strength and fluidity of my movements, and all of a sudden I am nothing but a shadow. Humans, this too is your fate. Look at your girl, look at her now.'

The shot had been fired by a man with red hair and a red curly beard. He said his name was Jack McKay and he lived in California.

'I'm a bounty hunter,' he explained, 'but thank God I don't hunt human beings any more, no thank you. For a few dozen stinking dollars you get yourself fired at by a cocaine-addicted gangster, to die in a dark cellar, or slip into a barn looking for some wild hooligan who runs you through with his knife in the wink of an eye and feeds you to the pigs. Big Bill O'Malley, you've heard of him, haven't you? The philosopher bandit of Chicago, former librarian, read Plato and Aristotle and all the other big guys, he stole funds from the Athenaeum to buy antique books, they found a heap of them hidden in a basement, and it was my job to flush him out of a bar on the outskirts of St Louis, you know St Louis? No, nice place, even without that fop Lindbergh, and before I can open my mouth he fires two dum-dums at me, this great intellectual, firing away. It was like that in Spain too, have you been to Spain? No? Shame, beautiful place, even if it is run by priests and that bastard Franco. I fought for the Republic, sorry, if a Boston Yankee like me doesn't fight for the Republic, what's he going to do? And yet I go home, plenty of my boys left in Madrid in shallow graves, and they take my passport away, I was a stationmaster in Oregon, have you seen the moors of Oregon when the quails coo at each other, head over heels in love? No? So what do you know about life?'

As he spoke, he skinned the puma that he had killed with a single rifle-shot. He used a Bowie knife, steel sharpened to a double blade. He slashed open the fur and stretched it to dry the viscous interior of the skin, before rolling the carcase into a ravine. The powerful flesh of the muscles that had been so terrifying just a few moments before now glistened red, dotted with horseflies and greedy ants. A yellow wasp tore off a strip of flesh and flew off heavily. McKay brushed it away with his hand.

'Coward. Five minutes ago you wouldn't have come

anywhere near, and it could have hurt you, small and poisonous as you are. Now you butcher it. The whole of life's like that. I fight, I come back, I haven't got a job: you're a communist, they say, off you go! So I have to work as a bounty hunter, they won't even have me in the army, too old, pal! Ask Franco's men if I was too old when I was running them through with my bayonet in Jarama Valley . . .'

He left only the head intact, carefully emptying it of its brain: 'I'll sell it to an embalmer, we'll get a few dollars from it and it serves as proof.'

'Proof of what?' asked H.S., who had sat down to get her breath back. The animal seemed only to have stroked her, no apparent injuries, just swollen bruises and deep scratches that the lieutenant treated with his US Army kit, bandages and disinfectants.

'I don't suppose you've got any morphine?' she tried to joke, her voice failing.

The puma had aimed straight for her, sniffing out the weakest prey, in the hope that we males would run off and leave her undefended. A wild animal's calculation that might have paid off – what on earth could the lieutenant and I have done without McKay?

'If I'd got Big Bill O'Malley, I was planning to send the money to the orphans of the Spanish war, hoping that the bureaucrats would hand it over to them, when a letter reached me, roughly signed "O'Malley", and a gift of a copy of Montaigne's *Essays*, not stolen this time, nothing precious, just a paperback but the ideas are still good. He apologised for shooting at me.'

McKay wiped his knife on a tuft of sage brush, blood and tendons dripped to the ground, and the ants went into a frenzy for them. 'So I decided to give up that job, thank you. Down in the south they pay you to kill mountain lions. The lions scared the workers who are building the dykes for President Roosevelt, God save him, still waiting for a while to declare war, while Hitler would have conquered Coney Island and eaten hot dogs on the merry-go-round. The settlers are coming by the coachload, and they don't want to see their children eaten by a wild animal while they're installing the ice box. Every puma head is worth twenty-five dollars. Not much, but McKay has to make a living too, *compañeros*. Goodbye West Coast, I'm heading south.'

'Do they often attack?' asked the lieutenant.

'The pumas? No, not if they can get away. God knows, I hate to kill them, I beg their forgiveness, but the Hopi Indians taught me to say, "I'm killing you, lion, but I have to do it to live." It's different in the north. The Lakotas hate pumas. "They're the only animals I don't understand. They speak a language more complex than English," my friend René used to say, and he was the last of the Nez Percé Indians in Oregon. This is the first time I've ever seen a puma attack a human being. I already had it in my sights, I was about to fire when you threw that stone and the animal pounced. I've killed more than a hundred of them, I won't end up in Wall Street but I make a living. And after the war . . .'

* * *

I can't remember what McKay planned to do, I've forgotten, because I remember my reaction to his phrase, 'After the war'. There we were, all spending our time telling each other what we were going to do after the war, work, love, families, meals, hunting with friends, reading in silence, pushing our children on the swing. None of us was living in the present, we were all stuck in a magical and ephemeral time. 'After the war . . .' and yet none of us would ever live so intensely again. Not the girl wounded by the mountain lion, nor McKay with his Bowie knife, nor me with my little radio hidden in my ruck-sack, and not the lieutenant, who was still clutching his tree branch, a faithful soldier who doesn't let go of his weapon just because the fight is over. In the midst of passion, all you want is domestic peace, family affections, peace. When you conquer peace, and you're happy with it, it's enough to hear the echo of gunfire, the flapping of a colourful banner, and suddenly your heart is filled with longing for adventure, chance and the action that means killing and loss.

McKay put the knife down, waved away an annoying fly, which flew towards the girl's neck and settled on a long horizontal cut. A little blood was oozing from it, and we hadn't noticed. The hunter leapt up like a man possessed. 'Disinfect it immediately,' he said to the lieutenant. 'We've got to treat it right now. Those beasts are beautiful, but their claws are infected with carrion.'

17

McKay had a little truck and we all crammed into it. The girl was extremely pale, and the pain made her oriental face look gentler and younger. She looked like a schoolgirl now, a sick child. The grit she had proudly displayed before had disappeared, and her coral-coloured lips were wan and dry. I felt guilty, as though I'd neglected her, as though I hadn't given her the care she deserved. It was too late, and I didn't know it: all through my life I've felt these premonitions, the sense of owing somebody something, when narcissism and vanity had distracted me for too long. I looked at the thin wound on H.S.'s neck, which I had kissed in the darkness. With her it had been love, and not a childish caper as with Zita or the face-powdered, sweaty and lipsticked whores during my time in the army. She knew how to take and to possess, she held her thighs tight with her hands and her knees, like a horserider.

The lieutenant handed her a cigarette, with perfect faith in the miraculous power of tobacco, and with every moment of pain or anxiety the Camel sprang into life, as though to ease the suffering of the world.

The girl smiled at him and inhaled with a shiver. I envied

the lieutenant, I always envied him. There I was ruminating about why I didn't know how to take care of H.S., while he got on with doing something, a little gesture of affection, of warmth, just a cigarette, but H.S.'s diaphanous face was reflected in the red embers, and she was drawing comfort from the cigarette. The lieutenant knew how to act, he had gone into the minefield, not drunk with rage as I was, but as a matter of free choice, he had adopted me as a prisoner, and he had lied to me, no doubt for some larger, magnificent plan of his own. Now I knew from the radio that he wasn't an American officer, but how on earth could I work out who he really was? He seemed somehow light to me. A man? An angel?

'Nino, you never told me you had a radio . . .'

He irritated me, as he always did with his astuteness. 'You've rummaged through my things, you've read my letters, I imagined you'd have found it in your searches.'

This time I was the one who was lying. I'd always kept the radio near me, it was my secret weapon, my last resort. I kept the earphone wrapped around my forearm, and the empty Spam tin that served as its base I kept in my pocket. Apparently frail as a butterfly, while I was on the run it had proved to be more solid than a rock. Only now, fearing that the lieutenant might see it, I had put it back in my bag: and he had managed to spot it.

'The first aid station. Here we are. We'll see to it that she's treated, but we won't spend the night here. I'll take you wherever you're going,' McKay announced.

The dust road had widened into a majestic tree-lined avenue. The front door to the hospital bore a gleaming wooden sign, on which I could read only a few gothic letters '. . . Health Department, New Orleans'.

There were pale bungalows among the sycamores and tall, plump magnolias, heavy with flowers. The lawn was perfect, every blade of grass aligned with the others, like the haircut of a recruit. All around, the five huge pavilions of the hospital spread out like a star from a central, circular nucleus, perhaps the refectory, the administrative offices or the operating theatre. The windows were covered with dense netting that made them look more like a prison than a sanatorium, but there was no sign of any guards, or barbed wire, or observation towers. The peace was complete, two geese walked elegantly across the lawn, and a group of women, all wearing the same blue apron that must have been the patients' uniform, were putting their embroidery into wicker baskets and setting off hand in hand towards the river. At the edge of the avenue there was a cemetery, small and tidy, the graves lined up in rows, without crosses or monuments. For a moment I mistook it for one of the many Confederate graveyards that the civil war had scattered around the vast fields of the south, but it lacked the inscriptions, the memorial stones and the battle epigraphs, 'Fallen for the Glory of the Confederation' or 'Lost with Honour in the War between the States' and names and dates of birth and death. Only a sequence of Roman numerals – I, II, III – distinguished one flat burial mound from another.

'A cemetery of strangers,' observed the lieutenant.

McKay picked the girl up and walked with her along a pavilion towards the heart of the star. Hornets beat against the gauze hung over the windows, a steady madness, numerous blows against the whole building, its structural harmony and the illness concealed within it. There was no sign of doctors or nurses. The doors of tiny cells opened on to the corridor, and no sign of life seeped from any of them. Just the dim light from the lamps, our footsteps and the girl's breathing. In the atrium, which the windows lit now with the light of the crimson sunset, there was not a living soul.

H.S. leaned against McKay, exhausted by her wound. The bounty hunter pressed her to his chest and called out in a powerful voice, 'Is there anyone there? We need help for our companion!'

By way of reply there came the sound of a violin, poignant, lonely, and accompanied by a bass voice: 'Stay with us, Lord, as evening falls, the walk is lonely in this bitter vale of tears, grey trees and mute nightingales, and the Serpent is the master of evil. You weep on the cross and abandon me . . .' The same blues as the poor sharecroppers in the minefield.

McKay crossed the hall and kicked hard with his toe on the half-open door, which let a blade of light flash into the darkness. 'Open up, mister, I'm looking for a doctor. The girl's hurt.'

The old hinges creaked and a blind man appeared. He brushed the strings of the instrument with agile stumps of fingers reduced to the first joints. The skin of his face was black, drawn, and from time to time his lids revealed blue eyes. He was about fifty, his frizzy hair completely white. He wore an African tunic that came down to his feet, and gripped the gleaming wood of the violin like a walking stick.

'Doctor ain't here. It's Sunday. The others are at the river for the procession. Blessing the souls of the drowned. Only one here's me, Orpheus, and I'm playing the violin. My soul has already been touched by the waters, in far-off times and places.'

'We're at the Hopesville Leper Hospital, the biggest one in the county, just outside New Orleans. I didn't tell you so as not to scare you. Orpheus is a leper, too,' said McKay by way of apology.

Orpheus smiled. 'The Gospel heals us through the Master's touch.'

He picked up his violin, brushing the wall with his sleeve, passed through the door and headed towards the infirmary. Without any hesitation, dodging the table that bore the surgeon's instruments, he opened a little cabinet, and took out a bottle half filled with a reddish liquid. They followed him and saw him drench two wads of cotton wool with disinfectant and massage H.S.'s wound, feeling his way around its edges with fingers pink from his illness. 'Is it inflamed?'

'Yes.'

'How'd she get it?'

'A puma. Looked as though it was finishing her off. Instead, it just injured her.'

'But its claws were infected. The wound is swollen.'

His bass voice filled with tenderness. He took H.S.'s temperature with the back of his hand and asked, 'Do my fingers bother you? Don't worry, they're not contagious.'

She looked at him and smiled. 'I've seen far worse, on people whose hands were sound as a bell.'

Orpheus took three white pills from a locker.

'The doctor will be back tomorrow. He'll probably have gone off for a drink at the village bar after the function, honouring the cross and Dionysus in a single evening. That's the best I can do.'

He poked his head into the yard through a little window uncovered by netting, and called, 'Pamela! Bring us up some tea.'

He walked H.S. to a clean and empty camp bed, its horsehair mattress folded back. He straightened it with a clean blow of his hand and covered it with a blanket. 'Don't worry, now, it's all for you,' he said and laid her down.

'Excuse me!' Pamela was a woman with Flemish features. Leprosy had gnawed away her lips and nose, but her beauty survived intact beneath her deformation, just as the face of an Egyptian statue looks wonderful to us, even though it has been eroded by time. She touched the girl's wrist and said only, 'Fever.'

The blind man rummaged in his chest again, ground some herbs that smelled like cloves in a white mortar, and poured the powder into a little pan. He mixed it with some brown oil, and heated it up on the flame of a Bunsen burner. The light from the fire rose brightly up the wall, casting grotesque shadows.

H.S. was pale, her forehead covered with sweat that trickled down her white neck. Pamela poured the syrup into a china cup, checked with her poor lips that it wasn't too hot, watered it down with her tea and filtered it through H.S.'s teeth. Hiccupping and spluttering, the girl gulped it down, and gradually dozed off. Pamela covered her with the sheet, wiping her face with a worn cloth.

'You're McKay, aren't you? I recognise your voice. Good puma-hunting? They pay you well? While you're hunting them, have you felt the spirit of the slaughtered mountain lions? The Indians believe it lives on freely for ever. I've felt it powerfully, especially in the summer, when the forest is dense with leaves and animals. It comes in through the windows and fills my cell with sounds and smells. If you breathe in hard you can feel it breathing out. It's even coming from the girl's wound. And what about you other people? That rustle is from military clothing. It's hard, chinos, I'd say. Officers? Soldiers?'

The lieutenant presented our old charade, which now sounded inane and incredible.

'I'm an officer with the US Army, I'm escorting this Italian prisoner to New York. I'm delivering him to the radio station, to broadcast to free Europe.'

'Deliver us from evil . . .' murmured the old man. 'Italian?'

'That's right.'

'Lovely language. Will you say *Sì* for me?'

'*Sì*?'

'Yes, but without the question mark. The way you answered

when your mother said, "Do you want your milky coffee, Nino?"'

'How do you know my name's Nino?'

'Oh, come on, all Italians are called Nino.'

He had the rich, clear voice of a young singer.

'Are you afraid, Nino?'

Yes, I was afraid that the girl would leave us, losing us for ever in that lovely leper hospital, the African violinist speaking endlessly of tears and grief.

'Do my hands disgust you, Nino?' He raised his stumps. 'We lose sensitivity in the nerves and our fingers wear away until there's nothing left. If I hold them over a candle I can't feel the flame.'

On the Island, the man who taught me about fishing and bait was Uncle Nardo, who had been injured while fishing illegally with dynamite, and now he mended his sail using only his first joints. In the war, in the desert, I'd seen more amputees than a Lourdes stretcher-bearer.

'Give me your hand.' Orpheus opened his blue eyes and took my left hand, holding it against his chest with his forearm. He stroked the lines on my palm. 'A long life, Nino, a long life, isn't that right? And fear inside you. What have you got locked in your heart?'

The man's stump ran lightly and agreeably along the line that palmists say belongs to the Heart. 'The Heart. I think you were wounded by love, Nino? A lost woman, a woman who will never forget you . . .' The old man ran his finger along the Life line, and once again up to the line of the Head.

'No, no, Nino, it isn't love. Are you on the run? And what are you running from, my friend?' He leaned nimbly over and ran his thumb along the uppers of my shoes, gauging the dust that they had collected with the same intensity that he brought to the crushing of the medicinal herbs. 'Why are you fleeing across the sovereign territory of these United States of America? You –' and the pressure became intermittent, a tapping of Morse code, a dot, two lines '– you're escaping from the war, from what you became in this century's carnage. Because –' Swift as a fox jumping on a sparrow, he grabbed the lieutenant's left hand and pulled it tightly to him. '– You're together?'

I looked at him in terror, but the lieutenant, who had never lost his cool during the days of our flight, stared at him steadily, sure that life and death would depend on the prophecy that we were about to hear. The old man narrowed his eyes. He silently ran through the labyrinth of fate contained in the lieutenant's palm. He jumped to the hollow of his thumb, went down to the base of his fingers and rummaged among the folds of skin.

He raised his own disfigured hand in warning. 'If a hand dies, the destiny that was tattooed upon it doesn't change: burning a map of a country won't ease that country's suffering. The marks of destiny are not our destiny. It exists even when we don't notice them, and can't interpret them. You want to know what they are? The signs, I mean. Destiny will appear sooner than you expect it to.'

'Yes,' replied the lieutenant enthusiastically.

'That's a "yes" from a far-away Europe, a fighting Europe. You've got big ideas, son, and big hopes. You have them too, Nino, but your ideas and your hopes are different.'

He held each of us by the hand, pressing his wrist against his chest.

'Leprosy is the only illness mentioned even in the Scriptures. It represents sin, and the Lord Jesus Christ seems more powerful and charitable when he cleanses the leper with his blessed hand than when he raises Lazarus from the tomb. And who isn't cleansed? When the procession returns from the river, the living souls of the poor creatures will come here, the ones who have abandoned family, children and work because the county doctor, staying a good distance away, eh! has given them a note bearing a hastily scribbled sentence: Hansen's Disease. Leprosy. Their families got them ready by night and dispatched them to this plantation. Some people have been here for half a century, some were born here, some got married and live in cabins along the river. A powerful river that can't deliver us from evil. We're the last ones, the negroes, the lepers, the blind, a straw dog is worth more. And yet I see, and the voices of the night speak to me, and they speak to you too, don't they, Nino? The warbling of the swallows in the spring, the roar of the mountain lions, the flow of the river and its creatures, the grass that grows among the graves, and the sap of the trees, which keeps the trunks as solemn as the columns of a cathedral. They are benign presences, here, all around me. Our plantation is populated by ghosts. Sometimes the cruel persecute the kind. You try to help the weak, but they don't acknowledge it, you're too remote, they follow you pitifully and ask for help. But you can't comfort them. The ghosts hold out their poor hands, tender and covered in sores, but how can you reach them? You wanted to grow, Nino, you wanted to fight, to see the world. And now? Now you're fleeing towards the past, what do you think you're going to do? Where are my fingers, Nino, where are the notes I used to play, filling the Church of St John the Baptist, when Reverend Orville prayed, "Lord descend on this urchin and make him a musician."

'How desperate you are, Nino, clear in your simplicity, behind a lost love. Not a woman, Nino, don't make a mistake or you'll lose your way, you're not in search of a beloved woman, you're looking for the innocent and all-powerful love you had for her. Innocence and the force of omnipotence. Cynicism is the distinctive feature of men and demons. But candour is divine. God is innocent.

'But you –' Orpheus adopted the tone of the preacher in the pulpit, like Father Xante on the Island with his Good Friday sermon, demanding penitence for our sins, and staring at the lieutenant as though he could see him. '– You're a man of mystery, you have plans, your heart is in war and in battle. Power: do you know what power is?' He gripped our hands tighter, and through his ribs I could hear his heart palpitating, a baby chick trying to break through the shell, a small, proud heart. 'Who takes power in his hands? The white men, of course. Which men dominate the others and why, my brothers?' His words emerged clean and precise. It was as though he had been waiting for ever to be able to deliver this sermon. 'Some people give up their family, the peace of the hearth, they don't see their grandchildren growing up, they live in terror of defeat, frantically busying themselves with everything, but forgetting the truth. You're driven to act to promote virtue and improve the world, and soon what's left? The defence of power. Power is a way of making goodness but it becomes an end in itself, the preservation of emblems, a crown, a medal, a queue of customers.

'You, Lieutenant, are you American? You say: I want power and I will administer it differently, I will take care of my neighbour. You wonder: if the kind and the courageous stay far away from power, keeping their hands clean, sitting still like dogs, then the cruel, the greedy, the evil will be the ones who rule. If the good man doesn't descend into the struggle that makes voices hoarse, distorts the gentle features of the face and twists the hands, the cynics and egoists will prevail. But the moment the good man engages in the struggle, he becomes painfully aware that in that ring – as a boy I was a boxer, a bantamweight and not at all bad – the winner is the one with the crueller punch. You have to adapt, you have to strike as your enemies strike, you have to pay the corrupt referee. The dream of goodness to come remains alive, but every day your hands get dirty and so does your soul. In the ring, the most ferocious thugs are the ones who sniff out doubt and goodness as though they were weaknesses. They tear into you, after blood.'

'So what do we do then?' the lieutenant asked softly. 'Doesn't staying outside amount to complicity? How can you enjoy domestic peace, poetry, music, books, in the shadow of injustice? Is the just man who stands aside not a wicked man? How can you fight and govern, without giving in to ferocity?'

'Are you asking me, son? What power do you think I've enjoyed? I used to play music, and now I have no fingers. I used to fight in the ring, and now I can't clench my fists. I used to read the ancient tragedies, and now I can't see. I preached the free word of the Lord in the fields of the south, and now I'm nothing but a trained bear in this plantation of the sick. Epictetus, the slave philosopher, was lame, deformed, and his only power lay in writing, leaving a warning of wisdom. He wasn't in charge of his own time, in which he was the lowest of the low, but he was able to educate the future. And this is the answer, my friend. In the domestic peace that you fear as cowardly, or in the ring of cruelty, from whose customs you flee, the just man preaches a word of wisdom in the hope that others will judge him by his fruits, and not care narcissistically for the prize, nor give in, frustrated by defeat. He entrusts his strength to others, the only way to preserve it for those who will come after us. Thus acts the wise man. Not me, I am old now, alone and ignorant. I have nothing left but these words.'

'You're teaching us,' H.S. whispered hoarsely.

'You? I wouldn't be so bold. I'm a dead man, a ghost, like the ones my mother pacified with candles and fruit in the cemetery of St Louis Vieux in New Orleans. She put out sea snails, little perfumed Costa Rican bananas and green limes, around beeswax candles, and invited the ghosts to give themselves up and go in peace. They listened gratefully, unhappily. I can't do that any more.'

'What do the ghosts teach you?'

'That you have to fight: there's no difference between being at home with your children and bringing them up to enter the great and terrible world, crossing swords with injustice. I'm not telling you to improve the world, too many people are making it worse by trying to do just that. I'm telling you to fight the evil inside you, carefully, as someone wades through a freezing winter river, aware of the direction he is going in, but ready to mark time on a steep rock lest he be swallowed up by the icy water. There's courage in walking and courage in stopping, in attacking and in drawing back, in sowing a seed that will yield fruit only after our death, and in tapping your foot with impatience as you look at the spring flowers that take so long to turn into summer fruit. Enter, if you wish and if you know how, the halls of government, but without the pride that immediately corrupts. Frequent those rooms without being their guests. Work among the powerful without speaking as they do. Check your route in secret, to be sure that you have not strayed from it by so much as a step.'

'But how can we heal evil if it's inside us?'

Orpheus took the lieutenant's hand again and pressed it even harder to his thin ribcage. With his rough palm he stroked his eyes and cheeks, an affectionate, paternal gesture.

'The truth is: for today you will be judged, and not for

yesterday. You will be judged for the world and ideas that you have touched today, and the hopes that you have consumed today. The Eternal One will judge you for today. Today what you want is goodness, isn't that so, son?'

'Yes.'

'Have you done wrong?'

'I had no choice, maestro.'

'There's always a choice.'

'I couldn't see it.'

'And now you want to erase the past with a piece of heroism?'

'Yes. Dry up evil at its source.'

'At the cost of your life?'

'Yes.'

'There is no source of evil, son. Without evil we wouldn't know goodness. Evil is inside us, you admitted that yourself. The elect no longer exist. The saints are sinners and the sinners can be saints.'

'So are we lost?'

'No. Goodness is seeking goodness. Are you a Christian? I am the Way, announces the great Teacher. My mother, who had known Africa, and who had been in fetters as a child, used to say, "It is better to go forward and die than to stay where you are and die."'

'Do I have a short time left to live?'

'They who fight for justice often have a short life.'

'Will I win?'

'Do you want the truth?'

'Yes.'

'Can you stare at it without going blind?'

'I hope so.'

'If you think that winning the battle is conquering the field of evil, burning its banners, occupying its throne, then no, you won't win. But if you're capable of understanding that the only just battle lies in being willing to fight on the path of goodness, day after day, with constancy and strength, then the question no longer has a meaning. Do your duty: that is victory.'

'I'd just like to be able to do it.'

'You do what you have to do, fate will decide whether to smile on you. May your victory be to walk the path of justice: to reach it is not the goal of human beings like ourselves.'

In the room, the atmosphere was measured out by the girl's laboured breathing, the metallic footsteps of McKay's boots and the mellow dialogue of the leper and the lieutenant. It seemed like a confession, an ancient medieval rite with the mystical monk and the valiant knight before a heroic mission, saving the Holy Grail, freeing a damsel in chains from a terrible monster.

Pamela stroked H.S.'s hand, and every now and again she gave her a spoonful of syrup, wiping away the red stream that flowed from her lips. As in a painting by Caravaggio, the light emanated from the faces, rather than illuminating them from far away. Our souls seemed to be revealed in their poverty, in their wretchedness, but with the marvellous stamp of divinity, intact and formidable as on the day of Creation. We were facing fate, none of us had missed the appointment.

'My friend,' said McKay, turning back to face the lieutenant, 'if you're intent on a test of justice, I'll give you a hand. I looked for it in Spain and it eluded me. You talk of power, you should see it in wartime, just to touch it is frightening. Death, devastation, torture.'

'And what about the girl?' I asked.

'She will die. The doctor will find her dead,' replied Orpheus, grasping my wrist tightly.

I felt lost. H.S. had heard nothing, she seemed to be asleep.

'And are we going to stand here and plot while she dies? Is that your justice? Not even being able to drag a doctor here?'

Orpheus stared at me with his glazed eyes. 'The puma's venom is in her and it will not leave.'

He suddenly stopped talking, and I didn't understand that this was the end of the flight into nothing, the end of my life as I had known it. Everything ends like that, we think we are leaving a beloved season only for a moment and we never see it again, we call to a loved one, her voice rings out alive for the last time. So the girl departed, although not without one final gift. She half opened her thin mouth – had I really kissed it, and in what time and place? What does it mean to kiss a woman, what is left after the moment and the encounter? Why are we jealous, what do we fear? Where now is the kiss that I gave to the girl? On my rough lips? In my long-sighted eyes? Or in the miraculous attic where history keeps the sword that Brutus used against Caesar, the mantle confiscated from Giordano Bruno and the kiss that Nino Manes gave the Japanese prostitute?

H.S. moved, stretching her skinny body, already old, already lacking the roundness that had enchanted me in the hot bar in Arkansas. Slowly she raised her hand and passed me a note written on missal paper. She opened her bright eyes and said, 'I want to walk with you under blossoming apple trees. Will you remember me, Nino? Read this note. I was going to give it to you when we got there. You, lieutenant, are strong and brave, but you're the one I fell in love with, little one. Will you love me for ever, Nino? Will you come to me in the darkness?'

The old man smiled at her. 'The apple trees are already around you. Close your eyes, don't be afraid of the dark: it will protect you until Nino comes back.'

H.S. hadn't yet decided to let herself die. 'Read the note now.' I opened it and held it towards the faint light: 'Captain von Luck is a dangerous Nazi saboteur, nationality unknown, Manes is an Italian on the run, perhaps a fanatical accomplice. You, H.S., are to tail them and hand them in as soon as possible. The US Army is aware of your difficult situation, with your parents in the camps for foreign immigrants, a life on the margins of legality. You have to get them to New York. Military Headquarters is convinced that attacking them in the open field is dangerous and will prevent you from uncovering the Nazi terrorist network active in the USA. We want to discover their accomplices, and capture them only at the end.'

'How did you get this?' I asked gently.

'A boy gave it to me. His name's Cheever. He approached me. I'm afraid he fell in love . . .'

The girl clenched her teeth tightly, and departed this world.

The old man became aware of death in the room, closed H.S.'s eyes with his ravaged hands and prayed the Lord's Prayer: '. . . which art in heaven . . . thy kingdom come . . . deliver us from evil.'

From the river, along the nameless graves and beneath the sycamores, came the procession of the sick. Each one held a candle that flickered faintly in their spectacles, *sed libera nos a malo*. They passed the pavilions of the leper hospital and came towards us like glowworms. They set down the wax torches in a long, gleaming line, they picked up the girl's body, bathed it with a big sea sponge, oiled her with balm and dressed her in their poor uniform.

The mark of the mountain lion appeared red and strong, blood-red but not threatening now, a coral necklace torn from the depths, a bond linking us to the kingdom of the shadows, the kingdom of silence.

18

The lieutenant spoke, and his words still ring out clearly to me as I tell this story, and the backwash of La Tonnara roars below me. It's not a memory, memories are faint, a film, celluloid scraps from the remembered past which we edit and stage as we see fit, easing sorrow and adding happier notes. It's not a memory: I hear his voice, just as I saw the ghosts in the Old Mill as a boy. If I had a tape recorder I could record it and reproduce it for you, and if you were sitting next to me, and are you really? you could hear that voice, so determined yet somehow childlike, with the certainty of children when they plant themselves legs apart, hands on hips, a smile on their tanned faces, announcing to the world, 'I'm going to do it this way, because this is how I want to do it.'

The lieutenant said, 'Friends,' and for the first time I became aware of his European accent, which until then he had kept hidden by means of his skilful metamorphoses: 'I'm an Italian officer. Corvette Commander Athos Pollini. I used to command submarines, I specialise in sabotage. I sailed the submarine *Tazzoli* and the *Leonardo da Vinci*. With the *Da Vinci* we established the Italian Navy record for ships sunk,

120,243 tons, the most deadly non-German submarine force in the war. When I was in action off the coast of Puerto Rico, saving two women from the sharks, when they were drifting on a raft after the sinking of the steamer *Doña Aurora*, a wave knocked me into the sea. My crew did everything they could to get me back on board, but the billows drove us apart. I was found by the crew of the *Hackwood*, and ended up in prison in Amarillo. I didn't know it at the time, but it saved my life. We were based in Bordeaux, at Betasom headquarters, Italian submarines in the Atlantic. On the way back to Gibraltar, after I was captured, on May the 23rd 1943, the *Da Vinci* was intercepted by the British torpedo-boat destroyer *Active*. It took a hit and went down with all my sixty-three dear companions and the new commander, my friend Gianfranco Priaroggia. My place was with them. My big brother lost his sight in Russia. The younger one, the soccer ace, is a prisoner in one of these prairies. I believed in the fatherland, I thought war was a sport, like yachting off Elba with the wind in your sails. Until I finally understood, as a prisoner. My plan is simple, I know you won't betray me. I've escaped to get back home. I'll be the first escaped prisoner to do it. By pretending to be Nino's guard I'll get to New York and from there, together, we'll be able to board a neutral ship and reach Europe – Portugal or Spain. I'll ask to go back to the north, to the Republic of Salò, via France and Switzerland. I'll be welcomed by the Duce. The war is going badly for us, and a propaganda coup like that, a saboteur at large in America, is extremely valuable. Mussolini will want to give me a medal, interrogate me about what I've seen in America, about the morale of our troops in detention there. I'll say that I have some secrets to reveal to him personally. When we're on our own, face to face, I'll kill him. I'll kill the tyrant who has destroyed the fatherland. If I have my regulation pistol, I'll whack him. If they search me as a precaution, I'll cut his throat with my dagger if I have to. If I have nothing else I'll strangle him with my bare hands, then jump on top of him and finish him off before they kill me. I'm prepared to die, none of my comrades has survived, so why should I? At the camp the Gestapo must have suspected something, they must have heard something from a spy. Talking to the submarine crews, on the other side of the barbed wire, I must have said one word too many critical of the dictatorship. Rumours will have gone around, accusing me of being a bomber. The two American officers who wrote that note to H.S. are on our tail, Nino, we only just escaped them the day she brought us to safety. I still don't know why she did it. Now she's paying for her generosity, a capital offence in wartime. This is my plan. I know you'll think it's mad, and that you're ready to advise me to forget it, hand me over to the Military Police and wait for the end of the war drinking orange juice and eating omelettes. My father was a diplomat and hated the Duce. My mother was American. That's how I speak such good English. Look.' And from his battered wallet he drew a black-and-white photograph: his father in evening dress, and his mother, so like her son, elegant and fearless, an orchid between her fingers. 'It's for love of them that I don't want to go home, to the ruins of Florence, and see my youth and my country in a state of shame. I must try and confront evil. I'm a man on his own, and I know how little the life of a man on his own is worth in battle. But I'm oppressed by the shame of surrendering to evil without raising my hand against it. Help me.'

'I'm with you. I'm still your prisoner, and I'll cover you as far as New York and beyond if you want. I heard on the radio that they're looking for you. You're right, the Gestapo in the POW camps have fingered you as a terrorist.'

'You can take my truck,' said McKay, 'or if you prefer I'll give you a lift. We won't be so conspicuous.'

'What are they going to say about the girl?'

'They'll interrogate me and the patients here,' interrupted Orpheus. 'I'll say you weren't involved, and she came here on her own. The doctor will confirm that. He's a drunk, he wants to hang on to his job, and he won't want the military inspectors to know what's been going on.'

I felt ill. Everything was clear, everything was ready to go ahead. The girl was to be buried at dawn, according to the old man's instructions. 'I'm the mayor of this dead town. I take care of marriages and christenings,' he told us. 'I sort out quarrels and administer justice. I receive remittances and family correspondence. I'm the guardian of civilisation among the lepers, and when the food donations arrive, I distribute them in an equal way so that none of the bungalows goes short. The girl will be buried in the nameless field. The lepers don't want to leave traces of themselves in this vale of tears. They're afraid that a doctor or a tramp might read their name on the memorial stone – Smith, Alvarez, Manasse – recognise the city – Boston, Baltimore, Memphis – and slander the family to their neighbours. To protect their own dear ones, who were often the first to report them and exile them here, go nameless to Purgatory. Because after living with leprosy none of them deserves to go to hell.'

'We can't abandon her like a dog,' I said anxiously.

'You can come back and find her once the war is over. She'll have number XXXIII, it belonged to a rich girl who died many years ago. Her fiancé's father forced him to leave her the evening before their wedding, and when he was a very old man, and had been left a widower by the woman he had married, he came back to get her. He gave her a merciful burial close to home, in Charleston. This grave is empty. She'll go there. Thirty-three is the number of years that Christ lived, he'll protect her.'

'Protect her from what? From whom?' I cried angrily. 'We can't protect her, we can't take her with us to New York. She saved our lives, she could have reported us, and this is how we treat her?'

The lieutenant gripped my shoulders with his hands, tanned from our journey.

'It's not our fault, Nino.'

'We brought her face to face with that animal.'

'Life wouldn't leave her alone. She gave as good as she got, like a fighter. We all succumb, Nino, the only possible revenge is to go down as we are, without losing ourselves. She knew how to do that.'

'We killed her. You with your escape bid, I with my love. You remember the yelling in the minefield? I was consumed with jealousy, because the two of you had made love the night before.'

'We had?'

'Tell the truth for once.'

His green eyes grew very dark. 'The truth. As though telling it were enough. The truth that we can't understand, perfect, inured to our souls, what's the point? You want the truth? Yes, we made love. You had awoken her soul, you had made her feel alive again. Then you had fallen into a deep sleep, you were delirious. I was desperate. The Military Police were after us, they would take me back to camp and the Gestapo would have finished me off in a bag in the dark, my friend. How they worked it out I don't know. Perhaps I was betrayed by the forgers who gave me my papers, or perhaps they were startled because I'd managed to escape without telling them. I kissed her, we were siblings in desperation, the Reich, the Axis, Berlin, Tokyo, Rome, reduced to three unfortunates on a straw mattress, clinging to one another in the face of evil. You blame me? Don't you understand that the fact that we both slept with her that night makes us brothers, like at the minefield? Stay with me. But take care: my flight is dangerous now. They may think that I killed the girl so that she wouldn't report us. You were in Hereford, in the hardliners' camp. They'll say you're in league with the Republic of Salò, they'll say you're a fascist. Poor Nino . . .' He looked at me, really like a brother. 'You have a degree of courage that I envy.'

'You envy my courage? You were in the submarines, all your mates were killed. You want to kill the Duce, you've got all the armies of the world against you, and you talk about my courage? You . . .' I looked for words without finding them. 'You're mad, but you're a hero.'

He smiled as though I was a child. 'The heroes are in Europe, Nino, they're fighting in cellars. I didn't understand anything, I followed the road that had been chosen for me, deceiving myself that it was really mine, and you know why? Because I thought that excelling, doing your duty properly, was the right way to take charge of life. I never reflected about the meaning of my life, until now, looking at H.S. I would have ended up dead, my bones picked clean by the fish at the bottom of the Atlantic like my crewmen, I couldn't even have given an answer to my guardian angel, the one who watches over me and lights my way, if he asked me, "What have you done with the life that was given to you?" I could only answer, "I don't know." On my last mission, when I was shipwrecked, I escaped the sharks by climbing aboard a drifting American sloop. It was empty, and under the rowlocks I found a Bible abandoned by a missing midshipman. On the first page he had written in pencil, "You know, Lord, all the heroes are dead," followed by the signature, "Rick".'

He looked at me affectionately, running his knuckles over my hair, back and forth. A favourite gesture of my father, on the Island, before he set sail. Hadn't I perhaps been looking for him in Barbaroux, hadn't I dreamed that he would be my mentor, the dear father I hadn't had, stolen from me by a shipwreck that had made my mother a widow and me a boy bent over my algebra, with eyes only for Zita? Wasn't I looking for my father in the lieutenant, too?

'Yours is true courage, Manes. You studied, you fought with distinction in Africa, you chose the camp of the hard cases and, when your girl wrote to tell you that she was leaving with the professor, you escaped. You could have got drunk for a week on smuggled wine, humiliated yourself, thrown up, yielded to hatred or grown resigned: "So what's happened? I've saved my skin. Many people haven't, when I get back I'll find another girl." And instead you remained true to the life you chose, scattered with defeats, in war and in life, without giving in. You humbly started over again. Tenacity and humility are the virtues of the travelling hero. The rest is the desire for power denounced by Orpheus. My mission is a desperate one. You're crossing the great republic that defeated us, to start a new life. You won't get the girl back, you know that. But the pilgrimage has changed you. You remember the time you spent questioning me? "What does Odysseus dream?" you asked me. I have an answer to that, I've never told you it, whether out of sleepiness or exhaustion. Listen. When Troy has fallen, Odysseus loses all his comrades. In exile out at sea, he has to win back his besieged kingdom in Ithaca from the suitors, and go with an oar on his shoulder, in penance to Poseidon for blinding his son Polyphemus, the fierce Cyclops, and peasants who have never even heard of the sea will use the oar to hold their vines up. You too, like Odysseus, know that you will find the void when you go home. Nothing left of your former self, Zita gone, youth gone, studies gone. You have joined forces with me, you have taken risks, you have come all this way by fighting for your life. A hero always fights for life, Nino, only fascists shout "Long live death." You have the courage to go on deceiving yourself, brandishing your candour like a weapon. It's people like you, Nino, who inherit history and, if we're to believe the Scriptures – and during these most recent days of mine in America I have discovered that I am a true believer – the Kingdom yet to come.'

'But, Lieutenant, wait. Athos?' For the first time I uttered his real name and it sounded strange to me, something out of *The Three Musketeers*, Athos, the most melancholy and intelligent of the king's swordsmen. 'Your name's Athos, isn't it? I just wanted to get back to my parish and hear the *Suscipiat Dominus* at my wedding. You're sorting out your papers with dignity. I'm escaping on my own behalf, you're fleeing for a noble purpose.'

He didn't reply. The lepers, guided by Orpheus's violin like members of an orchestra following the conductor's baton, laid H.S. on a naked bier and hoisted it on to their shoulders. They walked along by the pavilions, went back down the stairs and out on to the lawn towards the cemetery. They were wearing wooden clogs, tied by a leather strap. To keep their balance, they followed the steady rhythm of their soles, a slow percussion. They laid her by grave number XXXIII, freshly dug, the grass hadn't grown yet on the red clay. The lieutenant and McKay stood to attention. I didn't, I've always found military ceremonies gloomy and disheartening. But when Orpheus resumed that sharecroppers' blues that we had interrupted when H.S. was still alive – 'Stay with us, Lord, as evening falls' – I burst into tears. It was a song without hope. The blind man's bass notes expressed pain and suffering to the Eternal One, without rancour or illusion. Without yearning for the redemption to come. Pain was presented as a gift, without expectation of a reward, with the grieving humility with which H.S.'s body was consigned to the earth. When the grey stone bearing the numbers XXXIII covered the girl from sight, the procession melted away.

We had to get moving again, the American officers were bound to be near the sanatorium. There was no longer any pretext for pretending to be what we weren't: the lieutenant with his true name and rank, Commander Athos Pollini, reconnoitring for his attempt on the life of the Duce, but hunted by the Americans, and I, his accomplice to some extent, who had escaped because of an incredible love story. McKay, a soldier in the war that had been lost in Spain, would hide us in his truck. I can't tell you whether he was doing it in the spirit of a republican anti-fascist or out of an instinct for adventure, the frontiersman helping the tramp, the hopeless hobo, when the cops, the railway guards, patrolled the wagons travelling across the Great Plains. The rebel with the banjo around his neck against the cut-throat goons.

'Why don't you talk to Cheever and that other guy? Explain to them that you're trying to kill the tyrant, he's their enemy now, they'll let you go, they'll cover you on your mission, you'll see. Reach an agreement. The American army is full of decent volunteers who are making serious sacrifices for freedom. They're not making a fuss, they're just getting on with it. They're republicans, brother.'

'Who's going to believe me?' replied the lieutenant. We all still called him the lieutenant, Commander Athos Pollini remained a ghost. 'No one. They'd send me to the camp until the unconditional surrender. Theirs is a serious war, not an adventure. I have to do it on my own.'

Orpheus didn't want to let us go. He had read our futures and interpreted our past, he was holding our companion hostage, but when it came to saying our farewells he turned with a frown, stroking the ground with his violin and disappearing under the magnolias. Pamela walked him as far as the gate that we had passed through, unawares, a few hours before. We were already far away, and Orpheus appeared behind the metal grille that protected his window. He pointed to me with his stump and called, 'Guard your lives and you will lose them, lose them and you will find them. Climb into the sycamore, my friends, to see the Lord if you ever pass by!'

To escape surveillance, McKay drove us in a long, lazy detour. He headed south, along the Florida swamps, towards Okefenokee, where the sky was always grey, the road empty, the lemonade hot and the alligator soup tasted of blood and soil. Our pursuers had lost us at the leper hospital. They hadn't worked out that we were here, perhaps the people they had questioned didn't want to send two elegant officers to this place of tears. The south was accustomed to everything, no one asked any questions of our bizarre trio when they sold us a Coke from palm-roofed kiosks.

I was sleeping on the truck's loading platform, which was stuffed with sacks. The bumps from holes in the road, the dust, the flickering sun didn't wake me up. Like a beast of burden, no pain could drag me from the heavy sleep into which I had fallen. Only one memory has stayed with me from those long hours, one late afternoon. A violent jerk made me start, and in my half-sleep I thought, damn, the liberty ship. I hated sleeping with my feet dangling out of my berth beneath the waves on the Atlantic crossing as they deported me to America. I sat up. Leaning out of the window, McKay, his red beard blowing in the wind, was negotiating with a wizened bosun. The truck was secured to a barge by a shiny chain. We were floating gently down a big brown river. McKay was saying, 'A dollar a head? Madness, I won't pay more than a nickel for each of them.'

The impassive sailor manoeuvred his way along the river with two long poles, one bend after another, occasionally paying attention to a bamboo fishing rod that he had propped up on the deck. The smell of the water was intense, like the river itself. A black snake, eyes like periscopes, was following us at a constant distance. Bright, transcendent light widened the sky above the majestic river path. I heard the chugs of the diesel engine carrying us to the opposite shore. I looked at the sun, we were finally heading north.

A wet-winged black cormorant flapped over to a sandbank to swallow the carp it had just caught. The helmsman looked at it enviously and spat into the river. I knocked on the window dividing my platform from the driver's cabin. 'What river's this?' I was going to ask. Once again, the lieutenant read my mind. 'This is Ol' Man River. I said we'd see the Mississippi, brother. Next stop New York City.'

19

The two muddy banks of the river, covered with green bushes, quickly disappeared, as though the Mississippi were turning into a metal sea, to make way for the houses of New Orleans. The crawfishermen's boats pitched along the current, their helmsmen battling the heavy pull of the water that rushed furiously towards the estuary and the ocean.

Louis Cafard knew that his manoeuvre had failed. In some café somewhere, among doughnuts and cups of milky coffee, his adversaries had eluded him. Not thanks to accomplices, only General Matthews insisted on believing in the Nazi network in America. No, they had camouflaged themselves in the countryside, like egrets, the white herons with the serpentine necks that fished for eels in the swamp. The south had swallowed them up, turning them into ghosts raised by the heat on the tarmac. In the morning, when the cocks crowed to warn that the sun was about to awaken the nation, they turned into shadows. And in the evening, when the bats darted through oak trees they reappeared, invisible to everyone except the dead in the cemeteries, victims of malaria or smuggling, shot down by the pistols of the Union soldiers, a fantastic past that he, Cafard, should have brushed aside when it, instead, had mocked him.

A truck came towards him, yellow fog-lights ablaze. He remembered his far-away European flight: by managing to get away on his own, had he won? Or had he rather been a coward, incapable of a last stand like the Greeks at Thermopylae? He threw his cigarette into the big river, where a toad swelled, croaking as loud as a calf before diving arrogantly into the water. His hopes of capturing the fugitive had gone up in smoke. He and Cheever had hooked up with the girl called H.S., he had spoken to her, had left a message for her. Taking those two men by force could be difficult. General Matthews in Washington recommended: 'No shooting, no journalists. I don't want to see headlines like "Terrorist unit at large in the United States". Take them in silence, no gunfire, no vainglorious suburban sheriffs calling in the reporters.'

H.S. had said yes, had respected the orders, the fugitives had been sighted and photographed, both of them, but on the day agreed for their capture, when she should have answered the public phone in a railway station on the Delta, she had disappeared. Her promises had come to nothing, while her brothers had been transferred from the front line in Italy, and her parents declassified as 'non-dangerous aliens', and sent home to Los Angeles.

Cheever was worried. 'Perhaps they've eliminated her, they've discovered that we're after them.' He said no more than that, but Cafard had worked out that he was in love with H.S.

Desperate young men will unreasoningly yield to passion, they can easily be bowled over by an image.

Now that their contact with the girl was lost, all that remained was to catch the fugitives at all costs, adopting a rational plan in order to refute once and for all the fairytale version their bosses insisted upon, convinced that the network of Nazi infiltrators was a threat to the USA.

Cafard had spent a long time interrogating Commander Pollini's brother. 'My brother's an anti-fascist, there are three brothers, one wounded at the Russian front, me, the imprisoned soccer player, and finally the submarine commander.'

Summoned once again to a hut after their first meeting at the camp, he had arrived with a bleeding eye and a swollen face.

'What happened to you?' Cheever had asked.

'A mid-air collision, a bad mistake. And the ref didn't even declare a penalty.'

He had done nothing more than answer the questions, yes, yes, no, no, as though collaborating no more than his uniform would permit. In the doorway, Cafard had pressed him. 'Why did they beat you up?'

'Misunderstandings, Major. You treat us very well, but our lives aren't easy.'

'Your brother is risking the firing squad. Washington thinks he's a spy. Nazi Captain von Luck.'

Cafard's tone had struck home. Simone Pollini – that was the footballer's name – loved his brother Athos, and seeing him in the clutches of death, in a war that was already over for himself and his brother, gave him a twinge of sympathy for the steely officer. He came over to him, turning his back on the door that opened on to the camp. He stood to a kind of attention. 'Gentlemen, my brother is not a spy, nor a terrorist. Don't ask me how he thinks and what drives him, but trust me. He wouldn't harm a hair on anyone's head. If you get him in your sights, don't shoot, ask him to surrender, he isn't violent, I assure you.'

Cafard believed him. If you ever listen to a real killer – and he had listened to too many, giving him information in the bars of Budapest when he was on secret missions – you come to recognise the timbre of sincerity. That was why Cafard despised General Matthews and liked his young escort, Cheever. Because cynics can't tell cruelty from sincerity, and in war, over time, they will get you into trouble. Cheever didn't know what to believe: in his adventurous life, he never knew how to tell good from bad. He understood that Cafard had silently formulated a judgement, and he in turn tried to find one of his own, failed to do so, and shifted with embarrassment in his chair, his mind on H.S.

'Don't worry, Mr Pollini,' said Cafard, in Italian, certain that they'd missed their rendezvous by now. Now he had to stop the two men before they disappeared into the New York crowd. He had no doubt that they would catch the men, he made it a matter of principle never to have doubts during a mission: but in his heart he doubted the justice of this expedition. He felt flabby, disappointed, already succumbing to the post-war calm. Then he was sorry he couldn't simply abandon the mission, acknowledge that he was beaten, send his warrant card back to Washington. His code of ethics stopped him from doing so, war had to be fought to the bitter end.

'My brother's intentions aren't cruel, sir,' Pollini had replied. But Cheever wondered: who was that other drifter, Manes, escaping from Hereford Camp 1? And what if he was the real boss? If he was the saboteur we're looking for? But perhaps his jealousy had been aroused by the tenderness that had appeared in H.S.'s eyes when he had asked her about Nino.

Cafard reread the secret dispatches about U-boat sightings off the Atlantic coast. He didn't believe in the existence of an undercover army in the USA, but he couldn't rule out the possibility of a submarine landing a unit somewhere on the vast eastern seaboard to prepare an attack in collusion with the two fugitives. He was worried that Pollini had been a heroic submarine commander, who had miraculously escaped the sinking of his vessel only because a wave had knocked him into the water, allowing him to be captured by the Americans. By the yellow light of his torch, he read through the information that had arrived via telex from Italy and England: 'To whom it may concern, Intelligence Div. Nav. Staff – Admiralty London S.W. 0.350 et al.

'Arrangements concerning the use and strategic deployment of Italian submarines in the Atlantic, established on 20 and 21 June 1939, between the commander of the German Kriegsmarine, Admiral Erich Raeder and the Italian admiral Domenico Cavagnari. Underwater fleet of the Italian Army, when the country entered the war on 10 June 1940, consisted of 113 submarines, the second largest fleet in the world after the Soviet Union in terms of number of vessels, and second to the United States in overall tonnage. It should also be observed that in 1939 Berlin had only 57 submarines, barely 26 of which could be moved to the Atlantic. From 1 September 1940, the Betasom Italian submarine base in Bordeaux went into operation, planning attacks in the ocean. Other units entered the waters off Gibraltar, despite the steel nets and mines laid by British defence. Accords with their German allies allowed the Italians to patrol the waters, and launch attacks on British and American convoys. Submarines have been dispatched from the bases, Maricosom and Betasom in Bordeaux, to Bermuda and Florida, the Caribbean, the Bahamas, Haiti and the Antilles, as far as the Brazilian coast. Unconfirmed sightings and sinkings locate Italian equipment further north, beyond the Carolinas and Long Island. On the other side of the ocean, the area covered by the craft and crew of his Italian Majesty from 10 June 1940 until 8 September 1943 occupies the zone from the Gulf of Gascony to Cape Finisterre, Spain, Gibraltar, the Canary Islands, the Cape Verde Islands, Freetown in Africa and Cape Palmas. According to the data so far at our disposal, 32 Italian submarines have operated within the area of hostilities in the Atlantic. 16 were lost in military action. 5 of these were captured by German armed forces after the armistice on 8 September, one was handed over to the British Royal Navy and 10 returned to friendly waters in Italy. The 32 ocean-going vessels sank 109 ships, a total of 593,864 tons. Another 4 ships and a torpedo-boat destroyer were damaged. It is highly likely that Italian submarines are operating out of German headquarters, or the headquarters of the Republic of Salò. They could be: 1. among the five boats captured by the Germans after the armistice; 2. among the nine vessels named from S1 to S9, each with a tonnage of 797, handed over by the Italian Navy to the German Navy. At the time of the armistice, they were based off Danzig, complete with Italian crews. Many men opted for internment in a concentration camp, but Germans and Salò fascists could have recruited staff loyal to the Duce, and put vessels S1 to S9 back to sea; 3. part of the so-called Ghost Fleet, vessels from the Betasom base believed lost at sea because of detritus and the unloading of large quantities of fuel, and in fact hidden in friendly or neutral waters, such as those off the coast of Spain. It is not impossible that vessels from the Ghost Fleet were under the orders of Salò, and available to transport German or Italian units to the American Atlantic coast. Some Italian raiders have joined forces with the Northern Republic, and many of them specialise in sabotage operations behind the lines.'

So the documents of the military bureaucracy contradicted the anxious candour of the younger Pollini brother. Cafard hated feeling at the mercy of chance. Preparing things, studying a plan, however unlikely it might be, gave him courage. Having to get up in the morning, switching on the car engine, rereading files, without a clear track to follow, made the hunt distasteful to him, as though he were on the high sea, and had to intercept, alone and swimming in the water, what remained of the Ghost Fleet of the Italians.

20

I barely remember anything about the Atlantic coast of the United States. From New Orleans to New York I slept in the back of the van, as though hypnotised. I was extremely exhausted, and the lieutenant's words made things even worse. Why did he see me as a hero?

I didn't feel like a champion. I dozed, despite the bumps of the truck, and the humps of the Appalachian Mountains that unwound before us. Every now and again McKay stopped to ask directions from a toothless boy, his blue jeans bleached from hard work. Urchins emerged from the bleak scrubland, ran around the truck and stroked its muddy wheels, as I myself had done as a lad when the first blue car of the bosses in La Tonnara rolled up among us for a day, its passengers beautiful green-eyed ladies wearing ostrich boas and scarves that blew about in the brackish breeze. They threw us copper coins, and my friends stacked themselves up in human pyramids, grimacing and laughing for just a little more. In the summer the boys dived from the rock of the Impisu to cries of alarm from the ladies, to catch the money that the gentlemen had languidly thrown among the seaweed. I rarely did. But one year, thanks to a clever dive, I did in fact come home with two jangling coins and my mother had given me an angry slap, a real thump, the only one I ever had in my life. 'We're not beggars, we work for a living!' And she had told me to put the two little coins in the poor-box at San Noè.

The baroness's coins had filled me with such joy that now, years later, I wanted to violate my mother's commandment and throw money to the dirty street children. But I had nothing on me, not a cent, not a dollar, nothing. McKay and the lieutenant took care of the kitty and the gas coupons forged at the camp.

Those are the only memories I have of that long truck journey. Between half-closed lids I saw the south of the Civil War slipping past, steering clear of Washington, where our presence would have aroused suspicions. We drove up through industrious Pennsylvania, where they were forging the weapons of victory. To avoid being spotted by the security forces, we headed north towards Albany and Canada, before heading straight south again, towards the magnificent place that is New York. In Poughkeepsie, echoing with foundries, McKay left us, and of him, too, puma-hunter and Republican fighter, I have only a faint memory. He gave us his truck, replying in a stentorian voice to the lieutenant's protests, 'I'm going to Harlem, I'm going to hop a freight train like a hobo. I've got a girlfriend, widow of a jazz musician, I'll stay with her for a while and then we'll see. Death to fascism, freedom to the people. *La lucha* will lead us to the future, *resistir y fortificar es vencer.*'

The lieutenant took the wheel. He followed the country roads, now green and beautiful, dappled with fruit trees – apple trees, cherry trees, dark plums – and herds of strong, healthy, black and white cattle, staring at us indolently. There were silos full of grain: no one would have believed that we were in a country at war. It was near one of those opulent farms that I must have regained consciousness. Having left the hot south, my senses became acute once more, and I was ready for the final act of my escape, New York, Empire State. I dreamed again of noble Odysseus: from the deck of his ship, stupefied as I was by fatigue and unhappiness, he glimpsed Ithaca and his loved ones, or the dead men he was leaving behind, salt-whitened, terrible, swollen, drowned. At the end of his adventures did he count his days with regret, or did he pine with yearning, praying to the eternal goddess Athena, his protector, that they might soon come to an end? What will the hero dream as he lives out a nightmare? Does he remorsefully evoke the ghosts of his comrades, lost one by one? What fears, what anxieties still shake him? He had gone down among the ghosts of Hades, challenging eternal death, and glorious Achilles had revealed to him the melancholy moral of the pagan world. 'Better to be poor on the earth than king of the fallen, Odysseus.' He had tried in vain to hug his mother, clutching nothing but air. Was that failed embrace not perhaps a punishment for the hugs he had not bestowed on earth, to Penelope, to Telemachus, when he had taken up arms against Troy despite their wishes, putting a king's duty before life's true affections?

I believed that the only anguish and the only residual joy in Odysseus' dreams were the cords that bound him, puppet-like, to his fate. What was the good of blinding Cyclops, if he couldn't win the day? Athena had brought him to these horrendous waters, glorious Athena had brought him honour. He had followed in her footprints: and back at the minefield the lieutenant and I had faithfully placed our footprints in those of the booted giant. Was it a sign of noble courage to accept one's own fate? Odysseus, I decided, as I lay motionless in the truck, dreamed of the assent that every one of us, man and woman, owes to fate. In his anguished reverie he, the noblest and most constant hero, understood that he was nothing, that he had accomplished nothing. His life, loving enchanted goddesses and pale princesses, was nothing, it was no different to that of the lowest plebeian, Thersites, whom he had beaten mercilessly beneath the rock of Troy, just because he had dared to insult the king. Odysseus had rained a hail of blows down upon him, using his heavy sceptre of power as a mace. The troops who witnessed the thrashing had understood its cruel symbolism, and order had returned to the Achaean camp. What had driven Odysseus to rage, so rare in him, was the unsettled awareness that Thersites might be right to mock the Greek princes. Their parade of plumes and gleaming bronzes, beneath the sun of Priam's city, was nothing but a farce. Odysseus, the hero whom generations of humans would admire for his wisdom, was nothing but a puppet, even more ridiculous than Thersites, in the self-important illusion of being a great weaver of destinies, his own and other people's.

His pilgrimage with the oar over his shoulder was also a penance for his haughtiness, his fear of humility. Far from the sea, among shepherds unaware of his epic journey, alone with himself, Odysseus was finally great. Unknown to the world, forgotten by the love and hatred of Mount Olympus. That is our moment of revelation: when we are lost to the world, and able to accept the fate of the void, a shadow among shadows, even before we die.

So the last monster to be slain was pride, the arrogance of victory, the powerful meanness that had led Odysseus to insult the injured Cyclops, bringing years of suffering down upon himself. And why? Having blinded the monster, Poseidon's son, he hadn't been able to keep himself from signing off the task with his real name, abandoning the humble and powerful guise of No-Man. He could have lived in the void, a man among his companions. By shouting, 'Recognise me, I am Odysseus!' he had condemned them all to death.

So Odysseus dreamed constantly, or at least that was what I thought I had worked out in the twilight of my flight. I too had tried to become a shadow, to become nothing, a bird of the Texan fields who neither reaped nor sowed. Had I shown my mettle in some task or other, had I given proof of some kind of courage? In the minefield, which madness had drawn me into, I had obeyed the foot-steps of the giant, like Orazio on the Island when he was seized by his fits of sleepwalking and wandered about on the church belltower, high above the cobbled church square, clutching the rope of the lightning conductor. The mountain lion had sacrificed the girl because she had seemed weak, whereas in fact she was a rock. In the leper hospital we had heeded Orpheus' arguments and allowed him to bury H.S. in the anonymity of grave XXXIII, along with my days of freedom without citizenship. Now my conscience was awakening, and like Odysseus I had to carry an oar over my shoulder.

I opened my eyes, woke up and heard the sad, friendly song: '*Rosamunda, tu sei la vita per me, nei tuoi baci c'è tanta felicità, più ti guardo e più . . .*' intoned by torn and battered people, whose only chance of happiness lay in avoiding the evil to come.

I quickly opened the window, and struck the side of the truck with my hand.

'Friends, where are you from?'

'He wants to know where we're from! We're from Italy, where else?'

'Prisoners, farmers?'

'POWs, yes, sir, *povieri*, poor POWs and we're doing our duty here in the United States of America.'

They were four young boys and an old man, four boys like his sons, the man as the father. Sitting on the edge of the white road, they were eating bread and baloney, the name the Americans give to our mortadella, and drinking from a bottle of wine, so cold that the glass was misted.

'D'you want a drop, mate?' asked the youngest one. The lieutenant eased on the brakes and the bottle passed into my hand. I took a long swig and freed myself from my sluggish dreams. It was strong and sharp, straw-yellow. The boy asked, 'And where are you from, Italian guy?'

I told him about the Island and La Tonnara. 'The south? I'm from the south, too, but I work in the north and the boss is Tuscan,' and with a slice of bread skewered with a knife he pointed to the old man, who was smoothing back his white hair. His jacket was splattered with many colours, ochre, red, burnt sienna, amaranthine, indigo, turquoise, two long banner-red splashes and lots of drops of ultramarine.

'You want to see the church?'

'What church?'

'The one we're painting. Father Samuel, the parish priest, is Irish. He came to serve mass at the camp, met the boss, he's famous, he's painted in Rome and Paris. He summoned up the courage and one day he asked him, "Boss, would you decorate our church? It's humble compared to the cathedrals you've painted, but it's still art and the glory of God. You can take all the helpers you want out of the camp, you'll be free, you'll have all the time you like." The boss hesitates, and we beg him, "At least we'll be outside!" To make us happy he says yes, but then he goes bananas. He needs brushes, paints, wants to leave the prejudices of the camp behind him, teach us the technique. All in all, from being a quiet, tranquil person he turned into a demon. He's never contented, he makes us work day and night, he sketches cartoons, mixes paints, invents things, yells at you every time you make a mistake. He uses the old fresco method in the daytime, every morning we soak the area of plaster that's going to be painted on, and he paints on it *affresco*, a face, a cloak, the head of a saint. If the area dries too quickly, we have to start all over again. Except that Father Samuel's chapel isn't enough for him, accustomed as he is to larger buildings. Then he taught us to cover the adjacent walls with a special kind of stucco, a marble effect, which he's invented himself and which, when it dries, becomes gleaming and eternal like Carrara marble, yes sir, the kind dug up by Michelangelo himself. As for him,' and he pointed to his thin companion, who was biting into the fattest loaf, 'he cut the stained glass. They carve the wood and prepare the terracotta. Look at the Via Crucis – the stations are drying in the sun. When it gets hot it gets as hot as an oven.'

I pulled myself down from the truck and found myself looking at the little panels of baked clay laid out along the wall of the freshly whitewashed priest's house. Jesus falls the first time. Christ was bent, one knee forward, the Cross weighing him down mercilessly, but the representation didn't have the sweet manger-scene appearance of the statuettes of the Via Crucis in San Noè. Here the faces of the Romans were contorted with hatred, and the crowd gathered around the tormented figure waving furious fists. One peasant was grabbing Jesus by the collar of his tunic, and a woman was clawing at him fiercely with sharp fingernails. In the next panel, Jesus was hoisted on to the Cross, his hands tortured by the nails, John at his injured feet, and the Madonna bewitched with grief, imploring, already defeated.

'Do you like it?'

I turned around: it was the voice of the maestro, busy smoking a Camel, gauzy with tobacco smoke.

'How many mothers have wept like that, in this war?'

'I couldn't say. The soul of each one is transfixed like the Madonna at Golgotha. Without the blessing of divine resurrection.'

'What will happen to your work when you go home again at the end of the war? You'll be leaving a masterpiece behind, in the open countryside.'

He didn't reply, instead pointing to one of his young craftsmen in a grey-green uniform, chiselling the letters of an inscription. 'You know that every stonecutter has his own precise calligraphy? In Rome I was able to recognise all the ancient Romans, from the grace of an O, the strength of a V. This boy of mine risks getting good.'

Many letters were still covered by a veil of dust, which the artist gently blew away, and on others the coloured moulds were placed: 'ITALICI MILITES IN MAXIMO NOVISSIMO BELLO CAPTIVI, HOC OPUS PERFECERUNT AD DEI GLORIAM ENARRANDAM ET MEMORIAM REMOTAE INFELICIS PATRIAE HONORANDAM.' I worked it out slowly: 'Italian soldier prisoners in the last world war carried out this work for the glory of God and in honour of their remote and unhappy fatherland.'

The man patiently ground out the letters to be refined, using a little brush to get rid of the impurities. Once an O was perfected, he turned to me, face covered with dust.

'Can I make myself useful?'

I hadn't known what to ask the maestro, he intimidated me with his scented cigarette and the tragic faces of his creations. In a low voice I asked the stonecutter, 'Where are we?'

'The chapel in Poughkeepsie.'

'And how far's New York?'

'You're going to New York?'

'God willing,' replied the lieutenant in his beautiful Italian, his eyes resting enchanted on the panels, the glass, the drawings for the frescoes ready to be copied.

'God loves the needy,' said the maestro with a smile, 'and it looks to me as if you could use some help. Come into the church and look at our work.'

The lieutenant followed me into the gloom. And, raising his eyes, as the painter climbed up on to a rough wooden platform, we saw before us a crowd of creatures and figures painted on the arches of the chapel. At the bottom was the cry of amazement of the shepherds at the Nativity, a presage of the suffering that was drying in the sun outside, in the Via Crucis. From the top, the angels came fluttering down in flocks, their wings entangled, like prisoners called to mess. Suspended between heaven and earth, a ragged Christ. Suffering but serene, a torn tunic over his shoulders, the colour of our uniforms.

'He looks like us, doesn't he?' said the boy who earlier had asked me if I wanted to share their wine and, entering the church, had piously put the bottle into a bag.

'But he's very beautiful, whereas look at us . . .'

'We're beautiful too: it's just that by dint of looking at ourselves suffering we can see only our grimaces. You know why I'm painting here? Because in this setting I can recognise our true faces, free of the stench of the queue for the latrines. I see you as you are, beautiful in your pain and expectation,' the maestro called down from the top of his platform, his fist clutching a sponge to dry an angelic face. 'We're beaten, confused, far from home, our life has vanished. And yet we will never be as dear to Heaven as we are in this misfortune. Back home, at work, amongst our families, certain of affection, even glory for some of us, bitterness and boredom will set in, and indifference will gnaw away at us.'

'You're an artist, maestro. I'm going to enjoy it all enormously and I never want to leave home again by so much as a footstep,' interrupted the boy with the wine, cheerful and sure of his opinion. His voice was clear, like that of gunner Beretta – 'Shall we shoot, Manè?'

'We're strange creatures,' the maestro went on without listening to him, 'suffering forms beauty within us. Peace and serenity make us mediocre. When will I ever paint as well as this again? My masterpiece will be seen only by meek herdsmen from the valley, and it is to them, without their knowledge, that I am dedicating my life's work. At first I was anxious about it, but then I realised that only here can I remain with myself, me, the colours and beauty. I enjoy it, it seems to me to be the most formidable gift of this long captivity. Isn't that funny? My stonecutter carves his letters as though his life depended on it. Emperor Augustus himself couldn't have had more loyal craftsmen. Every technique that I have taught these boys they have learned, becoming maestros in their turn. They don't count the hours, they get no wages, they don't expect the praise of critics and gallery owners. They live in the studio, in the workplace, as in the days of Benvenuto Cellini. They nibble on an apple, they eat great plates of spaghetti, share white wine when they have any, and wait to go home, but they're alive thanks to the beauty that they're creating. Back in Milan I'll be a mummified old painter once again. Here I'm exploding with energy, like a boy with his first canvas. Work is our only reality. We're proud of this little bit of Italy that we've made one block at a time. Happy when the *camans*, who have locked us up for years like cows in a byre, stand open-mouthed at the sight of the angels we have drawn from our misery. They take their caps off, cross themselves piously, kiss my hands, "Well done, maestro! Well done, Italians!"'

I don't know why Major B, who would have been acclaimed as one of our major artists even at home, and whose work would have ended up hanging from a beam in his beloved Brera Gallery, addressed his thoughts to me. I was no longer as startled as I had been, that frescoed limbo of angels, shepherds and prisoners was the last station of my own Via Crucis. The maestro and the boys had taken a few square metres of universe and freed them from war, turning them into a kingdom of equality and grace, where the techniques of the past were handed down; a salon of the poor, revived from Renaissance Florence, admired by the powerful and enchanted victors. I too crossed myself: a homage to those who never surrender, who go on humbly fighting.

'Stay with us. I need a carpenter. What do you think? I can easily ask the camp commander to have you transferred here. I've painted his wife's portrait, and he says he never knew, until the day he hung the canvas on the wall of his hut, that he had married such a wise and beautiful woman. The miracle of paint! It makes us notice what we have in front of our eyes and fail to understand. Even strict Colonel Summers can recognise that.'

'I don't know anything about carpentry, Major.'

'You'll learn. Our community is alive because yesterday's pupils are today's teachers. We share the craftsmen's techniques, no one goes back to camp in the evening without having learned something new.'

I should have said yes. I could have asked the lieutenant, who stood staring at the angelic faces, closing his fingers like a lens, concentrating on a detail, to pretend to be my boss for one last time. To say that I had been escaping, that I was an actor-prisoner with a beautiful speaking voice, going to New York to read news to be broadcast to Europe. To leave me here at the camp, with the maestro, to paint the wooden ribs of the vaulting. At the end of the war, they would put my presence down to one of those errors by the military bureaucracy, which are quite capable of sending a whole unit to the other end of the world, let alone one harmless POW. Lost in the countryside of upstate New York, I would have planed wood, mixed paint and plaster, until peace was declared. Giving up my mad chase on the mighty ocean, leaving among my memories the mountain lion and the procession of lepers, tearing up Zita's letter and throwing it to the winds, letting the fragments scatter among the tall rye and the clover.

'So?' asked the maestro, laying his indigo-spattered hand on my shoulder. A thousand colours, the whole fluorescent rainbow decorating his fingers and his dry skin, an artist's tattoo. His turquoise eyes gazed at me serenely. The lieutenant left the church and waited outside.

'I can't, maestro. Thank you for your invitation, it would be an honour. But I have a task that I can't shirk.'

'So you really are escaping? You have my word as an officer that I won't report you. We're no longer at war with the Americans, but escape remains a prisoner's right, guaranteed by the Geneva Convention.'

'You have my trust, Major. I am escaping, it's true. Now I'm not sure. I'm confused.'

'Where did you set off from?'

'Texas, Hereford Camp 1.'

'Man alive! Texas? That's thousands of miles away. Not even Lieutenant Montalbetti travelled as far as that!'

'Montalbetti? That's a real compliment, sir. I thank you from the bottom of my heart, it'll bring me luck. Back home, Montalbetti is seen as a hero. He crossed the desert on foot, along the Texas–Mexico border, he was caught by chance at a customs post. The sandy wind made him lose his bearings, and he presented himself at the American checkpoint.'

'You've crossed the whole continent, not just the desert.'

'I let myself be transported by fate, like tumbleweed in the sirocco.'

'That's what we all do. What else can we do? You see Christ? That's the holiest face I have ever painted, I'll never paint a better one. It'll stay buried here among the farms of rural New York State. Do you think I could have done the same thing in Paris? Constantly being interrupted by phone-calls from a girlfriend I'd met only the previous evening, chirping into the receiver about a contract to be signed, at all costs, that very afternoon? It's solitude, an empty day that needs to be filled with courage, a jailer who can confiscate your palette and paints on a whim, for the slightest infraction, perhaps because he doesn't like the look of you, to give life and suffering to that holy face. You lose everything and rediscover yourself as you were as a boy, pure and intense. When everything returns to us, we will lose ourselves. It would be funny if it wasn't so tragic.'

'I lost myself, but I didn't find myself again.'

'You? You haven't even started!' he laughed, and rubbed my shoulder as a trainer might reassure a nervous sportsman. 'What's your name?'

'Nino Manes, Major.'

'Are you sure you don't want to stay with us, Nino?'

'No.'

'Nino? Nino?' The lieutenant's voice filled the nave. His shadow stepped into the light, his uniform still uncreased even after so much travelling, impervious to exhaustion and dust. 'I've made friends with Nino, Major,' he said.

'Then I'll leave you to him.'

'He shouldn't stay but, if you like, his papers could be altered, as you know.'

'I think he wants to follow you.' The maestro's eyes grew serious and penetrating.

'Follow me? I'm almost at my goal, if you could be so kind as to let me make a phone-call. I'm very fond of Nino, he can make up his own mind. The war's about to end.'

'Father Samuel has a phone. We prisoners aren't allowed to use it, but you won't have a problem. You're an American officer, aren't you?' the major asked curiously.

'Maestro, you're Italian, aren't you? Please help me. If I was talking about a phone-call for the mission, I could introduce myself with my stripes and requisition the phone. It's a personal call, not a military one. Do you understand?' The lieutenant's smile would have disarmed the most treacherous *caman*. The major sighed kindly. 'Let's see what I can do, Lieutenant Romeo.' And he walked back into the sacristy. Passing beneath the altarpiece, he stopped suddenly, and scraped away with his fingernail a grain of red that must have struck him as excessive. He looked at it carefully and let it slip to the floor, perplexed that a tiny imperfection might have interfered with his work.

The lieutenant walked arm in arm with me, in the shade of a rough confessional, where the workers couldn't see us. 'Take the maestro's offer. The war's over. He'll keep you here at the camp, our papers are good, the commander has it all sewn up and the prisoners on the Atlantic coast will be the first to return to Italy. Particularly this group, as a reward for the good work they've done. They're nice people, you'll be fine. Your journey testifies to your strength: don't test fate again. Okay, mate?'

'I'm coming with you.'

He pressed me harder against the little wooden kiosk, with its power to cleanse eternal sin. 'Do you trust me?'

'I've never crossed minefields with anyone else.'

'Listen to me now. You know who I am and you know where I'm going. So you can report me and that'll be that. I'll face a court martial, but thanks to your testimony I'll escape the firing squad.'

'You know I wouldn't do that.'

'I know. We're brothers in a mad flight. And we're proud of our madness, all this way for a girl and Mussolini! We've lost our companion, we weren't able to defend her: I can't shake off my remorse, I don't want to lose you either. You understand?'

'No.'

'If you really want to see Zita, then stay. In a few days you'll disappear, you can see that there aren't any guards out here, and if you stay, your pursuers will be completely baffled. Hang out for a while at the docks in Brooklyn, try and find the family of Italians that seems to have been helping fugitives, and fate will be on your side. I have the American sleuths after me, they're after a German saboteur, I'm going to have to get through some pretty tight security checks in the next few hours. We're going to have to finish this last stage, the decisive one, as our true selves: you, an escaped Italian, are happy-go-lucky, while I'm a wanted man, thought to be a terrorist camouflaged as a Yankee gentleman. It's the moment of truth, Nino.'

'The truth is that we're going together.'

He gripped my shoulders as the maestro had done, and pushed me against the confessional. The grille that filtered the penitent's voice pressed cold against my back. 'Nino, I have some bad hours ahead of me. I have no secrets from you now. The person I'm trying to call in New York, if she's still alive and free, is a woman. She belongs to the secret organisation with which we were in contact from the submarines, to coordinate the recovery of our units, we hoped to infiltrate lots of them. Spies: people who don't receive a message for years, but stay on the alert every day. When I call, they'll mobilise immediately with blind faith. They don't know I'm now going to use them against the Duce: if they knew, they'd cheerfully disembowel me, the last sacrifice to the cause. I would face the noose, no question, whether I'm unmasked by the Nazis or captured by the Americans. Stay out of it. Hide here until peace is declared, or try to escape on your own: you're lucky, you know that.'

I stroked his tanned cheek. 'Make your phone-call, Lieutenant. We've got here together, and we'll get to New York City together. 57th Street, remember? We'll split up there.' I smiled about myself, about him and about everything else, and shoved him cheekily into the sacristy.

The maestro was speaking to a fat Irish priest who haughtily lifted the heavy Bakelite receiver of an imposing telephone, and dialled a prefix, asking the operator for a line. Then he passed the receiver to the lieutenant, with a bow. The lieutenant thanked him and smiled, covering the receiver with his hand for the sake of discretion. The priest and the painter walked compunctiously away.

The lieutenant murmured and I – weren't our fates now conjoined? – stayed confidently beside him. He seemed to start the conversation by reciting numbers, like a school student answering a maths test, and then came a few phrases about the weather, a sick aunt and some fresh eggs that were getting scarce while powdered eggs were inedible. Then, with a laugh, a few words in German, the ingredients of a recipe. I didn't understand any of it. There was a click to indicate the end of the conversation, and a word of thanks to Father Samuel. What kind of parents must the lieutenant have had, what education and fine manners must have accompanied his childhood and adolescence, among ambassadors, suave debutante balls, skiing in Cortina, swimming off Portofino at dusk, American high schools. And all to end up lost in this absurd plot in Poughkeepsie, among wooden barracks that smelled of resin and old mechanics vulcanising truck tyres. Without losing grace, barely touched by fatigue and ready to waltz with his dancing partner.

'So?' he asked me suddenly, no longer willing to waste time.

'How long will it take us to get to New York?'

'We'll be in Brooklyn in four hours. My lady-friend's waiting for me. Are you sure you're coming?'

'Yes.' I sat down to catch my anxious breath and looked at

the faces painted by the Italians. One fresco to the side, with some patches of plaster still damp, showed two delicate boys holding a slender Jesus by his worn cloak.

'But I know them!' I said with surprise.

'The models? They're my studio assistants,' the maestro replied.

The wall showed the soldiers trampling on them, and Christ had the face of the maestro, but younger, and sadder. 'I was like that before the war. I hope that Heaven will forgive me for being so brazen. You know the story of Emmaus, son?'

'No, Major.'

'Jesus has died and risen again. On the road to Emmaus he meets two disciples and they talk together for a long time, but the boys don't recognise him. Only at sunset do they notice his charismatic presence, and ask him to stay. "Because night is falling," they say, "and we have sadness in our heart." I too asked you to stay, and you decided to leave.'

'Maestro, what you're doing here is beautiful. The Americans will remember us POWs as people who knew how to live.'

'They know it, son, don't worry. And if they didn't know it wouldn't matter. Work is our method, beauty is our goal. Will you stay?'

'I have a job to finish, maestro. And the beauty has fled from my life.'

'Beauty lies in the search for it. He who pursues it will never lose it. Don't become resigned. Stay faithful to her, and this mirage will cheer you up.'

I leaned over and kissed his paint-spattered hand. He put his left hand on the back of my neck and stroked my hair, blessing me.

'Save your skin. Whatever you and your friend are trying to accomplish, it's too late to die.'

The Italian workers filled the truck with all kinds of good gifts: wine, bread, cheese, tins of Spam and condensed milk, enough to feed us on our journey across the waves.

As we left, the maestro hoisted himself on to the scaffold, intent on his masterpiece once more. The lieutenant smoothed his fair hair over his forehead. 'Here we go, Nino Manes. It's time now to resign yourself to your fate. Not much time left to decide what Brutus' missing line might have been in Philippi. Now or never,' and he accelerated.

The yearning song of '*Rosamunda, tu sei la vita per me, nei tuoi baci c'è tanta felicità*' rose up mockingly from the fields around us, sung by hundreds of uniformed farmworkers, who had left our homeland for hard American labour. It was the last time I heard it sung by Italian prisoners, POWs, *povieri*, imprisoned in the USA, a hymn to the dignity and strength necessary to live without power, free men in captivity.

21

I never saw Manhattan by daylight. It was the island I would
have liked to visit more than anywhere else. On one of his
shelves Professor Barbaroux, damn him, had the photograph
of Italian workers building the Brooklyn Bridge, indifferent
to the power of the river and the brick pier that towered above
them. The *caman* Carraway had worked in Manhattan. He
told me about the Apollo Theater in Harlem: 'When the
violinist Pedro sneezed, the dancers all took a deep breath,
because the air was full of cocaine. There's life there, son,
women, music, a crowd, unlike this stupid camp.' I had imagined sailing from those piers to break into Zita's wedding,
arriving just in time as she was about to say yes, as the priest
raised his hand in blessing. And I called out from beneath
the fresco in San Noè, with the pale face of the boys stopping
Christ in Emmaus in the church of the Italians in upstate
New York. A melodrama, certainly, but my life has always
mixed tragedy and comedy, so I never got my Puccini-inspired
entrance on my island, and I never drank beer in the smoky
bar somewhere behind Macy's, where the barman Tom,
Tommaso, a friend of Carraway's, would have let me drink

free all afternoon, and that's a promise, in exchange for his greetings.

The lieutenant turned on to a minor road, a mule track among the fields, and reaching my hand out of the window, I clapped on the metal of the truck, like a cavalryman rousing his mount for the final charge. Our little road terminated in a modest jetty. The sun had set, and a November fog had risen from the sea to engulf everything. Shelter Island, the black sign read. Perhaps it had gleamed once, but now was pink with sea salt.

A barge ran from the jetty to the island, which we couldn't make out in the mist. Its guttural whistle alerted the other boats to its presence, making me shiver. Just a few dozen miles had carried us from the sun-drenched afternoon of Poughkeepsie to gloomy night. The landscapes were constantly changing like that; turn a bend and ice and snow made way for torrid desert. It was more voluble than the human soul.

The barge crashed noisily against the peeling wooden jetty and juddered to a stop. The bosun was chewing tobacco, high up in his cabin, eyes intent on spotting dangers in the fog. He lowered the gangway. 'Are you getting on? Hurry up, it's the last one tonight,' he told us in a hoarse voice, and without waiting for a reply he pulled his hat back over his neck, like an old tortoise.

'And you?' the lieutenant asked for the last time.

'I'm with you.'

'I'm going to a place from which there's no coming back.'

'We'll see.'

'Turn yourself in. Go back to the maestro.'

'I'm coming with you.'

'They might kill us.'

'Who?'

'All of them. We're friends of the people who are pursuing us, and enemies of the people who want to help us.'

'Then don't throw away the only friend you've got, the only one who knows that's what he is.'

It was the only time the lieutenant seemed to acknowledge that I might be in some way superior to him. He accepted my passion, he envied my love story and he always treated me as a brother, a puppy. Only when he said he was friendless, and I protested, saying I was ready to follow him, did he give me a serious look. 'Let's make a pact.'

'What sort of pact?'

'If I ask you to go because we're finished, listen to me. I've seen too much blood. Spare me yours.'

'Understood.'

We boarded the ferry. The deck, painted blue and white, held only one other vehicle, a truck whose load was covered with a filthy tarpaulin. The bosun came down to untie the rope, and the ferry steered through the metallic grey of Long Island Sound, bobbing on the waves, clumsy as a flatiron. I saw that the sailor was enviously eyeing our Camels, and threw him a couple.

'Where are you going?' he asked by way of thanks, spitting out his chewing tobacco.

My English had improved in the course of the long journey.

I no longer feared casual conversation as I had at the bus stop in Hereford. I had learned to reply with a question, the way people on the run tend to do.

'What island are we heading to?'

'There's no passenger port there. It's just for them,' and he nodded his head towards the covered truck.

'And what island is it?'

'The flat one? Can you see it? You've got good eyes, son. That's Potter's Field. You'll have read the Bible, you're baptised and you're a god-fearing man, I hope?'

'Saint Noah will surely protect me.'

'You know the story. Our Lord Jesus Christ is sold by the traitor Judas Iscariot, for thirty pieces of silver. Having repented, Judas hangs himself, and the assembly uses the thirty pieces of silver to buy Potter's Field, for the burial of the dead without families or a homeland. We do the same in New York City: the poor and the comfortless dead are buried on that island, that God may forgive them. The convicts of the Tombs act as gravediggers, you don't know what the Tombs are? Why that's the name of the prison in Manhattan, my boy! Where do you come from, that you know nothing? In exchange for a breath of fresh air and a day out of jail, they dig graves and silently bury beggars, strangers, the sick who have died with no one to look after them. It's one of those days today, we leave the coffins we're transporting, and then we head back for Shelter Island. Are you military men? The anti-submarine base is down there, but there's no point asking if that isn't a military secret. Everyone here knows. Let's dock here. Hold on tight.'

He finished his cigarette, stuffed another quid of tobacco into his mouth and chewed.

The island, a strip of yellow sand and thin pine trees, appeared to be deserted. A grey bunker, bearing a faded red and blue United States flag, blocked our view. The ferry stopped, and the little man threw a rope in the direction of a rough wooden bollard, clumsily coated with pitch that dripped like tears towards the water of the bay. Two young men wearing grey prison uniforms appeared out of the fog, identical in every respect, height, sad faces, silence. They caught the cable and secured it to the pier. They were the right age to be called up, some sort of crime had taken them from the front where their contemporaries were being slaughtered, and they had to unload corpses by way of compensation.

There were three coffins, badly planed, lids fixed on with a few steel nails, looking more like wooden shrouds than funeral caskets. The two prisoners struggled to hoist them on to their shoulders without smashing the thin wood and finding themselves embracing a corpse. 'Lift!' 'Careful!' they encouraged one another. On the ends of the coffins, the planks were mottled with black, and the boys moved carefully lest they be contaminated by the effluent. 'Mind out!' 'Up a bit!' The big communal grave had been freshly dug from the clay. The corpses were stacked one on top of the other, goods in a closing-down sale.

The three new coffins clattered on top of the others, squashed on to the pyramid, and the boys began to call one of their mates from the bunker, 'Hey, come on!' A tall, handsome man arrived, took a fat piece of charcoal from his pocket and began to trace names in elaborate gothic calligraphy, the only sign of elegance on the island. 'Lazarus, Emma, Eleonore,' he wrote elaborately, and I lamented quietly to the lieutenant, 'H.S. didn't even get a convict's tombstone. Just the number XXXIII.'

'You'll go and give her a name and a date, after the war,' he said, trying to reassure me.

The prisoner writing the names on the coffins polished his handiwork with his cuff and lit a match to check his precision. In the flickering light he declaimed to the deserted air, 'Lazarus, why don't you get up, brother? Where are you now?'

His companions sniggered.

'Have faith, brother.'

'The dead don't rise.'

'Yes, they do: they'll be the first to face God.'

The calligrapher rapped his knuckles on the knotty wood. 'Arise and walk, I said! You see? There he is, there he stays.'

He leaned forward to brush the coffin with his lips, as though speaking to the corpse. 'Lazarus, *iam fetet.*' He stinks already, and he doesn't move.

'When will they close the grave?' I asked the sailor, a little unnerved.

'The common grave stays open until it's filled with corpses. Then they cover it with a bit of earth and leave it to rot. Potter's Field is big, there's room for generations of desperately poor people. Every now and again policemen come, local cops or FBI bosses, and exhume a corpse, for an inquest, a murder. Three months ago it was revealed that one corpse was the scion of a dynasty of millionaires, the Buchanans of Connecticut, knifed while drunk in a bar. They carried him off with all honours, as though that changed anything for him. We catalogue the names carefully, yes, sir. As to the prisoners, you can see: acting the clown among the corpses is better than languishing in a cell in the Tombs, in jail.'

An old man came out of the bunker. He signalled to the sailor with a yellow lantern, making wide circles in the fog. The thick fog obscured the tops of the trees. The backwash of Long Island Sound thundered out regularly: Jay Gatsby's father had sneered at it as 'the most domesticated body of salt water in the western hemisphere', and yet today it was giving a menacing roar, like a December night in La Tonnara.

'I'll be back in a minute. Don't move,' said the sailor, spitting black saliva. He shook his head and headed towards his colleague, whose eyes flickered sadly in the torchlight. As soon as the fog took him from us, swallowed up by the mystic breath of reverberating light, the lieutenant gripped me by the wrist. 'Now!'

Two jumps and we were in a rowing boat, the varnish gleaming with dew. The lieutenant pointed me to the seat in the prow, and with the cadenced pull of a practised oarsman he drew away from the pier. Not even the sound of the lapping water betrayed us. We had been on the run for thirty-nine days and I had never felt lost. Whether you're in prison or on the run, there's a sense of belonging and identity. The prisoner hates his jailers, detests his cell, the mess, the routine, the timetables, the relentless days. But it all assigns a role to him. He knows who he belongs to and why. What he lacks is happiness, not a sense of himself. However low he may have fallen, he exists and he is bound to others. The fugitive is a puppet, secured with invisible wires to the camp he has left behind. He moves further and further away from it, he tries to stay out of the clutches of the guards, but he knows he's on a list, he knows people are after him. At every waking or sleeping moment, the investigators are preparing to catch him. And if he managed to shake them off completely, if he were capable of erasing every footprint that he might have left behind, he would still know that his name was held, carbon-copied, in that dossier on a metal shelf, he would feel that his flight, and his existence, were real. No one might ever open it, just as no one would ever read the names 'Lazarus' and 'Eleonore' in gothic letters on the shattered coffins. But it still exists.

In the fog on the island of the dead, on the other hand, I was in the void. I felt the lieutenant's oars pulling at the water with the rhythm of a metronome, a dull splash, the hiss of the air, another splash. From the island there echoed the scrape of the prisoners' spades, the hoes digging into the earth, the impact of the freed turf, then the sound of metal again. I didn't know where I was bound, and I didn't even really know what plan my boatman had in mind. All thoughts of love had vanished with the girl killed by the mountain lion. I too was a wild beast, I followed scents, the need of the moment and nothing else. If Lazarus had risen from his grave, summoned by the Lord to speak to me, heedless of the convicts' jests, I wouldn't have been at all surprised. In fact I wouldn't have batted an eyelid if the Lord himself had emerged from the fog to save me, walking fearlessly on the water as he had done at the Sea of Galilee.

The lieutenant had rounded a little promontory covered with scrub and brambles. He whistled lightly, two notes, one high and one low. Mozart, I knew it, the Piano Sonata in C major, KV 279. From the scrubland came the same notes, one high, one low. The boat hit the sand and we jumped into the mud. We couldn't see a foot in front of us. Holding my hands outstretched in front of me like a blind man to keep from falling, I spotted a face that I will never forget. Leaning against a tree was a slim, pale woman, half hidden by the fog. She was wearing a black overcoat and holding a piece of string tied to two tinkling copper keys. Her eyes emanated utter calm, as though at a single glance she could tell every past and future detail of your life. She entered you with her grey-blue eyes, the look of a bookworm deciphering an archaic manuscript. She stared at me and the lieutenant, as though it were perfectly normal to meet on this deserted beach. 'Heil Hitler,' she said clearly.

It was horrible. I had witnessed death on the battlefields, felt the anguish of prison, and never had evil been closer to me, the dogged evil of that colourless woman, sister to the rotting tree trunk that she leaned against, and her greeting, 'Heil Hitler', which had devastated the old continent, and laid waste my life.

The lieutenant didn't reply. With a blow from the handle of his oar he knocked out the bottom of the boat, threw in a slippery mass of mud and pushed it away from the shore. Gurgling and bubbling, the sloop sank to the grey sea bed and we were marooned on the island.

'Call me Frau Becht. Who's he?' said the woman.

'An Italian comrade. He helped me escape. He wants to carry on to Manhattan,' replied the lieutenant. There was a military inflection in his voice that I had never noticed before, honed by the barking of orders in the U-boat engine room. Now he was pretending to be German.

'I've got a boat to go to Brooklyn. We'll give him money for the subway.'

Barely glancing at me, she walked away, saying to me in English, 'Getting to Manhattan will be child's play,' and strode briskly down the mud path.

It was a very quick walk. The little beach that opened to the west hid a round fishing boat. The engine was already running, but not a soul could be seen on deck. We boarded the craft in silence, Frau Becht sat at the controls and pointed us to the cramped little cabin in the prow. I picked my way through lobster-pots of wood and rope. The lieutenant came nimbly after me. From dry land, as we were rounding the quiet coast, I could still hear the rhythm of the hoes in the cemetery, and the sound of a bell, perhaps struck by the man with the lantern to alert the sailors, or the sailor for his two dead passengers. The notes were the same – or at least that was what it sounded like to me in my dizzy state – as the ones whistled as a signal by the lieutenant: Mozart, the clarity of happiness, reason and virtue, the genius courageously confronting death by composing a requiem for the many Lazaruses in the communal graves, the ones that Jesus would not raise. 'Arise and walk. *Domine iam fetet.*' A shroud of beauty raised against the darkness and the fog around us, the banner of the human race, our true standard. Two notes, no more than that, and the shores appeared miraculously far away. We left the bronze bell behind us, and headed without any bearings towards a group of dirty yellow lights that crowded together like sickly Pleiades.

Since then I have always wanted to return to Potter's Island and leave bright flowers for Eleonore and Lazarus. But the nautical charts of Long Island Sound deny its existence. At the American consulate a pleasant girl rummaging through a pile of cuttings was startled – 'Dead poor people are buried somewhere quite different, in New York. You must have imagined it, or dreamed it, or you're getting mixed up with another American war cemetery . . .'

'Not at all,' I replied to her happy, wholesome, healthy midwestern face. 'I saw the cemetery, I heard the convicts digging in the sand, the lieutenant's shipwrecked boat must still be there somewhere, sunk in the mud, and the bronze bell must ring out on windy nights, those two notes from Mozart's C major Piano Sonata.'

That was many years later. Now, as I shifted around in the cramped and fishy cabin, I became aware of the warmth of other bodies beside me. My eyes grew accustomed to the darkness, and three men introduced themselves quietly to the lieutenant: 'Georg Datsch, sir.' 'Richard Hochhuth, sir.' 'Heinrich Stavinsky, honoured, sir.'

Without surprise in his voice, the lieutenant interrogated them in German and English. There was tension in his throat, but before I could understand, Frau Becht leaned over the hatch and said, 'You're very fortunate, my friends. They are saboteurs who arrived today on the last U-boat to cross the Atlantic. They have brought four cases of explosives and eight thousand dollars in cash. With your guidance, Captain von Luck, they'll strike a home run. It will be the last battle on this side of the ocean. And we will win it.'

22

My beloved Spanish godfather, Uncle Fernando, is dead, and
Nunu, his wife, is dead with him. My godfather opposed
fascism, and after the war he travelled to Catalonia to work
with the Americans, selling cleaning compounds for railway
boilers. He smoked Edelweiss cigarettes, he had an even
temper, and used to clap me on the back by way of greeting
– 'Be good, Nino, be good.' Margherita is dead, the demon
cyclist, on the bend by the fountain where I used to keep the
brake on hard for fear of the abyss below, while she used to
hurtle down, sending the gravel flying towards the glistening
sea, and kind-hearted Saverio died the kind of terrible death
that seems to be reserved for the pure of heart. Uncle Totino
is dead: on Sundays he used to take us shooting at the range,
and with his blue eyes would enchant the girl who ran the
merry-go-round, while we little savages burst balloons and
fired at tricolour targets. And Uncle Totino is dead, no longer
does he dry tasty tuna hearts in the sun, putting them back
in the cool of the brick cellar and slicing them wafer-thin
before leaving them to macerate in virgin olive oil. Trying one
with your tongue, you got a taste of blood, of savagery. Uncle

Massimo died staring at the portrait of the king that hung beside his bed, surrounded by little flags gathered from the cemeteries in the Himalayas, during his arduous flight from the prisoner-of-war camps of Yol. Aunt Maria is dead; she was said to have been the lover of the poet D'Annunzio at the Hotel Excelsior which belonged to Gardone Riviera and his sister, Aunt Emma, known to us as Cyrano: after funerals she used to entertain the children by pulling clownish faces, to make them smile through their tears. Aunt Vittoria is dead, buried with the blue uniform of honour of the Red Cross, having saved the lives of dozens of freezing soldiers, survivors of the retreat from Russia. Otto is dead, the German forgotten by the *Wehrmacht*, who stayed behind to join the tuna fishermen. And Uncle Nardo, who freed me from a squid-fishing hook that had got stuck in the palm of my hand, by opening the skin with a penknife as though peeling a lemon, ignoring my wails. 'To teach me to swim, my father threw me fully clothed into the cold January sea, so shut up, Nino.'

Grandfather Giovanni is dead: malaria contracted while working in a corner of the Island that was like the Wild West. He had to defend the tracks of his railway from bandits, and chase them away from the carnival celebrations.

'Station-master, you're a bastard,' the cut-throat said to him.

'Could be, but you're still not coming to the party,' and he barred the door.

Giuseppa is dead, and she really will sit on the right hand of Our Lord: who ever saw her doing anything wrong? No saint can match the goodness of a life devoted to others. Dino, the vet, is dead, his boat is no longer tossed about on the high, foaming waves as he heads out to sea, to my mother's cries of horror. Pinuccia is dead, so quickly and so unfairly, her heart full to the brim with the love of an eager, happy life. And Grandmother Adele, who travelled to Rome to get her pension, the heels of her poor shoes echoing out around the huge, gleaming marble corridors of the Royal Ministry of Transport, Railway Headquarters, one bureaucrat after the other passing the barely educated widow from one desk to the next, until she reached his Excellency the Sub-Secretary in person. Looking at that intrepid woman in her widow's weeds, demanding the pension for three children, 'It's my right, Excellency,' the sub-secretary thought once again of the years long ago when he had been sure that he acted out of a sense of justice and not for cynical, worldly reasons as he did today. He signed without a word.

Grandmother Anita is dead, she who used to paint the frogs jumping out of the ditches at La Guadagna, the brilliant green creatures slipping lithely out of the mud. And Grandfather Attilio no longer confides discreetly about the girls he kissed in Bologna and his concerns about the design of the castle on the hill, stolen by an envious rival. Candela is dead, and where is his red motorbike now? And Chicco and Max, brought down by Maltese anti-aircraft fire while elegantly pirouetting in their beautiful Macchi plane. Aniello is dead, the man who taught me to call all certainties into doubt, and used to raise his glass of white wine to the sun to check its colour, and Gaetano, who knew right from wrong: he looks straight at me from the photograph on the wall and, when I slip up, his eyes are the worst punishment of all. Misha is dead, the most intelligent man on the Island, burning ideas with his pipe tobacco. And Livio who gave me steak with asparagus and asked assiduously, 'So, what's happening? What's happening?'

I'm making the list in a notebook that someone left behind at the end of the summer, and slowly covering the lines. Ignazio's mother is dead, the most graceful and subtle of women, how could anyone have failed to love her? When Ignazio's helmet was hit by shrapnel and he lost his memory for three weeks, I saw her weeping when I was home on leave. Grazia is dead and I look for her with my eyes wide open, almost every day I think, 'Hey, must tell Grazia . . . I'll just give her a call . . .' and Grazia is dead and there's nothing left to say, or everything, but I can't, or perhaps I can, perhaps there *is* a way of talking to the dead: Odysseus knew it, that was his dream, he didn't manage to hug his mother in hell, but in his dreams, there was his mother alive, in front of him, open and beautiful. What has died within us that keeps us from speaking to the dead? '*Sunt aliquid Manes*,' spirits do exist, said Sextus Propertius: but if they do, what are they? And what are we?

Ernesto is dead, noble and defeated, capable of mocking the enemy who finished him off after the ambush. Inigo, the great cardsharp is dead, and so is Laura, his wall-eyed companion. Maurizio, Paolo and Giovanni are gone. I look at the photograph showing my companions from class 2A and register the ones touched by the war, recruited, injured, deported, missing, fallen. There isn't a face that wasn't affected. Nanni, Marranchino and Mandorla are dead, swallowed up with the fishing boat *Spavaldo* in the Sicilian Channel on the stormy night of December the 24th 1942, a tempest that left the coastal parishes covered with stones. I'm thinking and writing, but where is the *Spavaldo*? Professor Arturo is dead, and Professor Nino, and Bosco who taught me to repair crystal radios: and how would I ever have known how to use my receiver in the little tin without his lessons? Erina is dead, and Marchioneschi, who shot wild pigeons with his 1891 musket: if you think that sounds easy, just try and lift three kilograms of iron and wood in an arc intersecting with that of the skimming bird, don't let your aim be deflected by blast and recoil, and still hit your target. As far as I remember, in the Royal Army only Rigoni Stern managed that, in Russia in 1943, and two deserters immediately stole his fabulous musket.

No one is left on the Island. In the summer the kids come, filling the empty houses, and the young waiters who pour chilled spirits by night and snap starched white cloths on to two-ply tables in the daytime. The beaches are crowded with innocent, happy bodies from the first of June to the first of September. Then the steamer whistles and leaves. The last young waiter jumps aboard to sail towards his next seasonal job with his tub of scented hair-gel, while the last girl ties her wraparound skirt over her tattooed skin, shivering in the mistral. The steamer whistles, and three of us are left on the Island: Virginia the schoolmistress, a hundred and one years old last birthday, who wants to die here, George who turns on the radio lighthouse for the sailors and opens and closes the watertight doors at the power station, and me. Why I have stayed, I don't know. The summer tourists come, and among them, poor no longer, my friends' children and grandchildren. They stop below the house to say hello, to introduce a little French fiancée, to point at me as though I were the last albino gorilla, asking, 'Nino, tell us about your great escape from America.'

And every summer I tell the story, and the littlest ones wait their turn, but when the August heat arrives they shrug their tanned shoulders, they get tired of me, the lieutenant, Zita and Professor Barbaroux and Hereford Camp 1 and go to the beach, with a girl and a sinking moon, to make men of themselves.

Zita is dead too, and Professor Barbaroux with her. They left together on the *General Bourbaki*, Barbaroux's motorboat, the day before the wedding. Inigo told me he saw them arguing on the patio shortly before, Zita saying, 'Give me time, I want time . . .' and Barbaroux phlegmatically replying, 'The decision's been made, there's no reason . . .'

Inigo remembered, 'He pushed her on to the boat. Zita was yelling with fury, as only she could, and Uncle Nardo said, "Why's Zita shouting? I don't like that professor, never did. He nicked her off Ninuzzo. Let's go and see what he's doing," but in a rowing boat and at his age, poor man, how could he go after the *Bourbaki*? He rowed, but in vain.'

So swears Inigo, but Laura, his wife, laughs and says with

her squinting expression, 'What nonsense, Zita was happy, she wept for you, Nino, but then she showed me her trousseau: "Not only am I the first university mathematics professor in Italy, but I've got a trousseau, Lauretta, can you believe it? Aren't I lucky?" and the poor soul laughed.' But I can just hear that throaty laugh, and imagine the white embroidered sheets that Zita showed her friend, stretching them out in the sun, white veils pointing to a happy future. Where are they, who took them? Who ever slept among those embroidered linen sheets?

'She wept for you when you were in prison, Ninuzzo, but she wanted to marry the professor, and I myself with these very hands –' And she showed them to me, knotty and tanned, adorned with a gold ring. '– I myself drew the outline for the bridal veil, and I embroidered it for her, and instead I had to arrange it in her coffin, at San Noè, when they buried her drowned and swollen body.'

Jealousy still tears at me, rage fills my breast, as though I could fight a duel with a ghost, old fool that I am.

'The boat,' Uncle Nardo swore to me, 'sank in the shallows of Città Fenicia, you remember? I used to go out there to fish for octopus, in season, with Father Xante. I always told you, Nino, beware of the landward wind down there, it's treach-erous, it drives the turquoise surface of the water like sand in the sirocco. Once, when you were very small, the landward wind rose up at five o'clock in the morning and I pulled the boat on to dry land and put you back to bed, and you cried that you wanted to go fishing for *todari* and I said to you, don't mess with the landward wind, Nino. That day it turned into a storm, why on earth the professor went out in it I have no idea, I wanted to stop him and your Zita was shouting. Barbaroux knew the sea, he knew it very well, he was an expert: what made him go out with that wind, Nino, I couldn't imagine.'

No one knew. Aunt Dima, kindly soul, told me, 'Barbaroux had got a cargo of guns from Yugoslavia, from the Partisans, the order had come from Mommo Li Causi, who had carried them across the Balkans on a mule to a safe harbour and all the way to Italy. The plan was to send them on to Tuscany, because the Allies were stingy about issuing weapons that winter, 1944, General Alexander's proclamation, you remember? There was TNT and ammunition, lots of things that were supposed to get to Spain from Russia, and had been held up in Belgrade when Barcelona fell in 1939. That was why poor Barbaroux had gone to sea in that inferno.'

Even if the story of the expedition was true, why had Zita followed him? And why did people say that she was shouting as she boarded the *General Bourbaki*? My mother – and why shouldn't I believe her amidst that chorus of lunacy? – gave another version, which for a long time I hated, and which I now treat with some respect, especially when the pain becomes too great for the old man I am today: 'Barbaroux, I tell you, Nino, was the devil incarnate, the Satan of Manasseh, the demon Mastema that Jesus purged in Hell, *requiem aeternam*. He seduced our Zita, and sent you across the sea in chains. You, poor thing, were suffering in America, while he dragged her who knows where, when the Archangel Gabriel in person intervened, he used his holy sword to whip up the whirlpool in the sea and prevented the consummation of those obscene nuptials. Then San Noè, showing mercy towards the mortal remains of the child baptised at his font, brought her back to shore, after forty days and forty nights in the vasty deep,' said my mother, using a phrase she had been taught at school, 'the vasty deep'. 'Horribly bloated, she was. Not the professor, not him, he was cast into the volcano where his heart will bleed for all eternity.'

So many times I have closed my eyes, alone on the Island. First I sought the dreams of Odysseus, now I count souls. Gigi is dead, who used to strike the delicate sea bream with his harpoon beneath the water. I couldn't even throw that heavy harpoon out of the boat, but Gigi sent it flying into the sea the way Laura's needle passed through Zita's organza. I'm the only one on the Island who sleeps, Virginia the schoolmistress keeps watch at the window, studying the ghosts of her pupils, and George, at the lighthouse, ensures that the sailors stay away from harm. They watch intently and I, who would like to sleep obliviously, muse restlessly about Zita and Barbaroux, their final crossing, the hidden weapons, the row people said they had. What had united them in that marriage that I could do nothing to prevent, that marriage that was never celebrated?

I close my eyes and hear the wind whistling beneath the deserted porticos of La Tonnara, rattling the anchors abandoned on the pebbly volcanic beach, rusted by the salty air like my old bones. I hear the backwash down by the jetty, and the woodworm squeaking in their blind tunnels in the swollen shutters. The shutters need to be scraped down and varnished, but there's no one to do it. Everything on the Island is decaying, fading, all the wood and metal groans in the winter. Is that when I sleep? I know that the wind reveals the bright stars in the black sky. The man who tried to hunt me down in the last century, Major Cafard, knew all their names, knew every astral route. I close my eyes tight and if I could I would close my heart, which beats against my wool mattress and wakes me from my slumbers once again.

What were Zita's last words? What was her last thought? When she understood that she was finished, and the waves closed over her head? A skilled deep-sea swimmer, when did she abandon her elegant stroke and give up the fight? I have tried to drown myself to find out what it's like to die of water. I allowed myself to sink to the bottom in the shallows of Città Fenicia, and breathed in water through my mouth, like bitter air into my lungs, but my body's natural instinct kept bringing me back to the surface, spluttering, breathless and purple in the face, alive and superfluous. While Zita died in the water, and the waves stripped her flesh for forty days.

What did she feel as she left the life I felt was mine? Is it fair that the information we need the most should be withheld from us? What do I care of Eternal Life and Perpetual Light if I cannot know what for me, only for me, Nino Manes, is the cornerstone to the universe, the very foundation stone of time and wisdom? Whether the dying Zita, before her tomb sealed over her dear head, thought for a moment, just a moment, about me. All worldly honours, the salvation of my soul, I would give in return for this: a book, a scribble, a message in a corner of the cosmos where I could meet Zita and ask her about her thoughts.

I brood in the darkness, and rack my brains. I know what I was doing the day Zita died, I have a calendar on my kitchen table, thin sheets of paper and big red numbers. With a pencil, I've linked her last days with the days of my flight across America. I was in Potter's Field, on the thirty-ninth day of my escape. It was then that she sailed off into the Mediterranean, our very own sea, for another forty days. The waves sent her to the bottom and raised her to the surface, the currents, violent, gentle, brought her back home to the pumice beach. In my sleep I try to couple my every moment with hers. She died while I was at the Island of the Dead, she was sinking to the coral as I sailed Long Island Sound, the current dragged her to the shallows as I entered New York and perhaps a gull flew over her while I was in St Noah's in Brooklyn, the church that bore the same name as my own parish, listening to Father Giganti's sermon. When Cafard and Cheever came and sat in the pew next to me – 'It's over, son' – and the women recited 'for us now and at the hour . . .', she was still lightly floating.

That's what I say, and that's what I think, and age is pressing and a more troubled sleep of anxiety and worry closes my eyes. I'm the only one who sleeps on the Island. Every now and again I am woken by the trapdoor of the warehouse where the fishing nets were stored, clattered by the wind in the silence of the night. It rang out like that beneath the heels of Aunt Celestina: but she too is dead, and no longer buys the five-*soldi* ice-creams. 'The ten-*soldi* ones are too big for you, Nino, and you'll be full up' – and her sister, Aunt Ciccina, is dead and no longer gives tips on card games to her nephews and nieces. The whole island is calm, the only sound of suffering is my soul, running through the list of memories past. Salvatore, who died in the lap of his gentle mother, and Anna's twin who lost his footing on the soft pumice path, swallowed up by the volcano. Max's favourite son, Giovanni, who was never well, the one the boys threw heavy, wet balls of salt at, up by the old warehouse. He went home humili-ated, white in his hair and on his eyelids. He lived a few days more and then he left us: he was an innocent.

I list my mates who fell at the front, may God bring glory to my unfortunate fellow soldiers in Africa, and Ferrucci, from the camp bed next to mine in Hereford, may Heaven save him. When the list seems complete, or the pain weighs too heavy on my chest, I get up, and then there's no one sleeping on the Island.

I make black coffee, and the roasting smell reminds me of my grandfather being called each morning to mix the beverage in a pan for General Garibaldi: 'Manes, we can do without a lot of things, but never miss my coffee.'

'Have you ever missed one, General? Even in Rome, in '48 . . .'

Cup in hand and oilskin over my shoulders, I go down to

the jetty and face the damp breeze. The darkness still unites land, sea and sky. Sand crunches under the soles of my feet, the sound of the desert, from the Sahara to Texas. I've devotedly completed the register of the dead, but without getting an inch closer to them. I could scream, groan, cry out for mercy: no one would hear me. At the lighthouse, George has his headphones over his ears, and the schoolmistress hears nothing but the roll-call of her best class, the class of 1932. I fall to my knees and wait for the sun to announce the dawn of a new day. I wish General Garibaldi would appear, noble and alive so that I could make him coffee in his mess tin before the battle, the fight to the death for freedom, fatherland and justice, either you win or you fall beneath the tyrant's grapeshot. But all my friends are dead, all of them, the heroes first, and their true loves with them, and the kind aunts and the intrepid fishermen.

I'm the only one left, and General Garibaldi doesn't need my coffee. Tonight, once again, I will think about Africa, the dreams of Odysseus, Brutus' forgotten line, a falcon proudly clutching a rattlesnake among the crystal dunes of Texas. I beg to return intact, the fugitive Nino Manes, POW, *poviere*, of those forty days in 1944. But my entreaty will not be satisfied.

23

The memory struggles to recover those reckless days, when life and death and fate are all a motion apart. You jump to the right as your companion throws himself to the left, you escape the shrapnel, he catches the impact of the explosion full in the chest. You blindly deliver a bayonet blow, aiming in the dark where you think the enemy might be, the barrel of his gun already aimed at you, and you feel the flab of his abdomen and the scorch of the gunpowder, the deadly shot landing uselessly in the bunker ceiling, far from its target: your face. And when, back in the warmth of home, you try to remember the story of your adventures, everything grows opaque.

So forgive me, kind readers who have followed me this far, if I have only a fragmentary memory of the epilogue to my pointless flight. From Potter's Field onwards, the fog surrounding New York seeps into my mind. I see people, I listen to words, I hear gunshots and rapid footsteps on the cobbled streets of Brooklyn, but is it a story that I invent for the kids in the summer, or is it something that really happened?

The names of the Germans in the cabin are preserved in

newspaper cuttings of the day, yellow as parchment: Georg Datsch, Richard Hochhuth and Heinrich Stavinsky. They solemnly introduced themselves: 'We're the last Atlantic unit in the war, sir. We've lost our contact, he was supposed to be coming up from Florida, but either he's late or he's been intercepted. It's terrific that you're here, in American uniform and willing to help us. Our plan is a simple one.' Datsch, who must have been the man in charge, nodded towards me. 'Who's he?'

The lieutenant replied calmly, 'He's with me,' and Datsch, looking away from me, said, 'Sorry, my friend, too many of your people have betrayed us. So . . .' and he unfolded a map of the zone, marked in red. My eyes had grown used to the damp darkness of the boat, and could now make out the men around me. They were Germans, in civilian clothes, their pin-striped jackets and trousers then fashionable among American office workers. Their hair gleamed with brilliantine, their spectacles were rimmed with silver.

'What do you have in mind?' asked the lieutenant. I knew his voice well by now, and in it I heard a note of concern and fear.

Hochhuth spoke, with the sibilant voice of an asthmatic. 'It's our last chance. We're going to attack –'

Datsch broke in: 'I'm doing the talking. You know that.'

Stavinsky nodded. 'Without orders we're screwed.'

They were nervous, acting out a part they had learned some time ago. They were familiar with one another, they spoke simultaneously, like convicts or submariners, people used to spending the day together.

Datsch looked tired. He offered the lieutenant a cigarette, embarrassed to find himself facing an officer, and the lieutenant was soon taking long draws on it, and filling the cabin with aromatic smoke.

'We want to create fear, sir. We want to terrorise the Americans. We're . . .'

'The last mission, commander. That's us. The last one,' Hochhuth said in his halting voice.

'We need help, sir. We need orders,' Stavinsky explained, and he leaned nervously towards the lieutenant.

I tried to read the emotions on my friend's face. That's the first time, isn't it? The first time I've called him that. And at this point my memory comes to my assistance. It was only then that I saw him as a friend – or rather it was only then that I felt he was a friend, because I couldn't discern his features in the gloom. The faint light filtering from the porthole in the prow shone on the wall behind his neck. I imagined him tense, thinking about how this terrorist unit would change our mission to get to Europe. His every movement was noble, and I felt a certain affection for him. His plan, secretly elaborated in the damp stench of the boat, was surely designed to achieve justice. He was speaking in German now, he had changed identity once again. From American to German without a hint of embarrassment, with true Italian panache.

'I'm U-boat Commander von Luck. Of course I'll help you.'

'Our commander was supposed to be arriving from Florida to tell us our target, chosen from a range of possibilities. I know the objectives, but he, who had landed off Key West for safety's sake, was going to give us our final orders. We have over eighty thousand dollars in cash, a lot of money, sir, we're rich, we've got four cases of explosives, weapons and papers.'

'You speak good English.'

'We emigrated to America before the war, Commander. The Führer let us back in as part of the repatriation programme in 1939. After receiving our training, we were chosen for this mission. Once we'd landed, we contacted the secret network in America and Frau Becht told us that you, a U-boat commander and an expert saboteur, had escaped from a camp and got to New York. Please help us.'

'What is your goal?'

'You know Walter Kappe, Captain?'

'Kappe of the *Abwehr*?'

'That's right. Kappe of the *Abwehr*, military espionage.'

Datsch was shrewdly studying the lieutenant, who was perfect in his simplicity. 'I did my officer's training with him.'

'At the Farm?' Hochhuth asked him breathlessly.

'Is it still called that? Sure, at the Farm.' The lieutenant turned towards me – what was the expression on his face now? I could see the outline of his features, I heard the beating of the engine in the fog and the keel of the fishing boat cutting through the ocean waves that lapped in the bay. 'Nino, the Farm is the code name of the training centre, I'm sure you have something similar in Italy: it's forty miles from Berlin. The head of the Farm is Kappe, but we all call him . . .' and the lieutenant broke off, waiting for the new arrivals to remember the nickname of the head of the *Abwehr*.

Hochhuth took a breath, but Stavinsky stopped him with a jab in the ribs. Datsch smiled. 'You're testing us, sir. A sound procedure. I was doing the same in alluding to the Farm. That's what professionals in the secret service do. You passed the test with flying colours. So I can tell you that Kappe is known as Pastorius. And do you know why?'

'Franz Daniel Pastorius, the leader of the first group of German emigrants to America, in the seventeenth century. Kappe hoped to send a unit of saboteurs on board a U-boat every six weeks. I escaped only recently, and I've had no news. Did he do it?'

Datsch and his men looked at one another, convinced. Hochhuth gave a stiff salute, arm outstretched in front of him. 'A pleasure to serve with you, sir. You are the most senior officer among us. Please guide us. Kappe's plan will be accomplished.'

The lieutenant gravely shook their hands. 'You can speak openly in front of Nino, he's a loyal comrade. Now tell me about your mission.'

'Richard, the files,' Datsch commanded, and his man, happy to be useful, opened a leather folder.

Datsch showed the lieutenant his Social Security Card, which looked authentic – I'd learned to recognise them at Camp 1. From shiny leather wallets they took their identification papers: Selective Service Registration Card, with their fake American names, George John Davis, Edward Kelly, John Thomas, and photographs showing faces which, in black and white snapshots, looked exquisitely American, genuine Yankees.

'What do you say? Are we real Americans?' Stavinsky asked, proud to have regained his identity as an emigrant. 'Our objective is to frighten people, but also to sabotage production, particularly of aluminium. American aviation is bringing us to our knees, if we slow down the flow of aluminium we'll stop them. Fear and aluminium, those are our two targets.'

Datsch trustingly displayed the papers to the lieutenant.

'The factories producing aluminium and other light metals crucial to the aerial campaign seem the most obvious place to start.' He looked up from the files, looking through the darkness for Stavinsky, who spelled out: 'The Aluminum Company of America in Alcoa in the state of Tennessee, with branches in East St Louis in Illinois and Massena, here in New York State . . .'

'Other notable plants supplying strategic material for aeronautical production include the Philadelphia Salt Company in Pennsylvania, which supplies criolite,' Hochhuth wheezed. They were a well-prepared unit, each of them well informed about a series of targets, to protect the group if they were arrested separately. 'But to spread terror we could also strike aqueducts and the big Jewish-owned stores.'

'The best thing would be to sabotage the locks on the Ohio River, between Cincinnati and St Louis,' Datsch continued. 'With a bit of luck we could flood the plain, or else we could blow up a hydroelectric power station in the Tennessee Valley, or on Niagara Falls. To block the railway network, on the other hand, possible targets might be . . .'

Hochhuth broke in, his breathing growing more and more

difficult. '. . . the Horseshoe Curve Interchange in Altoona, in Pennsylvania, which, if blocked, would paralyse the east of the USA. If we blow up the Hell Gate Bridge, we'll halt communication between New England, Canada and New York City. On the other hand, if we strike further south, between Chesapeake and the Ohio Railway, we'll freeze coal distribution. What do you think?'

The lieutenant started checking the papers, picking up information. 'Have you got a network out there? Contacts? How are you going to travel? And how do you plan to get away once you've struck your targets?'

They listened to him with their heads bowed, amidst the rolling waves. Datsch spoke: 'We don't plan to get away, sir. It's the last mission. We're going to stay here. We're in civilian clothes, if they catch us they'll send us to the electric chair as spies. Otherwise we'll fall in action. There's no escape route planned for this enterprise. But we're not asking you to stay with us till the end. Just to guide us and tell us where to strike. We'll do the work, you'll be able to hand yourself in or stay out in the wilderness. There's no point sacrificing yourself again.'

'If I'm with you, I'm with you all the way, no half measures,' the lieutenant said in a voice so convincing that my heart clenched: had he gone back to the other side? Did he want to end his days with an act of sabotage in the American continent?

Frau Becht threw open the wooden door, and a cold gust from outside penetrated the foul air of the cabin. 'We're about to disembark. There's a backwash, and an unidentified landing stage. Once we've cleared it we'll set foot on land. Ready to whistle?' She slammed the shuttered door and was back on deck.

The lieutenant requested another cigarette, and the light changed once more, while Stavinsky rubbed hard at a yellow wind-resistant match. 'Friends, let's not talk about travelling. My companion and I have had the Military Police on our backs as well. To take the train to the Midwest with four cases of explosives and documents, even perfect forgeries, would be an act of madness. As to the choice you have, whether you stop production or sow fear, it's a simple one. Even if we stop a factory for a few days, what does that give us? One plane less in the sky over Berlin? Much better to frighten those damned Yankees, make them tremble, bring death and blood to their tranquil metropolis, as they're doing every night over Dresden and Hamburg. Let's strike right here in New York, but not the targets you know already, and which you say your inside man knows as well. If he hasn't shown up for his appointment, it may be that he's been captured. And the list along with him . . .'

'You're right!' exclaimed Hochhuth, glancing feverishly at his companions, who were nodding in agreement.

'We've got to strike at an unexpected target. To grab the world's attention. The shockwaves must reach Germany, our brothers and sisters . . .'

'Brooklyn Bridge,' suggested Hochhuth.

'The Statue of Liberty,' said Stavinsky, but the lieutenant, who was now in charge of the unit, replied, 'Those places are under constant guard. We won't be able to disembark with dynamite at the Statue of Liberty, and we couldn't take out Brooklyn Bridge without a lot of preparation. We'd have to spend hours submerged in the East River mining the pylons, we'd die of cold, we'd be dragged away by the current, or someone would see us. Let's keep it simple . . .'

'What about attacking the subway? A bomb at Times Square, at the 42nd Street stop, would have a devastating effect,' Datsch chipped in. 'I used to pass that way every day on my way to work, before the war. It has lots of levels, if you mined it well they'd come crashing down on top of each other like a stack of flapjacks . . .'

'No, they'd just close down the network, and say there had been a railway accident. It's the source of information that we've got to strike, friends, not aluminium. If we're going to sow terror, the news of our enterprise has to get all the way around the world. I think I know just the place . . .'

'Where?' And this time I was the one who asked the question, in a doubtful voice, which must have sounded like that of a new recruit wishing to assert himself, to show the veterans his determination, but to the lieutenant and me it just sounded doubtful. 'What on earth's happening?'

'Nino knows the place too,' and before I could murmur in surprise 'I do?' the lieutenant continued calmly, 'We'll attack the building I was pretending to take him to, as a cover for our escape. On 57th Street the Americans have set up a big radio station to transmit the news in every language across war-torn Europe. If we blow it up they'll have to interrupt broadcasts for at least a day. The Swiss will pass on the news from Geneva, and Berlin and Salò will be able to spread it to great propaganda effect.'

'It'll be even better,' said Datsch, 'if you've got documents that let you get into the radio station. You could even break into a studio during a live broadcast and announce the raid. And then we'd blow up the building. How much will it take, Stavinsky?'

'How many storeys, Captain?'

'Six or seven, I think.'

'Which floor are the broadcasting studios on?'

'The top floor.'

'We could mine the ground floor to inflict serious damage on the building without dragging the boxes all the way to the top. We'll say they're machinery. You and Nino could carry a bag of time bombs and destroy the studio right after the broadcast.'

'Fine. And I'll blow up a few cars in the street with delayed-action bombs, to spread panic when the firemen and the ambulances arrive,' added Hochhuth.

'We'll show up all together. Nino and the lieutenant will go up with the bags and the explosives. How much time will it take you to get them ready, Hochhuth?' Datsch asked.

'I'd just have to prime them. I keep them separate from the detonators when they're in transit, and once we're there it only takes a few minutes.'

'Fine. Once the proclamation's been read out, Stavinsky and I will leave the explosives in the foyer and switch on the timer. Meanwhile Hochhuth will blow up a few cars at a strategic position to hold up the emergency services. The Führer will be proud of us. What's the right time of day for the operation?'

'Early in the morning security won't be so aggressive. I'll say we got here on the dawn train, and no one will care. We'll land at the pier on 72nd Street, and it's just a hop from there. What about the boxes?'

Hochhuth pointed to them, small and square, like boxes of tools, nothing that couldn't be hidden in the boot of a taxi without arousing suspicions.

The lieutenant jumped up on deck and had a whispered conversation with Frau Becht, pointing to the coastline. I could see him through the purple porthole, and his face seemed gloomy to me. I no longer knew what part I was supposed to play in this new plan. The lieutenant had taken the helm, and I couldn't stay below any longer, suffocating down there. The air was heavy with damp, and clung to my light clothes, but it woke me up like a drug.

The lieutenant was alone at the controls of the fishing boat. 'What's going on?' I asked.

'These men are dangerous. They're going to create havoc. They're convinced they're going to change the course of the war, and they're going to add innocent blood to the carnage. I may be able to stop them.'

'What about me?'

'The moment you set foot on land, beat it. We're lucky we've got this unseasonal fog. Take the subway and slip off to Brooklyn. Frau Becht has told me how to trace an Italian family that's willing to help Italian fugitives. They're called Terranova, they're in Brooklyn Heights, just mention their name at the Café Ferdinando. Sit down, order a beer, and they'll immediately work out who you are. If they can't get you on to a ship, they'll hide you until peacetime. If the worst comes to the worst, Nino, hand yourself in to the police. Tell the truth, that you escaped for love, pile it on if you have to. They won't complain. Keep your mouth shut about this lot or you'll end up on the gallows.'

'These people have seen me, they know my name. If they get caught and talk, they'll accuse me.'

'They don't seem like traitors, they're determined fighters. If they do get captured, and they certainly will, they'll go to the scaffold shouting, "Long live the Führer", and they won't confess.'

'I don't want to leave you in their clutches. That woman's face . . .'

'You don't think I'm ahead of them? Come on, Nino.'

'Why don't we report them? We'll end up back inside, but at least we'll avoid carrying out the attack.'

'Forty days ago the Gestapo in the camp had its informers depict me as a Nazi. Now I'm travelling with three real spies, armed to the teeth. The men who are after us will never believe me. They'll hang us to justify hunting us down.'

From his expression, intent on the route among the canals that lead from the Harlem River to the majestic Hudson, I understood that he wanted to stop them all by himself, and make his contribution to the cause of freedom. He looked happy as he steered the fishing boat, with the brackish waves of the Hudson splashing the keel, bringing the sea air from the bay of New York. He was a boy again, he was back in a time when life and battle were a chivalrous code, an adventure, free of insults, lies or betrayal. Even in the most squalid battle he wanted to show how pure he was.

'You know what the Americans say? Nice guys finish last. All my life I've been trying to overturn that stupid saying: Nice guys win, the only victory worth having is a clean one, otherwise what's the point? I told you my mother was American, didn't I?'

'Yes, but you never mention her.'

'She died when I was a child. She used to tell me stories about Benjamin Franklin using his kite to catch lightning, and his ancestor who defended the Indian tribes against unjust treaties. That damned sense of fair play comes from her: and look where it's got me this time, Nino.'

He bore left, towards the first lights of the city that were coming towards us, reminding me strangely of a barbed-wire fence. 'You see the Empire State Building there, Nino? It's on 33rd Street. Now count up northwards to 57th, is there an aerial? There is? Keep your eye on it, that's our goal, that's the radio station I was planning to take you to. And in front of us we've got the ocean, Nino, and home. Just beat it, remember: Terranova family, Café Ferdinando. You can't go wrong.'

He turned the tiller and the fishing boat moored at a narrow jetty of boats and heavy barges. Frau Becht poked her head into the cabin. 'We're there,' she said.

We got out one by one, the men from the unit unloaded the material in silence, and there was no need to flag down a taxi as I had imagined. Hochhuth opened the bonnet of a limousine parked not far away, tied the starting wires together and fired the engine, fiddling with the gears at the chrome steering-wheel and, stopping at every red light like a good citizen, drove us through the darkness to our goal.

No patrols, no guards, a yellow light illuminating the words 'US Army Radio World System'. Forty days after my escape from Hereford Camp 1, we had reached the end.

24

Organising an act of sabotage is a task that requires precision, like mending a chronometer. Preparation and solitude, checklists, everyone intent on his own task. Testing the fuses, calculating the resistance of a wall. Tallying up the amount of surveillance done and to be done, unexpected encounters with the chaos of events, a sleeping guard who makes the job easier, a nervous recruit who shoots instinctively, sending the perfect plot crashing to the ground. The savagery of the delusion, in a dawn raid, that your own attack will be definitive, win or lose.

How benign those Germans had seemed to me, like a group of Tyroleans on a tour of Venice. And how quick and sharp they were now, their every movement perfectly judged. The lieutenant was silent in his calculations, which made me extremely worried. Could he have changed his mind, did he want to die on the side of the barricade where he had begun the war? Why, all of a sudden, had he mentioned his American mother? To tell me that he would die here, in the womb of his original homeland, or that he was renouncing that side of the family, to fall faithfully beneath the warlike banners of the Axis?

His advice had been reasonable, to take the subway and slip away to Brooklyn, hibernating until peace came. But my fate was linked with his, and I waited inertly for fate to cut the thread. At La Tonnara, Christian faith and pagan memory coexisted, Orazio the sacristan warned me not to do wrong – 'The Archangel will pass, and blind you' – while Barbaroux firmly believed in the Parcae, who weave and sever the threads of our fate. I had grown up willing to believe that the Angel flew above us brandishing the sword of justice, that every spring on the Island was home to a lovely nymph, while the mighty sea, our source of life, was ruled by a stern king.

I felt as though I wasn't responsible for my own movements that day, as though I was following someone in front of me. I could die, I could end up in the electric chair as a saboteur, or else I could escape: my power to choose was gone. I allowed myself to act, I shadowed the lieutenant, helping him if possible, but helping him to do what?

Hochhuth parked the car, uneasily eyeing the No Parking signs – 'I got lots of fines before the war' – got out and told us to walk ahead. Then he bent down as though to tie his shoes, and instead I saw him inserting the tubes of explosives under the chassis of two cars. The ones he chose were dusty and covered with leaves, their owners had probably left them there a few days ago, and there was little danger of them turning up while our mission was under way.

'Go, Nino,' the lieutenant whispered, but I shrugged. 'I'm going in,' I said, and made as though to enter the dark hall.

'Have you got your radio with you? Yes? Fine, tune in to the frequency of Armed Forces radio, you know it, don't you?'

A solitary guard was dozing, his glass of milk half drunk on the table, its remnants whitening his moustache.

Suddenly aware of the lieutenant, he stood abruptly to attention. The lieutenant handed him his papers, God alone knew how he could have kept them safe on that long and dusty flight. The guard grumbled, 'It's early, there isn't anyone in the offices. You're going to have to wait.'

'And are you going to make us wait here, like two rookies? We've just got here from Texas, with precise instructions, I'm going up. If you're not happy about it, call your superiors' – and, turning to me, his voice cheerful once more – 'Let's go, kid.'

He didn't call the lift, and I was sorry about that because I'd never been inside one, and I'd have liked to feel myself being carried up through the void. Instead we climbed the broad, gleaming steps four at a time, until we reached the floor where the radio studios were.

Two secretaries, wearing pressed auxiliary uniforms, were puzzling over a crossword and paid us no attention. The lieutenant looked up at the broadcasting studio with the red light outside it, a gently flickering bulb. He smiled at the girls. 'Live?'

'Mmm,' said the prettier of the two, a brunette who seemed intrigued by the elegant lieutenant.

'Europe?'

'Live news, 12 Greenwich.'

'Fine, then we're going in,' and he pushed down the handle.

The girls jumped up together, like puppets. The brunette shouted, 'They're broadcasting live, you can't go in.' The blonde, stocky and resolute, switched on a microphone, asking for help. 'Security, we've got an intruder.'

Apparently enjoying himself, the lieutenant said, 'Nino, go and call the guys down below. After the war we'll have to ask these young ladies to dance. Watch out for the lift, security's on its way.'

I flew. If he'd asked me to throw myself out of the window and into the dark street outside, I would have opened the shutters and hurled myself out. Nothing touched me, everything was like coloured cotton wool in front of my eyes. I looked at the first flight of stairs, the steps were more brilliantly polished than any marble I had ever seen before, and from the corner of my eye I saw the little lights that indicated the storeys reached by the rising lift. The lieutenant had guessed correctly, security preferred to take the easy way up.

The lieutenant silently tied up the girls, and I tied up the lazy security guard, the secretaries with two brightly coloured scarves and the security man with a big cleaning cloth. Inside the studio no one had noticed anything, and the voice emerging from the speaker alternated with music coming from black vinyl 78 records.

The lieutenant waited for the new piece to begin, it was a big band tune, I clearly remember the rasp of the trombones, the happy blast of the trumpets, the nostalgic swing of oboes and clarinet. He pushed the door open, smiled at the protests of the boy on the console – 'You can't come in, Glenn Miller will have finished in less than a minute, and then it will be my turn again' – and silenced him by producing his revolver, raising the barrel and saying with a smile, 'Don't say anything funny or it's goodbye from you, my friend. There's a new programme this morning. Get set, go . . .' The big band ran out of energy and the lieutenant approached the microphone that hung from the sound-proofed ceiling, as though he was going to bite it. He made a twiddling gesture with his thumb and forefinger. In response, I took out the radio, fiddled with the crystal, put on the earphones and, among the whistles of space, tuned in to New York.

In all the houses in Europe where people were listening, on that day in wartime, a moment of silence was heard between the music and the lieutenant's emotional voice. In the huts in the woods where Partisans and the Maquis were awaiting their instructions, in the freezing cellars of the occupied cities, where a worn-out overcoat and a biscuit weren't enough to conquer cold and hunger, in the secret hiding-places of Jews suspended between freedom and the camps, that silence must have seemed interminable as they took a sip of ersatz coffee, or oiled a magazine-loader. That moment seemed endless to me, too, listening on my POW crystal set.

Then the lieutenant spoke: 'Guten Tag, good morning, bonjour and buongiorno,' in the languages that his father, his mother and a series of good schools had taught him in the enchanted world of his youth. And, speaking a magical idiom that no one had ever heard before, English, French, German and Italian all mixed up together in such a way that every sentence was perfectly clear, he was understood everywhere in strife-torn Europe. He told the story of his escape from the prison camp, he gave his own rank and serial number in the Italian submarines and his training in Germany, and he recalled his exploits in the Atlantic. 'Now I've taken this microphone, brothers and sisters, to call on you to revolt. Rise up now, rise up in force against those who have oppressed you and sent you to die in silence, putting us against the world we loved. To those of you who are in the occupied cities I want to say that the hour of liberation is nigh, and it will come. From that moment onwards a new construction must begin, on both sides of the ocean, to put an end to death and savagery.' Speaking now French, now German – 'I have an American mother and an Italian father, and yet I have escaped from prison in Texas to travel to Salò and kill the Duce with my own bare hands. One of us must put an end to the slavery that has afflicted us. My great escape has stopped here in New York, but I, a former Axis officer, say to you that this is enough. Kill the dictators, grab your freedom once again. Rise up, and hope. There is a season in which the forces of evil appear invincible and cast their dark shadow over the continent of men. It will not last for ever, my friends, it will not last for ever. However divided and weak they may appear, however humble and docile each individual soldier may seem, the forces of good are finally emerging triumphant, because they have truth on their side. Truth will win out, because evil, being based on lies, does not last for ever. Over time, like a plant rooted in infertile ground, it withers and dies. I won't be among you on that blessed day, but you will be there, and you will be fully conscious. Revolt against injustice, disavow evil oaths, assume the burden of those in pain, and sign up for a fight to the death. He who frees the earth from tyrants will be remembered with joy. One thing alone troubles me: that I did not bring my mission to its conclusion, that I did not strike the mad dictator who brought my country to ruin. Avenge me. And now a personal message from an anguished fellow soldier, please, broadcast it everywhere, your words must reach their destination.'

He smiled at the startled presenter, benignly gesturing to him with his gun to wait a moment longer, and called me into the studio.

I slipped off the headphones, which were wailing with feedback because they were so close to the transmitter.

'You heard that, Nino?'

'Yes!'

The lieutenant stood me in front of the microphone, encouraging me: 'Speak to her. Tell her you love her. Tell her not to get married and to wait for you.'

'What?'

'Don't be a fool. Speak to Zita, for heaven's sake. We're on air, we haven't got all day. Speak to her.' He pushed me heavily into the centre of the studio. 'As though she were here. She might be listening with Barbaroux, go on, do it.'

I closed my eyes, and there was the Island. The slower boats were still visible off the coast, you could follow them from the Old Shipyard, with a scapular to protect you from the damp. Zita had made coffee for the professor, and the warm smell filled the red-walled study. From his case, Barbaroux was taking the sheets of paper that recorded, in black ink, the equations that Zita was patiently copying out for publication. He took her by the hand and led her to the terrace to watch the boats, or perhaps two dolphins that were leaping cheerfully, wisely, animals sacred to the oracle of Delphi. We had stood together on that little balcony when the air was scented with Saracen jasmine. I was paralysed with fear, but jealousy and rage – we humans are so simple and innocent – brought passionate words issuing from my mouth. With my eyes shut I called into the microphone, 'Zita? Zita? Do you hear me? Do you recognise me? It's Nino, your Nino, Nino Manes. I've escaped, escaped from prison and now I'm in New York City. Don't get married, my little Zita, don't marry Barbaroux, because I love you and you love me. Did you hear the words of my friend the lieutenant? Freedom's returning, but what use is freedom, Zita, without love? I know you miss me, for two people in love closeness is all. I can imagine what confused you: Barbaroux is our professor, he fought against the dictator, he speaks fluently. But you don't love him, Zita, you can't love him. Wait for me. If this flight of mine ends well, today is the fortieth day that we've spent in the wilderness and, with God's help, I'm coming home, I'll find a way to persuade you. Wait for me, Zita. Even if they catch me, the war's about to end, you heard the lieutenant and his call to the armed forces, didn't you? And I'm coming back, I've changed, I'm mature, you know what a year in the desert means, in silence, and Africa, do you know what it's like to be alone and in love in Bardia, Zita, when the stars are so cold and so numerous that you feel you could reach out and touch them, and you have the roars of the lions in your ears? If a man loves a woman like that, that's what two deserts taught me, then she's bound to love him too. You may not understand, you may be confused, and you are confused. I know what you have to do, take our boat, it's still afloat, isn't it? Go down below the stone arch when the frangipanis are in bloom, smell their perfume and ask yourself if you could help loving a man mad enough to cross America for you and announce his love on US Army radio . . .' The lieutenant nodded to me – 'Cut' – and the enormity of what I had done made me feel happy and weightless, I started to laugh and the lieutenant laughed with me. The boy from the station looked at us as though we'd gone mad, and our fresh, cool laughter filled the eternal ether and the war-torn world. I hadn't laughed like that since 1940, the tears fell down my cheeks, hollow with weeping. I swung my hips and howled into the microphone, I howled with freedom, I howled with excitement. The lieutenant's noble words and my pathetic appeal had gone where our poor feet couldn't go, but now it barely mattered. We had mocked the dictators who had sent us to our deaths, we had matched the Americans in dignity, we were free like them, masters of our destiny, capable of inventing policies, declaring love, occupying space with our voices and now laughing till our sides ached while the whole world listened and was filled with us. No one could order us around now, no one could force us to march or carry out nefarious orders, no one could keep us behind a barbed-wire fence.

Datsch had gone up to check the security guard and the secretaries, and hadn't heard the lieutenant's appeal. Even now I don't know who it was addressed to, the Americans, the Germans, the other Europeans held hostage by dictators. Or perhaps he was simply speaking to himself, perhaps it was his farewell to life, to flight, to youth, lest he be swallowed up in the shadow, in perpetual silence, like H.S. at the leper hospital. Perhaps he had done it to make his mark on the future – 'You know, Nino, that the waves of your little radio,' he had said to me as we docked in New York, 'will advance for ever through the cosmos, radiating without a pause, and bring the message ever onwards; one day a man will invent a box to decode them on the edge of the universe, and listen to our voices.'

'Did you hear me? Were we on air? Were we cancelled?' he asked me, trembling with emotion.

'I heard you loud and clear, Lieutenant. And they heard you everywhere!'

'I told you we'd make it home.'

Datsch gestured broadly at us to leave. 'I don't know what your broadcast said, but well done. Now let's get out of here.'

The auxiliaries and the pale announcer were locked up in the studio. Datsch told us he had laid explosives beneath the corner support, and the whole wing of the building would come down in the explosion.

'I'll set the fuses. Where are they?' said the lieutenant.

The German looked at him in surprise for a moment, lighting the fuses wasn't a job – as I knew from my time in Africa, where I'd charged more than one mine at a time – that you took on voluntarily. 'Are you sure?'

'I hope you didn't see us laughing. Humour is the chief enemy of the saboteur,' murmured the lieutenant, and then raised his voice: 'Have no doubts about me, my friend.'

'No, no,' replied Datsch, but any trace of sympathy had faded from his voice. 'Let's get going right now,' and he hurled himself down the stairs.

'What are we doing?' I asked.

'We're pretending to charge these damned bombs and make our getaway. We'll disarm these guys in the street, and let's see if we can get a few dollars from them too, once we've ensured that they're harmless. We've got to stop them doing any damage. If we manage to get the cash off them, we'll fly to Italy.'

We'd reached the finishing-line, our insane broadcast would have every patrol in the city converging on 57th Street within a few minutes, and Datsch was completely unaware. The lieutenant was holding the fuses, and enough TNT to bring down the whole block. Behind the massive glass pane of the studio, the uniformed officer was struggling frantically to free himself. But the lieutenant, forgetting everything, was thinking about how to rob the Germans of the 80,000 dollars, use them to bribe a sailor, cross the ocean and try to kill Benito Mussolini. Ignoring the fact that even Salò knew of his plan by now.

He bent down under the tables, perhaps afraid that Datsch might be watching from the stairs, set light to some match-heads to make a hissing sound, and smiled at the prisoners by way of reassurance. Then he grabbed me by the elbow: 'Get out!'

In two bounds we were back in the hall through which we had entered a few minutes before, greeted politely by the man at the desk, who was now tied to his chair. One of his colleagues, who had come running at the first sound of voices, lay with his head on his forearm, stretched out on the gleaming formica of the office counter, as though weeping his heart out. Thick blood trickled from the back of his neck, and he was clutching the telephone receiver: the engaged tone rang out in the empty room, in a vain bid to give the alarm. Stavinsky was polishing his silver-studded dagger. Datsch was ready. 'How long before it goes up?'

'One hundred and eighty seconds.'

'The guys have switched on the engine. I hope the explosion will be heard around the world. Did you leave the microphone on, Captain?'

His voice was harsh, the subdued Datsch from the boat had made way for a fierce and unpredictable fighter. The lieutenant had dealt with worse. 'Left it on air? I turned the volume up to the max. It'll blow out the few windows left intact on the continent of Europe.'

Hochhuth had removed the booby-trapped car, parking in its place the one he had stolen on the jetty. A muffled sound of sirens was converging from the Hudson River, but I couldn't make out whether they were tugs signalling in the fog or the police, alerted by the security man before Stavinsky got to him with the dagger.

Datsch drove us along 57th Street, light rose from the steely river, scented and close. A sound of clarinets and a big band emerged from an open bar, the tender music of Glenn Miller once again. The Allies would win the war, how can you lose a war with so much wonderful music on your side?

The passers-by already on the way to the office had their hats on, it was 1944, there was an air of victory in New York. But Datsch's unit was dreaming of death. Hochhuth pointed to the chosen target, 'Army and Navy Recruitment Centre'. A queue of beardless boys with very short hair thronged outside the front door, laughing and smoking. Recruits who would soon be taking the steamer to Europe, in the final push against Hitler.

Earlier, the lieutenant had lagged behind, gestured to me by bringing his fists together and then pulling them violently apart, like someone breaking a thread. He had cut the fuse to the bomb at the radio station. The world would not hear the Nazi conflagration.

Hochhuth fussed skilfully with the detonator. Datsch passed him a wire, and they ran it through the boot of the car and fastened it to the box of explosives.

'What now?' the lieutenant asked calmly.

'Now,' Datsch replied, staring into his eyes, 'we blow up the car and send these boys to hell. The radio broadcast isn't enough. The explosion will spread panic. It couldn't be better.

From there we move on to the big stores. Before the day is over, we'll be dead, but New York will be ablaze, and the world will know that the Reich isn't finished. Not yet, my friend.'

I looked at the lieutenant as I had looked at Colonel Paoli, at a loss as the British bombs fell on us. 'Tell me what to do and I'll do it, tell me where to go with this head of mine, bursting with fear, and I'll do it, come what may, but this feeling of doubt is killing me.'

The lieutenant shook his head and startled me, as he always did. 'If it goes off here, it won't do much damage. The street is open to the sea. You may kill a few, but the shockwave will be harmlessly dispersed. They'll say a boiler exploded.'

'You're right,' Hochhuth agreed grimly, 'there's too much room.'

'What do you suggest?' I asked, really anxious to know what plan my companion had in mind.

'It's going to take balls, boys. The footpath is low, you see?' and he scraped it with the sole of his muddy shoe. 'Hochhuth, you prime the bomb, how long can you give me? One hundred and eighty seconds? It's not much. I need at least four minutes –' He glanced at his steel Vetta chronometer, he was the only one still wearing one of our magnificent Vettas. '– otherwise give me 250 seconds, or 300, even better.'

'Two hundred and fifty,' Hochhuth conceded, admiring the lieutenant's technique.

'You're always stingy, you firework-makers! Let's do it like this. You prime the bomb. When you're ready, I'll drive the car at the queue. You lot make off and we'll meet up at Macy's,

33rd Street, at the ice-cream and soda stall at eleven o'clock exactly. Nino and I will go in the car. When you feel us hitting the footpath, Nino, throw yourself out of the door and head east. I'll jump out of the driver's door and try to make it to the west, towards the river. After the bomb goes off it'll be harder for them to come after us. Is that okay?'

I wasn't exactly convinced, throwing myself out, explosives, escaping through an unfamiliar city, but now I was following him, and that was that.

'It's a good idea, but I'm going too,' Datsch insisted. 'It's our mission. We appreciate your help. But I've got to be on board. You go with them,' he said, turning to me.

'I take my orders from him,' I replied, looking steadily into his cold eyes.

The lieutenant nodded to me, his index and middle fingers open in a V, asking for a cigarette. I passed him one, and leaned across to light it over my fist. 'I'm going with Datsch, Nino. You run to the river. Follow the pier to the left, and when you see the sign reading 32nd Street turn left, it'll take you straight to Macy's. Have you got money?' And he handed me a few dollars, anxious as an older brother. He took another draw on the cigarette and distractedly threw what was almost a whole Camel into a courtyard just a few feet away from the recruitment office. It was a narrow redbrick yard, overlooked by the wooden water towers that dot the Manhattan skyline. An explosion in there would have been nothing but a shift of air, it would have had as much effect as a firecracker. Ex-fighters and prisoners were used to smoking cigarettes down to the last scrap of tobacco. Even when we were lucky enough to set a few packs aside, we still sucked the acrid smoke down to the bottom, for luck, as though sucking on the marrowbone of fate. The lieutenant never squandered anything, life in a submarine schools you in frugality. If he wasted a cigarette it was to give me a signal.

I looked at him, checking my intuition. He gave me a bewitching smile. Okay: he was going to send the car bomb in the direction of the courtyard and neutralise the outrage. How would he have got away with it? By throwing himself out of the car? Or did he want to go up with it, like a kamikaze fighter?

He said to Datsch, 'Let's go, buddy boy,' and climbed into the car. Hochhuth and Stavinsky headed west, towards the Hudson, and I was supposed to be running eastwards as fast as my legs would carry me, towards Broadway and Macy's. But I was rooted to the spot. A yellow bus full of children was accelerating along 57th Street. 'Jewish Relief for Children', read a sign on the side, and a little splash of green paint suggested the flight of a refugee child, escaping the war and arriving in New York, protected by the muscular Statue of Liberty. Behind the misted windows, the chubby-faced children, orphans who had been cast ashore in safety here without a moment to lose, were busy munching doughnuts. All of a sudden Datsch leaped aboard the car, took the wheel and lurched off. The lieutenant barely had time to throw himself in, and the car was already going at full speed. Datsch steered the car straight towards the bus, which was making for the river. He would collide with it, detonating Hochhuth's explosives and slaughtering the children of Israel in their belated refuge. Hochhuth and Stavinsky suddenly froze on the pavement and then, on second thoughts, turned on their heels to cover their colleague.

I started running hard along the sidewalk. Each stride was a kind of flight – 'You've got to calculate that a block in Manhattan takes a minute to walk,' Carraway had told me – but in the chase between the yellow bus and the black car, a few seconds was enough. I ran as I had run at Alborada, fingers spread for extra speed, lungs heaving, the muscles in my back tense. Prison had left me flabby, my legs weren't as vigorous as they had been. Flight gave me back my lost strength. Wasn't that the sound of bells in my ears? Wasn't I running at breakneck speed towards Orazio and the church square in the brackish mist?

The bus was ten metres ahead of Datsch's car, and I was twenty metres behind. The river was two hundred metres away. I don't remember if there were any streetlights, or whether the bus slowed down at crossings. I remember a three-man race: the children in front with their cinnamon doughnuts, the death-car in hot pursuit, and me, a ludicrous flying athlete who had just travelled thousands of American miles. I had no idea what I planned to do, but I was sure the lieutenant had already guessed Datsch's intentions. Did I want to die? Did I want to save the children? Or him? Without thinking, I was running towards the sea, whose opposite shore lapped against Zita.

The driver parked the bus on the jetty, parallel to the water. A schoolmistress was showing her pupils the New Jersey shore with its chimneys, and the Statue of Liberty peeped out of the fog. There could have been no easier target for a saboteur, aiming straight at the bus which looked enormous against the iron-grey backdrop of the river. Datsch must have smiled smugly at the chance to make his contribution to the war effort. Jewish children killed in New York, a conflict switching continents, the American mainland humiliated. I let out a high-pitched shriek and leapt on to the last pavement, hovering for a second over a pile of copies of the *New York Times* with a map of the European conflict on the front page, brushed past a café, a kiosk, leapt over fire hydrants, heard my own voice in my ears and the rumble of the cars, and saw one child turning round, perhaps bored by his schoolmistress, staring black-eyed at the car that was coming straight towards him, ten metres, five. The little boy opened his mouth, full of sugar and cinnamon, and shaped it into a circle of alarm; it wasn't fear, not yet, just a mournful amazement that there was no respite in suffering fate, that death, which he had dodged by a breath in his homeland, was now coming to get him in imperial Manhattan. I was half a block away, the explosion of the TNT, the fragments of the bus, the fire from the petrol tank, would have torn me to pieces along with the child, now blood kin to the lieutenant. I knew everything there was to know about artillery fire, I could throw myself to the right, one more step and I would be safe, the Hudson would absorb the conflagration, and I would escape as lightly as a sparrow. Instead I asked as much of my breath as I could give, and reached my appointment with the terrorist attack.

Reflected in the schoolboy's frozen expression I saw Datsch's car turning abruptly and brushing the yellow side of the bus with its mudguards. It seemed inevitably destined to blow up its innocent, solemn and tragic target, and yet all of a sudden it veered away, shattering the red rear light into a thousand pieces that flew into the air and rained back down as harmless confetti on the pier. I neatly avoided a truck – the driver slammed on the brakes and shook his fist. I was on the pier now, and the little boy had turned his eyes to follow the speeding car. Shoulder to shoulder, Datsch and the lieutenant were fighting for control of the vehicle. They clung fiercely to the wheel, one to deliver a death blow, the other to parry destruction. My final obstacle was a roll of hemp cable, coiled like a rattlesnake in the desert. I must still have been in mid-air when the little boy put his hands over his mouth to stifle a scream. The lieutenant summoned a hidden source of strength, his American mother revitalised him just as Gaia had strengthened the giant Antaeus when his enemies knocked him to the ground in hand-to-hand combat, and subdued Datsch, freeing the schoolchildren from harm at the last moment. The black Ford car crashed a few times, just missing a wooden box that hung from a winch above the river before shooting off the end of the pier. It flew over two badly moored little boats and looked as though it was going to make it all the way to New Jersey, skimming across the waves like a pebble. Instead it aimed its squinting headlights at the current, sent up a frothy fountain as it fell and vanished into the waves.

I reached the end of the pier and dived into the whirlpool that had swallowed up the car. The water was cold, but lit by faint sunlight. I followed the violent spiral of bubbles that whirled up with a gurgle from the riverbed. I plunged down as hard as I could swim, the icy current pulling me by the hair, I kicked my legs like a frog. It didn't matter any more, but I wouldn't come up alone. With the lieutenant, or dead.

My right hand banged against the roof of the car. I gripped the waterproof fabric tightly, and lowered myself towards the door. Opening my eyes wide, I couldn't even tell whether the Ford was lying upside down on the mud, or whether it was still sinking through the freezing water and dragging me with it. I held on to the chrome handle with my left hand and tried to yank it open, as the weight of the water tore open the roof of the car. The little oxygen I still had in my lungs escaped in bubbles, as though horrified by the water of the bay, and hungry for the effervescent air of New York. An inert body drifted towards me, bent in two like a newborn baby. I held it tight, lungs aching. I had only to touch the body's shaven scalp to know that it was Datsch. I let him slip through the roof, legs dangling, his stomach must have been full of water, too heavy to float. Dead. I thought of Queequeg, the whale fisherman in *Moby-Dick*, having to free his mate, trapped in the body of a sperm whale that is diving down into the ocean. I was stretched out on the passenger seat, bracing my feet against the door. If the car did turn over, this would be my grave.

The lieutenant's hand was wedged underneath the steering wheel. To free it, I gripped his soft belt and tried to pull myself up with the little air I still had in my lungs, our sole hope of life. My legs whirled around as once they had done at La Tonnara, and I felt the cold stripping my bones and joints, flaying me like St Bartholomew. The surface of the water was a long way away, it didn't look liquid now, it had condensed into a freezing slab of arctic pack-ice that sealed my own fate and the fate of the lieutenant who hung on to my wrist like a lead sinker. Despite the strain I climbed quickly, quickly. I thought I was going to shatter against the icy wall – if I hadn't time to get my head out the curtain would close for ever. Queequeg had done it, before finding proud death in the shipwreck of the *Pequod*. And what about me?

'It's over,' I thought, and nothing came to mind, not my mother, or Zita, nor even God, to whom I would soon surrender my useless soul. As I stretched upwards to gain the last few inches of safety or death, I thought of Orazio, the sacristan in La Tonnara. How would he take the news of my drowning in America? Would he pray? Would he remember me at the Novena for Our Lady of the Rosary, or would he reflect on my fate with a mixture of pity and scepticism – 'Always an odd one, that boy, but this time the race finished before the holy Alborada' – the blue smoke from his pipe sealing my epitaph?

I didn't want to disappoint Orazio, I wanted to see him again, I wanted to run on the cobbles, an eternal race against accursed, murderous time. 'Listen, Orazio, what fate awaits you if you get there before the Alborada explodes? Help me. Help me, *nunc et semper.'*

My mouth grimaced at its bitter impact with the air. I carefully rested the lieutenant's body against one of the dinghies, not immediately noticing the dagger that protruded from his slim shoulder. I felt faint. All around me the reports of Alborada rang out, *tac, tac, tac.* Did I get there in time, Orazio? Am I in time to bring my brother the hero back to life? *Tac, tac, tac,* the bangs of Alborada. I smiled happily, drained, fulfilled. I had kept my pact with fate, sweet indeed it was to die at Alborada.

Only after the war was over did I discover that the explosions ringing in my ears were the bullets of the Federal snipers as they riddled the car with gunfire, fearing that Nazis were still on board. If a bullet had struck Hochhuth's dynamite, the explosion would have taken their mission to its conclusion. But Fate watched over us that day, and over the children, and the Ford stayed harmlessly where it was on the riverbed. Datsch's body was never found. The current carried it towards the ocean and his beloved motherland.

25

We were perfectly hidden by the dinghies. The cops who had been firing randomly, lazily, at the wreck of the black car, to make themselves look like warriors, now surrounded Hochhuth and Stavinsky. One short, bald man levelled his revolver at Stavinsky, who was pointing vigorously at the water and shouting, 'Don't shoot, don't shoot!' They quickly understood about the bomb, and took a few steps back. The lieutenant put a languid arm around my neck.

'How did you do it? I was as good as dead that time.' His voice was free of irony, free of accent, it sparkled like the beam of bubbles that had drawn me into the whirlpool and down into the murky waters, ensuring that I didn't lose my way. Blood ran copiously from his shoulder, and his face was pale. 'This is going to hurt,' I murmured, and with one stroke I removed the heavy blade. My first instinct was to keep the dagger, just in case, and I stuck it into my belt like a pirate. 'No need for weapons now, Nino, throw it away. We're on our own, whether in water or in air, we need nothing now,' the lieutenant said gently, and threw the burnished steel dagger down to join its owner in the Hudson Bay. I stemmed the

271

flow of blood using my belt as a tourniquet, and bound the wound with my handkerchief, a present from H.S.

'I'm under your orders now, Commander,' he whispered. 'I don't know what to do.'

Neither did I. On the pier I saw the policemen hurrying to usher away the Jewish Relief children, sheltering them behind some large concrete blocks nearby and from there, one by one, sending them towards the coffee shop on 57th Street. The last one to pass by was the pupil I had seen at the bus window, still clutching his half-eaten doughnut. They couldn't see us, but the bomb disposal men would soon arrive to defuse and recover the car. Stavinsky seemed to be talking, while Hochhuth, silent and standing rigidly to attention, eyed the water to see if there was any trace of Datsch, and whether the rumble of the explosion, which would merely be symbolic now, might not bring their final mission to a close.

I could have called out to the FBI men, hoping that they weren't trigger happy, that they wouldn't want to shoot before asking questions, and finish us off right there on the pier. But I was in the water, it was too cold to think, the boat's engine gleamed, and there were rough waterproof tarpaulins in the bottom of the dinghy. I was a seafaring boy, and the sea made my decision for me. At that point in the Hudson, the sea bass swim vigorously against the current, and it is there that the lobsters of the bay have their lairs, because the early morning undertow tirelessly carries the brackish water northwards.

I performed a half-somersault to pull the lieutenant on board, sobbing and groaning, and hauled myself in with my aching arms. I untied the rope, wrapped the lieutenant in the tarpaulin to protect him against the cold and, staying in the lee of the pier, we drifted along the river. No one noticed, and soon we were passing by the great steamers moored by West 42nd Street.

My teeth were chattering. My friend had turned white. He opened his mouth: 'Where are we going, Commander?'

'Out to sea.'

'All the way to Italy in this little skiff? Yes, sir, set the tiller to the east.'

The engine jolted to life and the tank was heavy with gasoline. Now we turned our backs on the transoceanic ships. From the main deck of the biggest steamer, a lookout saw me and called out in Italian, 'Good luck, pal, may the Lord be with you.'

I waved and shouted into the mistral, 'I'm Nino, Nino Manes, an Italian from the Island, remember that!'

Past the Bay of Manhattan, the ocean wind and the surge of the foam drove the waves. I didn't know where to go, I was terrified. 'A plan, Lieutenant, a plan . . .' – and I looked at him, hoping that he might come up with something. He nodded with a faint smile to encourage me, do what you think best, you're making the decisions now.

I would actually have headed out to the sea, aiming the prow straight east, towards Gibraltar and the Pillars of Hercules, had Datsch not stabbed the lieutenant. So my sole strategy was to save his life. I shook myself out of the crazed joy that came from sailing after four years of exile on dry land. I breathed in the smell of salt, turned the tiller slightly to dock by a red brick building: 'Brooklyn Yards, Slow pace, Engine off.' I turned off the gas and reached a lonely jetty. A white coastguard minesweeper slipped slowly by. The lookout paid us no attention, his eyes lost on the horizon.

I climbed out of the boat, with the lieutenant leaning on my shoulder. The few steps that separated us from the street were covered with moss. 'Never put your feet on the green, always on the white,' warned one of my fellow POWs in Hereford, a Venetian sailor from Malamocco. 'Always on the black, never on the green as long as you live, Nino, or you'll slip into the stinking water.' But now I had no choice, the steps were all heavy with petrol-drenched seaweed. It was hard to keep my balance with my mate on my shoulder, heavy and silent. I wanted to go in search of first aid, but didn't know where to start – the whole district seemed to be exactly the same wherever you looked, house after house, windows, gardens, driveways with brightly painted gateposts, as identical as a prisoner's days. I glanced at the lieutenant's Vetta watch, it was still very early.

Ahead of me a congregation of black-clad women was walking towards a church square. 'La Madonna bedduzza . . .' I heard one small, white-haired woman saying in dialect. 'Blessed Virgin . . .' They were Italians, perhaps they'd be able to give me directions, perhaps they wouldn't call the police, perhaps I'd be able to leave the lieutenant in their care so that he could get to safety and make his way home after the war. Did they know the Terranova family, the ones who helped escaped prisoners? The anchor of the steamer from which the

Italian sailor had called to me was tempting now, so close. Once I had brought the lieutenant to safety, I would take the skiff, swing on to the chain like Tarzan, and my compatriot would hide me in the galley.

A silvery bell rang out. Under the water Orazio had inspired, and now his Novena was calling the faithful to prayer. It seemed to me that the vibrations penetrated the vastness of the ocean. Orazio was listening, Zita was listening. My footsteps struck the old cobblestones, just as my wet soles had slipped along the cobbles on the Island.

The lieutenant whispered, 'End of the line, Nino, leave me here. It's too risky together. Let's split up, my brother.'

I tried to sound encouraging. 'But I don't know where we are, I'm lost without you.'

'Look behind you.'

I turned my head slightly so as not to hurt him, and went on climbing the battered marble stairs. In the faint light I could see the powerful line of bricks and cables of the gothic Brooklyn Bridge, the stone aisles in the fog, an American cathedral, the stretched steel tie-beams, the strings of a harp that God alone could play.

'Do you know how long we've been on the run? Forty days, the same length of time that Noah spent in the Ark. The church on your island is called San Noè, isn't it?' said the lieutenant, and his voice was human again, colourful, not the voice of the living angel he had been in the sea when I had saved him from underwater death. That voice had been constant, this was the voice of a man fading away.

'Have you been counting them?' In wartime you always talk to people in their death-throes, to keep them conscious as you wait for help, or to console them during their final moments.

'If we're like Noah in the Ark after forty days, the flood will end today, and so will the divine wrath upon us.'

He struggled to lift his hand, and ruffled my hair as an experienced girl might do to her more innocent boyfriend. I'm a romantic islander, just as much now as I was then. I was moved. The bell continued to ring out, detached, methodical, summoning the faithful to their communion prayer. The lieutenant yielded inertly, drawn in by its shadows. My godfather Fernando had told me about Lot's wife, turned to a pillar of salt because she wanted to look back at the past, and about Orpheus, the gentlest of the heroes to have claimed the Golden Fleece, tricked by the powers of Hades because he had looked back to see his wife Eurydice as he was leaving the Kingdom of the Dead. Why does wise Orpheus turn around, and not wait patiently to return to earth with his beloved? Because he fears the new Eurydice, he wants her to be the same as the one who lived on earth among us mortals. The past kills, if we wish to preserve it with human eyes, if we lack the courage and the dignity to resign ourselves to the passing days. Lot and Orpheus are victims of the past. Did the steely Hudson River, which ran turbulently from Canada, kissing the bridge the Italian workmen built in Brooklyn, yearn to return to the north, where the grizzly bears had slapped its surface as they hunted for leaping salmon? No. It patiently poured all its immense force into the ocean before me, and waited to evaporate into clouds, condense into rain and finally return to the earth. With the eternal strength of one who knows the universe is sacred, its cycle more worthy of life than I, writing now in memoriam.

The bell fell silent, and there, emerging from a motorboat and climbing the mildewed stairs that I myself had climbed, were the two figures that I remembered from the sweltering heat of Arkansas. The confident officer and his young companion, moving brusquely now as though to show the world he was a full-grown man. They were clutching pistols, and between them, gesturing into the darkness, was Stavinsky, his blond hair clinging to his forehead. He called out in German, I didn't understand what he was saying, but the lieutenant gave a start. 'He's telling them we want to blow up the church.'

The younger of the two officers fired a quick volley of shots that ricocheted around the church square. Bent double beneath the weight of the lieutenant, I slipped into a courtyard. The lieutenant, on the alert now, said, 'The other man tapped him on the arm. He doesn't want him to shoot. He wants to take us alive.'

It would have been sensible of us to stop and give ourselves up, but you don't willingly abandon an adventure. We were still on the run: don't ask me why. It was our war, our mission, our life, and we followed it patiently.

I was afraid that they were about to capture my wounded friend, bring our journey to an end and kill us amidst this pitiful morning dew. We had been on the run together for too long not to move in unison, like a pair of tango dancers. 'To the right, to the right,' he said, we were back in the mine-field, together for ever.

'Halt!' called voices, footsteps running very close nearby.

Why didn't we stop? Because memory confuses us, dulls our senses and deprives us of our reason. One day, when we were still with the girl in the prairie, the lieutenant had boasted that he had been a champion cross-country runner at high school. I told him about my Alborada marathon. H.S. drew a line in the sandy path with the heel of her shoe, and pointed to a goal among the bushes, standing in front of us and holding out her white silk scarf. Under the sun we flew, fast, powerful, healthy, the immortal warriors that only young people imagine themselves to be. I took great strides and felt the soles of my feet striking the earth, and the lieutenant was close to me, I couldn't tell whether he was a shade in front of me or a shade behind me. We rolled hugging past the scarf that flew into our sweaty faces. 'I won! Long live Italy!' 'I won, greenhorn!' H.S. awarded two prizes, the scarf to me and a kiss to the lieutenant. And on we went: out of absurd loyalty to that race, and the memory of our flight.

The men pursuing us were on the ball. The older officer caught Stavinsky by the elbow and dragged him easily away. Quickly, silently, the sleuths cornered us, covering one another, calling out once again, 'Halt! Halt!' They wanted to take us alive, but their first gunfire had drawn the attention of a mili-tary patrol in Brooklyn, alerted by radio from Manhattan.

And they weren't keen shots. The moment they saw us they started firing, the only shots fired in their domestic war, and they would tell their neighbours about them for years, over glasses of mulled wine: 'Us? We were the ones who intercepted those Nazis, with our Smith & Wessons. The Intelligence aces were after them, sure, but we were the ones who stopped them.'

Two shots. The one meant for me, Giovannino Manes, missed its target and I skipped my appointment with the Eternal One for a little while longer. The bullet scorched my ear and shattered a pane of dark glass. The man who fired at the lieutenant was a better shot, or luckier, and hit him in the shoulder blade. His lithe, elegant body that I had admired so much was paralysed now.

He gave a jolt, and all of a sudden his athletic, swimmer's grace was lost. If I had charged towards the church door, I would have found myself in the middle of the firing range. It looked as though it was curtains for us but then, just a couple of feet away, I glimpsed the opening of the church coal chute, a subterranean, soot-blackened intestine. There was enough coal at the bottom to soften my fall. 'Hold on tight' – and I began to slide, protecting my companion with my arms. We looked like two little boys in a park cheerfully sliding down the banister of a flight of steps, laughing at the statues of the saints and horsemen around us. The coal sacks broke our fall. I opened a wooden door and from it, cadenced and consoling, came the rhythm of the Hail Mary. The priest intoned the words calmly, and the congregation dutifully replied.

I sat the lieutenant down in the back pew, and he leaned his head on my shoulder. He seemed to be asleep, and yet he was speaking fitfully, waiting for the chorus of women to cover his faint voice, and falling silent when the priest's baritone rang out alone in the apse.

'Nino, I told you it was the end of the line, didn't I? Listen, my father's address is in my jacket pocket, and my brother's is in there too, he's a prisoner in . . .'

'*Sancta Maria, mater Dei, ora pro nobis peccatoribus . . .*'

'I wanted to get back to the fatherland, too. The first man to escape the United States, the first and the only one. A hero magnificent enough to be admitted to the presence of the Duce himself. A hero who has seen enough of this mad war to fire two bullets into the Duce's bald head, and bring his dictatorship to an end. I wanted to kill the Duce, Nino, to redeem the Italian uniform and its military honour in the eyes of the world. Think of our guards, Nino. Their paper, the *Stars and Stripes*, would have dedicated a whole page to my action: "Prisoner crosses the United States and the ocean and brings evil tyrant to justice."'

'*Ave Maria, gratia plena dominus tecum, benedicta tu in mulieribus . . .*'

'I failed. My brother, the footballer, a fascist prisoner, had managed to warn me through that Nazi fanatic who brought us to New York. We had a code, if there was any danger he would say he'd had a soccer accident. We were hunted down, the fascists and the Gestapo sniffed out my plan. They're scared I'm going to reveal the names of the Nazi agents who've infiltrated the camps. And I don't even know who they are! They've exposed us by blackmailing some double agents inside the camp.'

He coughed and groaned, listened benignly to the *gratia plena* and continued. 'Tell my father I tried, and good luck with Zita. Don't worry about wisdom, you see how the wise end up? Shot down like mad dogs in Brooklyn. I could have gone back to Venice, Ninetto, I could have dived into the Lido and swum at sunset with the bells of San Giorgio behind me. No, I had to execute the Duce. From America!'

He smoothed back his hair, now nothing but a few wet clumps, and I stroked his head maternally. His failed adventure was a source of endless pain. He softened against me, eyes closed. 'What difference does it make, Nino, whether I rot in the camp or at the bottom of the sea like my submarine crews? There's no point in anything. But how proud and happy I was being on the run with you. In uniform, finally, on behalf of truth and justice, with the secret flashes of truth and justice branded on our souls. That's how you should behave in the army. But you, Nino, you know how to love, and how to act out of love. Never forget that.'

'*Nunc et in hora mortis nostrae amen.*'

The priest climbed into the pulpit. He was young, almost a boy, of Italian origin, olive-skinned, thin and with the merest hint of a beard. His stole hung loose over his shoulders, like a jacket passed down by a working-class father to his eldest son. My teeth chattered, the church was cold, one of my shoulders was frozen, and the other was sweating with the heat of fever and the weight of the lieutenant. We sat in the shade of the stained glass, where the exhausted women in their black veils couldn't see us. The solemn statue of St Noah in person, with the pale dove behind him, shielded us from the view of the street, which I tried to check by craning my neck.

The boy-priest leaned down from the purple parapet of the pulpit and cried, 'Resurrection!'

His boyish body concealed a prophet's voice. Calm and confident, fully aware of the fallacy of all the things we thought we knew.

'Why, sisters, did our Christian fathers and mothers abandon their belief in the ancient gods of pagan Olympus to convert to Christianity? Because of the resurrection of the dead preached by Christ Jesus. No longer were we lost slaves, no longer did we have to live a brutal life filled with pain and a few fleeting pleasures. There was an alternative to the endless yearning of pagan life, consumed in a flash and followed by an endless silent gloom: our belief in eternal life, that we will rise and sit next to God and the angels. When our forefathers slept, they slept the sleep of faith, certain of the life to come. And what of us, surrounded as we are by the requiems of war? Do we still believe, sisters, do we still believe we see eternal life, or are we resigned to mere existence, radio, cooking on coal-gas, our children's schools, our husbands coming home drunk on Saturday nights? How many generations swallowed up by the shadows, how many faces cut down between 1941 and the present day? I say to you: if you do not believe in the Resurrection, then you are dead already, and I am dead with you in this very church. This city and our suffering nation are a vast, open-air grave.'

'What kind of sermon is this?' murmured the lieutenant, rubbing his head against the padding of my jacket. 'The time really has come for me to bid farewell to this world, you can't even get a moment's peace in a church,' and he closed his eyes. From the other nave two slim officers appeared, clearly having handed Stavinsky over to the patrol. They couldn't see us in the faint light that poured from the stained glass showing the stations of the Via Crucis.

The priest raised his slender hands, and his booming voice stirred the congregation. 'How lucky our forefathers were. They had heard the word from close to, for them the Resurrection was close at hand, just as sleep is followed by awakening without any real loss of consciousness. We, on the other hand, must bury our dear ones, even the young ones taken on the field of war. The promise of eternal life recedes: where, when, will we finally see the Lord? That is the test of our generation, sisters: belief without hope. Leaping in the dark, with no one there to catch us, renewing our trust in the shepherd although his silence has lasted for centuries now, and the mocking forces of evil seem to be winning. Never despair. If you are able to recreate the eternal world of tomorrow in your heart, God will keep his promise. That pledge floats here among us. Let the struggle consume your faith, let your despair for your children gnaw at your belief and we will all lose our salvation. Renew your hope in truth, and you yourselves will be the shepherd, you will stand surety of the Resurrection.'

'What kind of sermon is this, Nino?' This time the priest seemed to hear the lieutenant, perhaps through vibration or magic, and instinctively our pursuers' eyes darted in our direction. In vain, protected as we were by the cold darkness.

'I have to bury men and women who have never had an ounce of power on this planet, I preach that the last will be first. But is that fair, sisters? Preaching a world to come to those presently in despair? You know the answer in your innocent hearts. I don't. I can't read it, whether out of greed, or inanity, or narcissism or an excess of penitence. Might it not be a sin for us to mortify ourselves until we cannot understand what we have within us? Perhaps –' The little priest raised his arms, and his tunic fell back to reveal two thin wrists, a tin watch dangling from a worn belt. '– Perhaps evil triumphs in power, perhaps evil has plunged us into this terrible war, because good has been outside for too long, at home correcting the children's homework, making pancakes for breakfast, darning socks. I spend my days with you. We live in poverty. But is that fair? Is our poverty enough to assure us of paradise? No! It is not enough. We must submit to the weight of the world and its injustices, but future redemption, the happiness to come, depends on our faith. If you don't believe in the Resurrection, which we cannot see, you condemn Him too, the Eternal One, to oblivion. He came to bring us life and instead we shall bring him death. Can you be as harmless as doves, and yet as wise as serpents? That is what the Gospel requires of you, to use even wickedness for good.'

The priest pressed his hand to his forehead, as though shaken by a sudden and terrible migraine. 'I don't understand, sisters. Sin makes me foolish. To oppose death, we must accept it ineluctably. But if we don't resolutely take up arms against the Evil One, the world will slide into chaos, that is the rule of the hard of heart, that is the end of hope. To fight for good, sisters, means being able to scour the battlefield for the weapons broken in the fray with evil, and sharpen them against death.'

His words were interrupted by a fit of cavernous coughing, and the lieutenant murmured, 'That little priest is telling the truth, like blind Orpheus, in New Orleans. Such illusions we have, Nino. Remember me, my friend.'

'Yes, sir,' I said stiffly, in response to my officer's final command.

'I care nothing for lost glory,' he went on. 'It remains intact. My victory lies in having taken up arms against evil, strong only in myself, both general and a private soldier, defeated by destiny. Whether you win or lose, the outcome matters for the living. The truth of our deeds lies in their origins in good-ness, in their existence for the sake of goodness. Any battle on behalf of righteousness will always be victorious, even in defeat. Any attempt to further the cause of evil will dissolve into nothing. That will be Brutus' last line. We've reached the end of the line, Nino. And didn't we meet by chance at a bus stop? You remember the Texas light? Beautiful. Two twenty-five-year-old veterans, pure in heart, free from power, finally ready to bend fate to our desire, our will.' He coughed gently, holding his breath so as not to be heard, clandestine even in his death-throes. 'Nino, the light of that Texas day continues on its way towards the cosmic customs posts. No one can erase our adventure, ever. Where our bones are, love and truth will join forces, and there we will be alive, young and handsome in the light of innocence, just as we were in Texas. Prisoners and yet, because of a pure deed born of our emotions, free men. No army is so strong, Nino, that it can conquer our souls, no plot so treacherous that it can pollute our goodness. The truth has an essence of its own, which is purified by pain, and not corroded by the rust of sarcasm.'

His words must have struck him as too solemn and, as he had lived, he didn't want to finish without a smile. 'The Americans are right, Nino: life is like a Hollywood western. The bad guys may win until ten minutes before the end, but before the closing titles the good lift up their heads once more, and save the day.'

By now he was breathing with difficulty. The priest had started talking again, but soon I lost the thread of what he was saying, distracted as I was by the lieutenant's breathing. 'This war is about to end, and we will win. But we will not lose our lives in the uncertain future. Soon those who hope will be treated as fools. The Old Testament knows no more grievous sin than to mock hope with a sneer. However much destruction we may find at home and in our ashen hearts, let us stay simple, let us not worry. In our disappointments, in our darkness, let us embrace the spirit of Lent. There are ideals at the end of the wilderness, not merely hopeless mirages. Men, St John teaches, choose darkness over light. Why? Out of horror at the mirage of a Resurrection that doesn't come. Out of terror that they might be disappointed by a hope of truth vanishing in the sunlight, like the Fata Morgana, bestowing her bewitching smile on the sailors as she drowns them. We search for truth, but the moment clouds obscure our vision of it, we take refuge in the lair of ignorance and cynicism, fearing that we might be deluded. We would rather put our eyes out with our fingers than leave our suffering behind. Don't timidly escape the light. Allow it to dazzle you, allow it to blind you as the Desert Fathers did. If this is our faith, sisters, don't yield to the fascination of nothingness, the forces of power and evil, and this will be your Resurrection.'

The lieutenant smiled, his eyes wide open. 'He's talking about us, Nino, do you hear? He's preaching this Brooklyn Requiem for us. The desert, you remember? The light, the sand reflecting thoughts and images, the wind scattering them in all directions, and the wild donkeys, the swift hawks, the sly coyotes and the languid snakes mocking our fetters. I still have a handful of that desert sand, a talisman that never made it across the sea. Take it in memory of me.'

He stuffed his fist into his pocket, filled it with fine, shining sand and let it slip into my hand with a caress. He stared at the vaulting of the church, which showed the open sky and the distant stars, and gave up the ghost. The rest of the earth that he was clutching slipped from his grip and fell to the paved floor like sand in an hour glass. When the final grain returned to the ancient mother Gaia, the lieutenant's time on earth was over, and I could weep without hiding my face.

26

The rest was easy. Our pursuers saw us: to this day, I wonder whether some divinity had hidden us from their eyes in the darkness of St Noah's Church in the United States. The lieutenant was dead, and the young priest gave him the last rites, while the women recited the *Requiem aeternam*. I was taken to a Military Police station by Cafard and Cheever. Sitting on a wooden bench was a boy with features so similar to the lieutenant's that my knees trembled with fear.

It was the lieutenant's brother, the brother of Commander Athos Pollini. We were led to a makeshift morgue in a damp brick cellar. Cafard asked the boy, 'Do you know this man?' The boy kissed its forehead, which was smeared with sweat and holy oil, and said, 'Yes, he's my brother, Commander Athos Pollini.'

And so our flight came to an end. After the war I tried to find out about Cafard and Cheever, what finally happened to Frau Becht, whether she'd ever been captured, and about the fates of Hochhuth and Stavinsky. I tried to write to Cafard a few times, but the letter came back marked 'Not Known at This Address'. When I opened it, I saw that the sheet of paper with my questions on it was gone. Had I forgotten to put it in, or had someone steamed open the glue, taken out my words and sealed the envelope without replying?

Cafard and Cheever, angry at not having been able to prevent Pollini's death, had me repatriated shortly afterwards, along with those prisoners who had collaborated with the Americans. I disembarked in Naples and stayed there for a while, the guest of a girl called Eloise who worked for American radio.

One evening she asked me, 'You were in Hereford Camp 1, weren't you, Nino? With the hardline fascists.'

'Yes,' I said, smoking an aniseed-flavoured cigar.

'Were you a fascist?'

'I didn't want to change banners. I didn't know a thing about politics, and there were communists at Camp 1 as well.'

'The *Marine Lion*, the ship bringing home the guys from Camp 1, is docking tomorrow in Mergellina, at 6.30. I read it in the paper today.'

They were my companions. The last to return. I went down to the docks at the right time, my pockets full of cigarettes. The ship docked in the morning gloom. The deck was packed with the faces of my brothers, silent, in faded uniforms, two of them ill and on stretchers. The other men looked tanned and fit, despite the hunger they had suffered over the past few months, when the Americans, horrified to see how the Germans had starved their soldiers in the concentration camps, had reduced their rations to a few calories a day, and the Italians fed themselves on snakes and locusts fried in brilliantine. A little band played shrill tunes by Verdi.

A captain gave orders to disembark, and the men who had been captured as boys in 1940 stood to attention on the pier. He took out a box of oranges, and announced, 'Welcome home. The Arrears Office opens at 10. You will receive any pay owing to you. After that you will get your rations. Before returning to your families, you will be confined to barracks for five days, punishment for not obeying orders to collaborate with the Allied armies.'

On his orders, they did a right turn and disappeared through the poverty-stricken streets of Naples. Could I follow them and speak to them after this final injustice?

One lad eyed my cigarettes. 'Please, sir, be so kind.'

I gave him the lot. The following day, with only the uniform on my back, I said goodbye to Eloise and set out on a big fishing vessel, the *Vulcano*, which was taking a group of refugees to the Island. Since then I have never left.

On the anniversary of my first kiss with Zita, the 19th of April, I row out of La Tonnara, whether the weather's fair or foul, and throw white frangipani flowers along the waves. They quickly drift away to the horizon, elegant as a word. Each year, rowing out to sea becomes more of an effort. Soon I will be celebrating my last farewell with frangipani, the flowers which in winter, the poet Lucio Piccolo tells us, are preserved in frail eggshells, to keep them safe from cold and death.

Hereford, Texas, 1944
Tonnara dell'Isola, 2001